THE REAL
LIDDY JAMES

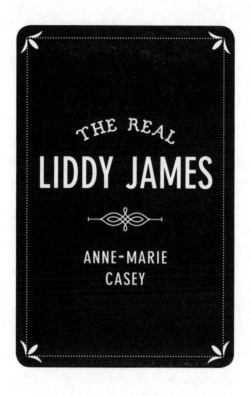

THE REAL

LIDDY JAMES

ANNE-MARIE
CASEY

G. P. Putnam's Sons

New York

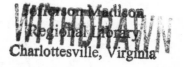

PUTNAM

G. P. PUTNAM'S SONS
Publishers Since 1838
An imprint of Penguin Random House LLC
375 Hudson Street
New York, New York 10014

Library of Congress Cataloging-in-Publication Data

Names: Casey, Anne-Marie, author.
Title: The real Liddy James / Anne-Marie Casey.
Description: New York : G. P. Putnam's Sons [2016].
Identifiers: LCCN 2016008415 | ISBN 9780399160226 (hardcover) |
ISBN 9780399574764 (ebook)
Subjects: LCSH: Middle-aged women—Fiction. | Divorced women—Fiction. |
Women lawyers—Fiction. | Domestic fiction.
BISAC: FICTION / Contemporary Women. |
FICTION / Family Life. | FICTION / Humorous. |
GSAFD: Humorous fiction.
Classification: LLC PR6103.A843 R43 2016 | DDC 823/.92—dc23
LC record available at http://lccn.loc.gov/2016008415
p.   cm.

Printed in the United States of America
1   3   5   7   9   10   8   6   4   2

Book design by Lauren Kolm

For Joe, always

And all the while, I suppose, he thought, real people were living somewhere, and real things happening to them . . .

Edith Wharton, *The Age of Innocence*

THE REAL
LIDDY JAMES

A FIG TREE GROWS IN BROOKLYN

Liddy knew Mrs. Vandervorst had been crying because she emerged from the corridor bathroom with her sunglasses on. There had been some confusion over timing, a not unusual occurrence during the holiday season, and Mrs. Vandervorst had arrived alone, so Liddy solicitously accompanied her to the conference room and settled her into a velvet upholstered armchair with a cup of camomile tea, which she had made in a white china teapot with loose buds, not a bag. The buds bloomed into pretty white flowers floating on the surface of the pale yellow liquid and the sight of this seemed to calm Mrs. Vandervorst, who sank back into the cushions a little and sipped slowly. Liddy hoped the woman would gather herself before the meeting began. She did not want any scenes this afternoon—accusations, counteraccu-sations, sordid marital mudslinging. Drama inevitably delays ev-erything. She had a twice-postponed interview with the *Times* at four that afternoon.

"What color is this?" said Mrs. Vandervorst, looking at the walls.

"It's one of those fancy country house colors. Mist on the Heather, it's called, or something like that."

Mrs. Vandervorst took off her sunglasses. Underneath, her eyes were stubbornly ringed white with ill-matched concealer, but the telltale bloodshot around her pupils remained.

"I like it," she said. "It's very soothing."

Liddy smiled. It was not the first such comment and she found it gratifying. Before she agreed to join Oates and Associates, in addition to the usual stock allocation, health coverage for her ex-tended family, and use of a driver on weekends, she had insisted upon a supervisory role in redecorating the offices and had been delighted that her arrival as a senior partner coincided with the expiration of the lease on the macho marbled space on Fifth. She had found this town house on East Sixty-first through a client, an-other forced sale after the demise of a third marriage of unseemly haste, and set about refurbishing it in the manner of a boutique hotel or luxury *gîte*, probably one in the south of France but with American owners so the faucets didn't screech like injured ani-mals when turned on. The other partners scoffed at the discussion of a "color palette," but Curtis Oates, founding partner and pio-neer in the new world of extreme prenuptial agreements (compul-sory face-lifts, monthly threesomes, or custody of children along gender lines, *no problem*) had dropped into her office one evening brandishing a line drawing from the Hirst studio as a thank-you.

"Very clever, Liddy," he said in the raspy Humphrey Bogart voice he had affected as a teenager because Leonora Mott, the object of his affection in 1971, had told him it was sexy. "You got a lotta class, kid." (Liddy knew this; she had worked hard to acquire it.) "Make 'em relax before we screw 'em."

Liddy turned to Mrs. Vandervorst and hoped she was relaxing, for she was certain to be screwed.

"Are you all right?" she asked, and meant it.

Mrs. Vandervorst looked straight at her. She had the sorrow under control now and so, left with disbelief, she kept digging the nails on her left hand into her palm hard, as if she could wake herself up.

"How do I get rid of his name?" she said. "I can't take it off like the rings."

Liddy glanced at the enormous pink diamond on the other woman's finger and, mentally scanning through her list of Mr. Vandervorst's demands, thought, *He wants the ring, my dear, the name he doesn't care about, because it didn't cost him anything.*

"You go back to your maiden name," she said.

Mrs. Vandervorst thought about this for a moment.

"I don't remember who Gloria Thompson was."

Liddy looked away to see if anyone had appeared in the corridor (Mudlark Blue on the walls, an arrangement of vivid poinsettias on a side table).

"*How can you do this to me?*"

"Sorry? . . ." Liddy was not sure if she had heard something or not. Mrs. Vandervorst had whispered, as she was a woman frightened of her anger and she did not want to cry again.

"Are you a mother, Ms. James?"

Liddy assumed her default low-register professional voice, designed to convey understanding as well as authority. "Yes, I have two sons."

"Then don't take my children away. They need me."

"Mrs. Vandervorst. They need their parents. A shared custody arrangement is *not* taking your children away."

Liddy glanced up at the corner of the room where a concealed camera, ostensibly for security purposes, videotaped all exchanges in case of a later dispute. *Perhaps conversation had been a mistake*, she thought.

"I'm going to find out where your attorney is," she said, moving to leave.

Mrs. Vandervorst stood up too quickly, and the camomile flowers in the bottom of her cup spilled onto the cream handknotted silk rug.

"It's *Christmas*, Ms. James, it's my religious holiday. I want the children. My youngest, Karl. He's only four. He barely knows his father. My husband travels for weeks on end and Karl cries when I'm not there. *Liddy*, you must work all hours. You know what it feels like to hear your child begging you to stay—"

Liddy turned. She was not frightened of her anger. Her eyes went beady and cold and her nostrils flared imperceptibly.

"Having reviewed your domestic arrangements . . . *Gloria* . . . I fear that a woman who left a lucrative job to bring up her children but who has availed herself of maternity nurses, day and night nannies, weekend housekeeping, and homework assistants for the past fifteen years can hardly claim to have devoted her entire existence to them."

"I didn't want it to be like that."

"Then who did? You say your husband is never there."

"I suffered from exhaustion after the twins."

"Yes. I understand you took a two-month recuperative break to a spa in St. Barts, where you improved both your health and your doublehanded backhand."

"How the hell do you know that?"

The change in tone was so abrupt that Liddy almost cheered. Clearly Mrs. Vandervorst had suddenly remembered who Gloria Thompson was: the brightest girl in her high school, a woman who spoke four languages including Russian and had an MBA.

Gloria realized that somewhere on Liddy's computer might be a JPEG file containing photos of her in white shorts with Carlos, the tennis coach, copies of her biweekly therapy bills, and, perhaps most worrisome, recordings of a series of ill-advised messages she had left on her husband's phone late at night that, if judiciously edited, might make "unstable" sound like an understatement.

"That's why your husband hired me," said Liddy, and headed for the door, where she paused. "I understand how you feel, Mrs. Vandervorst. You want to savage him and I probably would too, but believe me, the price of going to court is too high—and I don't mean the eight hundred dollars an hour you're paying Gillespie, Stackallan and Ross."

She gestured toward the table. "If you want to use the phone, you press extension one."

Liddy glanced at her watch as she marched up the corridor: 3:25.

"Where the hell is everybody?" she yelled into the reception area, where an enormous fir tree decorated entirely in white lights and silver bells twinkled splendidly. There was no reply save an extraordinary honking laugh that Liddy realized was emanating from her new paralegal, Sydney Grace, a young woman who had given no previous indication that she had any sense of humor at all. Sydney was doubled over in hysterics, her right hand clutching the sleeve of a long coat of dark color worn by the extremely tall man beside her, her left brushing a few stray snowflakes from his shoulders.

Liddy turned to the window in surprise. Outside, the first proper snow of winter was falling, and Liddy remembered there were seasons, and that she had not been aware of them for about six years, since her life had changed, since she began moving between office and home by luxury car, since weather became something she looked out of a window at.

"Did I miss something?" she said. Sydney looked up and opened her mouth, but Liddy spoke first. "Hello, Sebastian."

The tall man in the snow-flecked dark coat turned to look at her. "Hello, Liddy. I'm here to divorce the Vandervorsts," he said with a wink at Sydney, who scurried back to her desk collapsing into giggles once again. "I know you were expecting Mr. Gillespie, but he's got food poisoning—a dodgy oyster over the weekend—so I drew the short straw."

At this moment, Curtis appeared in the doorway of his office, grinning in anticipation. "Top o' the morning, Mr. Stackallan. How are you?"

"I'd rather be negotiating a ransom with pirates in the Malacca Straits," Sebastian replied.

"Thank you," said Curtis, genuinely gratified, before ducking back inside again.

From somewhere a tinny version of "Danny Boy" started playing. Sebastian began first patting the pockets of the coat, then his Donegal tweed suit (authentically matted with what could have been wolfhound hairs), until he located the iPhone tucked into a red sock beneath the bicycle clip on his right leg, above his brogues. He pulled it to his ear, his attention caught by the row of legal certificates lining the wall, in particular the one for a certain Lydia Mary Murphy.

He glanced at Liddy.

"Excuse me, Lydia Mary," he said.

"No one's allowed to call me that, apart from my parents. It's Liddy . . . or *Ms. James*," Liddy replied, but Sebastian Stackallan turned away to take the call. "Hello, Gillespie?"

Liddy took the moment to consider how annoying she always found him. And not in an *adorable* annoying way, not in a way sizzling with sexual attraction like the setup of a Preston Sturges movie or *Much Ado About Nothing*. She looked at his green tie, patterned with tiny shamrocks, knotted roughly beneath the face of a Celtic poet, with an aquiline nose and a sensitive mouth. She saw the one graying forelock of his jet black hair that he flicked absentmindedly away from his blue-gray eyes, his complexion so palely handsome that he seemed permanently to be in black and white.

No, she disliked everything about him, because she was a woman who lived in the vivid color of a constantly reinvented present, and she distrusted those who clung to an idea of a caste or the past. Sebastian was a foreigner's caricature of a sensitive, sexy Irishman and Liddy had learned in seventh-grade writing class that cliché always diminishes what it describes.

"Yes, I understand . . . *Holy Jaysuz, man, see a doctor!*" he was saying as he held the telephone away from his mouth. Liddy and Sydney heard violent retching before he hung up.

"It seems our client wants to agree to your client's proposal," he said, fixing Liddy with his blue-gray eyes, his stare no longer pale but icy.

"Shall I take you to her?" she replied, returning his gaze with wide-eyed innocence, unleashing her killer wide-toothed smile. She gestured for him to follow her down the corridor, where he might perhaps appreciate her perfectly proportioned figure in her plum-colored dress, the pencil skirt fitted to just above the knee, all the better to show off the long, slender legs that had walked unscathed through forty-four years, a solitary childhood, one divorce, and two pregnancies. But Sebastian was distracted and, as usual, appeared utterly indifferent to Liddy's considerable charms.

"Par for the course," he said, more to himself than her. "Nobbling our client at the status conference and terrifying her out of litigation. Straight out of the Curtis Oates playbook."

Liddy could not bring herself to defend her boss; Curtis Oates was, after all, a man so loathsome that even his adult children would not tell him where they lived.

"I've saved Mrs. Vandervorst a lot of money," she said.

"Fair enough," he replied, and Liddy was conscious that this had some sort of double meaning.

They were outside the closed conference room door now and for a moment Liddy was struck by how perfectly Sebastian fitted in with Mist on the Heather.

"We would have got what we wanted, just so you know," he said, "if we'd gone to court."

"There are no winners and losers in the field of marital warfare, Sebastian," she said, mostly because she knew it would annoy him.

He turned to her, the icy stare returning.

"Okay, maybe," she conceded. "You're always good at the big emotional appeal out of nowhere. The lilting Irish accent helps." This was true. She had often seen Sebastian command the attention of a noisy courtroom simply by adjusting the timbre of his voice. "That soliloquy you did for Judge Carson last month about the little boy with his backpack and his teddy on the plane. Genius. You can make the most absurd statement sound moving. Shame you never let fact or precedent get in the way."

He nodded. "You know what you're good at?"

He did not wait for her to answer.

"Making a complicated situation look simple."

There was something in his tone that went beyond collegial banter and into contempt.

"Someone once said to me that this business makes nice people do nasty things," she said, stung.

Sebastian laughed rather hollowly and moved his hand to grab the brass doorknob. "And for always getting what she wants in the long run, commend me to a nasty woman," he muttered, the beauty of his voice contrasting with his words.

Liddy flinched.

"Edith Wharton. *The House of Mirth*," she said, shocked by the force of her reaction, looking at him but remembering another voice entirely, in another place, at another time.

"Precisely," he said, but he was disconcerted. The laconic, erudite aside was something of a trademark of his; normally people responded with a knowing smile or a roll of the eyes. Liddy's eyes, however, had filled with unexpected tears and she spun away, raising her hand to her mouth. There was no point in claiming she wasn't upset, because she never cried in an understated, glamorous way, and was now red and snotty like a toddler. But before she could wipe her face with her silk jersey sleeves, Sebastian pulled a tatty, but clean, monogrammed handkerchief from his cuff.

"Liddy? . . ."

"I'm fine," she said, seizing the handkerchief and bolting toward the corridor bathroom, her sudden grief stuck like bile in her throat. He followed.

"I'm sorry. I was rude." His tone was gentler now.

"People have been much ruder to me than that," she said quickly. (She had no intention of qualifying the statement, although she could have said that she was sure there were small wax effigies of her regularly burned throughout the five boroughs.

And only the previous weekend she had been shunned at a spin-
ning class by a couple of furious first wives.)

"I can imagine."

She turned and looked at him, askance. He continued. "I
mean, it's what you said about this business. How many more
times can I watch wedding videos where the happy couple vow to
always smile in the sunshine or, worse, pick up guitars for their
customized rendition of 'Your Song' and know that one of them
was on the phone to me seventy-two hours later? My wife says it's
made me irredeemably pessimistic."

"Not me." Liddy paused for a moment and blotted at her eyes,
although she knew it was too late to regain control of the situation. "I believe in love."

Now it was his turn to look at her askance. They had been
acquainted for over fourteen years, so why she had chosen this
moment to say it she did not know; what she did know was that
the statement was true. Practicing family law had not made Liddy
cynical. She did not believe that most couples made those solemn
vows with their fingers crossed behind their backs; she knew
from experience that it was just, to misquote the old song, that
love and marriage did not always go together like a horse and
carriage. (In fact, in Manhattan, by conservative estimate, half
the time the horse bolted through Central Park and left the carriage overturned.)

And Liddy still felt empathy for the broken ones, the people
like Gloria, blown apart by divorce with no guarantee that the
pieces would ever fit back together. She hoped always that kind-
ness and friendship would triumph amid the wreckage, in the

end. But she could not deny that these days, as the economy plummeted but romantic expectations soared, negotiations were growing more and more unpleasant—as Curtis Oates was making a fortune proving.

Sebastian smiled.

"How very optimistic of you," he said, and though she expected this comment to prefigure a further apology, Sebastian waved good-bye to his handkerchief and headed back to the conference room to escort Mrs. Vandervorst from the building without as much as a backward glance at Liddy.

In the bathroom, Liddy leaned over the sink and splashed cold water on her face, avoiding the small puddles and pile of soggy tissues Mrs. Vandervorst had left behind. But it would be a good five minutes before the angry pink blotches on her cheeks faded, so she sat down on the armchair in the corner and rested her head against the toile de Jouy wallpaper. She tried to take a breath and count to five, but her mind wandered. Of course she was annoyed with herself for sobbing in front of Stackallan—although she had occasionally used vulnerability strategically, she knew tears always left professional women open to accusations of hormonal imbalance. But who could have predicted the extraordinary coincidence of his quoting Edith Wharton? The very words her ex-husband had said to her, almost seven years ago, in the terrible aftermath of what she had done; a scene she could hardly bear to remember and that she had made her mission to forget. Liddy could sometimes be a *nasty woman*, it was true, but up to this point in her life that fact had never made her cry.

For a moment, she pondered the possibility of hormonal imbalance.

Sydney came into the bathroom to deliver the news that Mr. Vandervorst had finally arrived, only to promptly leave to await papers at his office, but not before fiddling an overfamiliar arm around her waist.

"He's repulsive. Mrs. V's better off without him" was Sydney's opinion, but she did not continue for, smitten with Sebastian, there was only one man she wanted to discuss. "But Mr. Stackallan's so cute!" she said. "And that voice. I want to close my eyes and listen to him read. Anything. Even *Constitutional Law*, 17th."

Liddy said nothing.

"No one makes me laugh, really, but he was joking about my name. He says with so many American names, you can't tell if it's a girl or a guy, *a bird or a bloke!*" Sydney honked again.

Liddy stood up, smoothed out her skirt, checked herself in the mirror, and attempted to affect an expression of complete indifference.

"You know," continued Sydney, "*Mackenzie*, bird or bloke? *Campbell*, bird or bloke? Last week, he was due to meet someone called Roger and it was a woman!"

"That didn't happen," said Liddy sourly, walking into the corridor, thinking, *What is it with all the "sharing" today?* Curtis Oates, who was currently in reception barking at the girl to put on the Christmas "chill-out" album he had purchased on Liddy's instruction, would never make such mistakes.

"I asked him out on a date, but he said he was married. I said it didn't matter, and he laughed and said I was charming but far too young for him."

Sydney stopped and looked at Liddy uncomprehendingly. "I mean, what sort of a man says that?"

"Not me," said Curtis Oates cheerfully, flashing his pearly veneers and running a hand through his hair transplant. "Liddy, it's four p.m., the gal from the *Times* is here."

Over the speakers came the familiar organ introduction of "O Holy Night." The tune did not soothe Liddy, and, still discombobulated by the contemplation of her *not*-niceness, she knew the interview would have to be postponed for the third time.

"Oh, no," she said. "I can't do that now, Curtis."

"Why not? It's good for business. Remember to mention our growth areas. Gays and geriatrics."

"*Pfft* . . ." She exhaled. "It's the Style section. Do you ever read that? I won't do it. I'm not in the mood."

He looked over at her.

"Who gives a fuck?" he replied, and pointed toward her office before sashaying into his.

"Quick. *Look at this*," whispered Sydney, who had been googling. "I found a photo of Sebastian and his wife at their wedding."

Liddy glanced over because she couldn't help herself. Mrs. Chloe Stackallan had straight blond hair, high cheekbones, and tiny ankles. She wore her cream lace Temperley gown as if it had been made for her, which it undoubtedly had. She had a bouquet of lily of the valley in one hand, as the other rested casually on Sebastian's arm, and she was staring up at him adoringly.

It was like the cover photograph of *Perfect Bride* magazine.

"Wow," said Sydney mournfully. "She's . . . perfect. They look *perfect* together."

"Nothing's perfect, Sydney," said Liddy brusquely. "No matter how it looks."

This cheered Sydney up a little.

"You'd better go, Liddy," she said.

Liddy sighed. The journalist had told her that she wanted to discover "the real Liddy James," but Liddy had just seen her real self, and wanted that Liddy kept hidden.

It's showtime! she thought.

"I DON'T DO GUILT"

One of New York *magazine's top ten divorce attorneys, a best-selling author, and a regular contributor to the* Huffington Post, *Liddy James navigates the choppy waters of the Manhattan matrimonial law system with ease, and she does it in slippers. Corinthia Jordan has an appointment.*

The fact that Liddy James—mother, art lover, and senior partner in the firm of Oates and Associates—is relaxing in her glorious office on the Upper East Side, dunking chocolate cookies into her hot chocolate with her UGG-slippered feet up, is, she tells me, mainly the result of the newfound freedom she discovered in her forties.

"I spent so much of my younger life worrying what people thought of me, and let's face it, because I am a woman, worrying if they *liked* me, that it has been the greatest gift of aging to discover that I no longer care."

Her green eyes glitter meaningfully as she says this, and with her long, auburn hair and the fair, freckled complexion of a woman half her age—the genetic gifts of her Irish parents who brought her to America when she was nine years old—as well as the distinctive lope in her stride, which, she tells me, makes high heels impossible, James exudes a blithely unaffected but charismatic air. She leans back, a *tableau vivant* of magnificent midlife, and among her botanical prints, I spy a faded Polaroid of her with her sandy-haired sons, Matty and Cal James, ages thirteen and five, and an adorable scribble picture, emblazoned with superhero stickers, declaring BEST MOM IN THE WORLD. To my surprise there's no treadmill desk or selfies with celebrity clients to be seen. Only the shark line drawing in the corner gives any indication of Liddy's formidable professional reputation.

"Oh, that," she says, smiling when I point to it. "It was a present from a colleague." I ask her if she is known as "the shark" in the office and she shrugs. "You know the amazing thing about sharks? If they stop swimming they drown. They have to move forward to survive. I totally relate to that."

On growing up in a low-income family in suburban New Jersey, she says, "Look, my parents were twenty-one when they married and had me. They fled the economic deprivation of Ireland in the 1980s in search of a better life here, but it didn't work out exactly as they planned." James made her escape through education. She graduated first in her class at Stanford Law School, then had her pick of any top legal firm on either coast. She chose the legendary Rosedale and Seldon in New York, where she quickly rewrote the rulebook on precourt settlements, only leaving seven years ago when Curtis Oates made her "an offer she couldn't refuse."

Since then her career has reached new heights, including the publication of her controversial book *Equality Means in* Everything: *A Divorce Lawyer's Guide to Modern Matrimony*, which came out two years ago in a blaze of publicity that swept it to number one on the *New York Times* bestseller list. Does she regret how certain chapters were reported?

"There was certainly a lack of nuance about some points. I mean, I am a feminist, so to be portrayed as somehow anti-women was extremely hurtful. And seeking to punish a former partner through his or her wallet is far from an exclusively female pursuit! But I do stand by my view that marriage (and therefore divorce) isn't a meal ticket. Women can't pick and choose what gender equality means, and although I am well aware that nothing affects a woman's career trajectory like having children, the financial responsibilities of the home should and must be shared, as parenting should and must be shared. No able-bodied person should assume that the lifestyle they enjoy because of their marriage will continue if that marriage ends. In other words, *don't give up work, ladies!*"

One on one, James expresses her views so forcefully and articulately that resistance seems useless, but many people disagree with her views, commenting that until cultural expectations of a woman's role have changed dramatically, or women themselves are willing to relinquish the role of primary caretaker in the family, such a utopian vision of marital equality is impractical. How, I ask her, has she managed to juggle her own brilliant career with motherhood?

"Imperfectly," she replies cheerfully, then turns suddenly serious. "I was far too young when I first got together with my ex-husband (Peter James, a professor of English and American literature). I was a terrible wife and I broke his heart, but thanks to his fortitude, and that of his wonderful new partner, we managed a good divorce."

"So there is such a thing?" I ask. Her response surprises me.

"Personally, I still don't believe in divorce, particularly where there are children involved."

"What about prenups?" I ask.

She replies without hesitation. "My boss, Curtis Oates, vehemently disagrees with me, but I think that's like opening the exit doors of the plane before buckling your seat belt. If you've got doubts about getting married, don't do it. That's my advice."

And with this, she glances at the antique Jaeger-LeCoultre clock on her desk and shrugs in a disarmingly girlish manner. "I have to go. I'm making tuna surprise for dinner," and, interview over, she offers to drop me off at a work event on her way home to her magnificent apartment in a landmark building in Tribeca.

"Would you like to marry again?" I ask her as we sit in the back of the car.

"Who would risk it?" she replies, laughing. "Anyway, it's not on my radar at the moment. I am a single mother of two children, and the father of my younger son is not in our lives, so I don't have a minute of spare time. *Literally.*" Before I can ask another question, she says firmly, "Cal was very wanted but not planned," and I know better than to pursue the subject.

The snow is falling heavily now and James opens her bag and pulls out a light-as-a-feather I Pezzi Dipinti shawl, which she wraps elegantly around her neck. "You must have read the interview with President Obama when he said he had to limit the number of decisions he had to make in one day, so his suits are all the same color. I share his philosophy. My capsule wardrobe is black and white—although every season I buy one key piece, like this dress, in a color—but the bottom line is, in my life I don't want to think too much about anything I don't have to."

I am struck by how rarely one meets a woman so *bien dans sa peau*, a woman at the top of her profession, who so successfully juggles a complicated domestic situation with the extraordinary demands of her career. As someone who struggles most mornings to run a brush through her hair before the school run, I wonder: What is the secret to her superproductive existence?

"My irreplaceable nanny, Lucia, no personal life, and working late at night!" She laughs before continuing. "I accept I can't do everything and I don't try. I won't ever be one of those frazzled women in dirty sweatpants, making brownies at midnight for a bake sale. I like order, because I am a Virgo. And I guess I don't do guilt."

Rose Donato had a secret that made her happier than other women: she was an atheist who knew miracles could happen. This unshakable belief was born from the formative experience of her childhood, when her older brother Michael had fallen head-first off a rope ladder, and in the six seconds he lay crumpled and motionless on the playground tarmac, her mother had fallen to her knees for the brief moments before he blinked awake again. Afterward Rose, aged seven, turned to her mother and asked what she had been doing. "I prayed for a miracle," her mother said, before running off to holler at Michael, who was now balancing one-legged on top of a slide.

Rose was an unusually thoughtful and wise child, so once she knew that such things could happen, she decided to harness the power. She imagined that a person might be allotted only so many miracles in one lifetime, but in teenage desperation she squandered two in rapid succession; first, when she prayed that the line of pimples that studded her forehead like red pushpins would disappear (which they did, by magic, two weeks later), and second, when she *had* to get two tickets to the Jacksons Victory Tour, and in the line for returns a kindly woman gave her the front-row seats her son was about to throw away. She would regret this when, aged thirty-two, at a time when she was not so secretly obsessing about rings and reproduction, Frank Pearson, who had been her room- and bedmate for ten years, casually left her for a woman he had met on the 6 train. The miracle of her rent-controlled apartment in the West Village and the senior lectureship she loved seemed like nothing after this, and when, three years later, she fell irrevocably in love at the first sight of Peter James, newly appointed professor of English and American literature, only to then meet his wife, the incomparable Liddy, she became convinced that she had used up her allocation.

For five years she and Peter worked side by side, sharing milk cartons and ideas on semiotic literary criticism, as Rose discreetly avoided promotion and other suitable men. She reread *Great Expectations* and cherished her unrequited passion, until one day Peter appeared in the common room, gray-faced from sleeplessness, and told her that he and Liddy had separated. Rose reached out her right hand to touch his, the first time she had dared to be so intimate, and he looked at her as if for the very first time.

She was forty years old that day; it took a year for him to want her, and so, when she moved into the town house in Carroll Gardens with the fig tree in the garden, and after three miscarriages in rapid succession, she abandoned her dream of a child and accepted it would be just the two of them. And soon it did not matter, at last she had him, it was the *enough* miracle—and of course there was his child too, Matty, whom she had first met as a tall and winning seven-year-old boy, and whom she had decided to love as if he were her own. And while their relationship had never become the one she had fantasized about, she dutifully cooked and cleaned and cared for him, which, from her outsider's perspective, seemed at least ninety percent of what parenting was really about.

"What are you reading?" said Peter. It was a bright February morning and he had walked into the kitchen to kiss the top of her head, but stopped at the sight of her, her hand leaning against her cheek, her soft beauty framed in the winter light of the French windows as if she were posing for Vermeer. "You look completely absorbed."

Rose gulped. She had woken early and, unable to lie still, had half dressed and crept down the stairs, kidding herself she would get a head start on a paper about Shakespeare's *Coriolanus*. But in fact, after an hour or so, she had stopped, too eager to read the Style section of the *Times*, which she had bought yesterday evening and had not yet had a moment alone to peruse. Cup of coffee in hand, Rose had crept across the room to the innocuous brown bag, slung across a wooden chair, whose contents seemed to be summoning her with an insistent *read me, read me* until she gave in and pulled the newspaper out, although as she did this she knew she should have waited until the apartment was empty. Liddy James, one of *New York* magazine's top ten divorce attorneys, stared out at her from the front page, sitting, legs crossed, on a desk, hands by her sides, her face tilted up in a smile just the right edge of rictus but still ever-so-slightly fake. Rose began to read in case there was anything she needed to know about, and it had indeed been so absorbing, she had not heard Peter's arrival, his socked footsteps on the stairs, the thump of his elbow against the warped wood of the kitchen door they had resolved to fix three years ago.

She stood up, attempting to stuff the newspaper nonchalantly into the table drawer. It was no good. She was being furtive and he knew it.

"What is it?" he said, walking toward her, curious now. Rose was the least furtive person in his acquaintance and she could never not tell the truth, even when she probably should.

"It's Liddy's article in the *Times* yesterday. D'you remember? She warned us about it before Christmas."

Peter reminded himself that his determination to ignore Liddy's self-promoting interviews (which inevitably portrayed a version of their marriage designed to fit whatever she was selling) had served him well in the past, and as she had recently reminded him with typical candor, the royalties from her book were paying Matty's school fees and might even cover college. But there was something in Rose's face this morning, a different brushstroke across her forehead.

"What did she say?" he asked as he sat down, resolutely pouring his cereal and forgetting to kiss the top of her head.

"Oh, more or less the usual." Rose paused. "She compares herself to Obama. . . ."

Peter groaned and rolled his eyes, anticipating what humorous aperçus his colleagues might be practicing on their way to work.

"And apparently she was a terrible wife."

Peter looked up. *"Is that all?"*

Rose shook her head. "And she says she broke your heart."

He was silent in an unusual way, so Rose felt the need to keep talking. "I don't know why she has to do this."

"Yes, you do. Because it makes her feel powerful. It's a good line, a good story, and people want to read it. People like you, I might add. Where's Matty?" Sudden anger had consumed his appetite. "It's quarter of eight. I can't be late this morning. *Matty! Get down here. Now!*" And he marched into the hallway.

Rose hoped Matty was dressed. Though Peter might say his sudden bad mood was all her fault, it was really Liddy's yet again, and when confronted with his son, the living, breathing embodiment of Liddy, down to the shape of his eyes and the music of his rare laugh, you didn't have to be a therapist to guess what might happen.

"You go, then," Rose said, calling after him. "I'll walk with Matty. It's a beautiful morning. And I've got an appointment at the doctor's at nine thirty."

Peter picked up his bag and coat and left with a sharp double bang of the front door. Rose sighed and stood up, wincing slightly as her knee twinged, and hauled it up the stairs, where she knocked on Matty's door.

"It's time to get up, Matty," she called.

"No!" came the muffled shout from inside the room, so she opened the door, braving the intense odor of growing boy and stale shoes, and switched the light on, cruelly pulling the duvet off him with a flourish.

"Up! Now!" she barked, marveling at how their interactions,

once so fluid and fulsome, were now reduced to words of one syllable. Liddy had remarked on the phone to her just last week that it seemed Matty had been invaded by an alien body snatcher who had only one expression, sullen, and only one word of English, *no*, and while Rose laughed politely, she wished Liddy and Peter would talk about it. She saw how they both mourned the passing of their perfect little boy and how hard they found this teenage stranger, full of new hairs and hormones, to deal with. By contrast, Rose had come to learn that her ability not to lose her temper with Matty might be directly to do with her not having given birth to him. She did not take his outbursts personally because she did not see his behavior as any reflection on her own.

"C'mon! Hurry! I packed your school bag, I charged your phone. Don't forget to tell Miss Walsh you need an afternoon slot for your piano lesson next week, and you've lost your library book so I've stuck twenty dollars in your jacket pocket to cover it."

He shook his head and grunted something unintelligible before picking the duvet up off the floor, rolling onto his side, and curling into a ball underneath it.

"Matty!" she said, exasperated.

"Can Dylan and Jack come over tonight?" came his muffled response.

"Yes, if their parents text me. *You have to get up now!*"

Suddenly, from downstairs, the front door swung open.

"Rose!"

At his father's voice, Matty leapt out of bed, picked his clothes off the floor, and hurried into the bathroom, not quite so teenage yet as to brave paternal wrath first thing. Rose came down the stairs once more. Peter was standing in the doorway, hangdog. Rose smiled.

"You didn't have to come back," she said.

"I wanted to say I'm sorry."

"No. I'm sorry. I shouldn't have been reading it. It was insensitive—"

"I can't believe she said that. It's so *personal*. And in the *Times* . . ."

But it was the truth and they both knew it. They just wanted it unsaid. Liddy had not just blithely broken Peter's heart, she had shattered it; but Rose had spent a year picking up the tiny pieces so the two of them could stick it back together.

"She makes me look like a *shmuck*. . . ."

"She thinks I'm wonderful," Rose dared, and wrapped her arms around his neck.

"Something must have happened," said Peter. "It doesn't sound like her."

"What are you talking about?" said Matty from the bathroom door, a toothbrush sticking out the side of his white frothy mouth.

"Your mother gave an interview that upset me and I over-reacted," Peter announced. Rose smiled forgivingly and hoped Matty would appreciate what a fine example of taking responsibility for negative emotions his father was giving him.

"Is it the 'broke your heart' thing? Mom told me about that. She said she was sorry. She was in a funny mood that day and she probably made a complicated situation look simple."

He went back to the sink. This was followed by the exuberant gargling and spitting noises he had been told innumerable times to avoid, but Rose and Peter were too intrigued by his comment to admonish him.

"I love you," said Rose to Peter. "Go, or you'll be late."

In the background now, the sound of Matty pissing, like a horse onto a metal gate.

"Close the door, for Chrissake!" shouted Peter, then whispered, "How do you put up with us, Rose? And why are you seeing the doctor?" He pulled her close. His hand rested gently on her hip.

"Annual physical. My age. My knee."

"Is it the change of life, Rosey?" said Matty, emerging, a slick of hair gel plastering his fringe to his forehead. "Melinda's mom's having that and she's turned into a monster."

"C'mon, son," said Peter, chivying the boy out the door before they could find out if this might be the morning Rose's legendary placidity deserted her. "I know you haven't eaten, so I'll buy you a bun on the way."

"Cool." The boy grinned, suddenly looking like a little child again. It was so confusing, this cusp time, thought Rose, for Matty and for her. He was quite right, of course, the change was coming. She had been feeling it for the last couple of months. The two of them were trapped in their mutating bodies, wrestling with the extraordinary confusion of feeling young while growing older.

"I resent so much of our time being taken up talking about her. That's it, really," Peter said quietly.

"I know," Rose replied, and he left again, Matty in tow.

Although Rose did indeed resent having to talk about Liddy

quite so much, what she really resented was that in all the talking, Peter never *said* anything about the relationship, dismissing it as "ancient history," although "secret history" was more accurate. But, over time, she accepted that all new partners are forced to navigate the complicated terrain that their predecessors leave behind. That what Liddy had left behind was more like scorched earth, and because she was vivid, extraordinary, unforgettable, and all these things in all ways, Rose had to fight not to become a sort of puny, satellite moon rotating in the gravitational pull of Liddy's blazing sun. For this reason she had told her mother that, if they ever got married, she would never take Peter's surname, as she could not face being the second Mrs. James when the first was quite so *first* in everything. (This comment conveniently sidestepped another conversation, which was why, despite their obvious domestic happiness, the marriage had not yet happened. Peter seeming resolved not to make what her mother referred to as "an honest woman of her.")

Similarly, there had been the issue of what Matty might call Rose, or rather what Liddy might "helpfully" decide she could be called. On this, Rose felt some relief that she was not formally his stepmother. After all, as a person who looked to literature for a map of life, she would shudder and think, *Who wants to be the Wicked Queen torturing Snow White?* It could not be helpful to the millions of children who ended up in blended families that the image of stepparents imbued in their nurseries was almost inevitably the black horns of Maleficent looming over the crib bars. Thank goodness Matty had suggested "Rosey" almost by accident when they were playing a game, so Liddy's suggestions of Aunt Rose, which sounded like a dowager, or Mom2, which sounded like something out of a Disney movie about a family of androids, could be ignored in a way Liddy herself could never be.

Rose had often noticed that if there were lulls in any conversation she was having, all it took was for Liddy's name to be mentioned for interest to be revived. There was always something to say about Liddy, and as Rose's doctor, Barbara, strapped the cuff of a blood pressure monitor around Rose's upper arm one hour later, today proved no exception.

Barbara had resolved not to mention the interview in the Style section, but because she was also a single mother of two and having a bad day, when it fell out of Rose's bag onto the floor, she picked it up, glanced at it again, and could not control herself.

"Liddy James. Superlawyer! Supermother! What a bunch of baloney! With the irreplaceable Lucia, the driver, the personal trainer, the chef delivering the meals, and, no doubt, the life coach on speakerphone once every two weeks, I'm amazed she ever sees her children. *And* you seem to look after Matty most of the time."

Rose looked up, astounded by the accuracy with which Barbara had portrayed Liddy's life, although, of course, Barbara had been Rose's doctor, and then her friend, for over twenty years.

"Liddy agreed that Matty would stay with Peter Monday to Thursday, to be close to the school," Rose said. "And she's flexible if he has a soccer practice or a playdate on a Friday night or something—it was all decided with a child psychologist after they split."

"Just as well she doesn't 'do guilt,' then," continued Barbara. "*Huh!* Of course she doesn't. She's forgotten what it's like for the rest of us. Guilt is our hobby. It gives us a break from the exhaustion. You ought to see the online comments!"

The cuff gripped Rose's arm, then seemed to sigh out. Barbara checked the reading.

"Perfect," she said. "You want to know the truth, Rose? Liddy couldn't have her life unless she shared custody. I'm telling you. If she really was a single mother with her job and two kids, she couldn't cope."

Rose attempted a noncommittal shrug.

"She looks good, though. Has she had work done?"

"No," said Rose. "She says she wouldn't ever have plastic surgery—she once represented this guy whose wife left him when his nose fell off."

"Typical. It's only women who look like her who announce things like that. I'm not talking lifts, or even fillers. I bet she's had this thing where they inject your own blood into you. The Vampire Facial, it's called. 'Totes appropes' for Liddy, as my daughter would say."

Rose couldn't help giggling, suddenly mischievous. "I would like to know one thing," she said. "What's tuna surprise?"

Barbara paused as she expertly pricked the vein on the underside of Rose's elbow with a needle. "The surprise is she actually cooked something."

And she drew three vials of viscous blood from Rose's arm, stuck different colored labels on each, and took out a pen to mark them.

"When was your last period?" she asked. Rose shrugged and said ruefully that she thought that ship had sailed, pulling out the receipt from Duane Reade on the back of which she had scribbled her symptom list (swollen ankles, sore boobs, lethargy), so Barbara handed her a plastic sample jar and ordered her to pee in it. When Rose returned, the hot little pot in her hand, Barbara was still staring at the photograph of Liddy.

"I think she should be worried. She's got that thing, that thing characters in plays have, pride before a fall. Right?"

"*Hubris,*" said Rose, thinking. "An overestimation of one's own competence or capability."

"Yes," replied Barbara, sticking the thin paper strip into the sample pot and glancing at her watch. *"Hubris."*

"After *hubris* comes *nemesis* and then comes the fall," continued Rose, delighted to change the subject and adopting the beguiling academic tone she used on her students. "It's from Greek tragedy, like in *The Iliad* when Achilles, extremely prideful, drags poor Hector's body over the ground outside the city walls of Troy, and fate deals with him pretty swiftly afterward. I was thinking about it this morning, because I'm teaching *Coriolanus* again this semester. Another great man brought low by his hubris. I think he's somewhat misunderstood, though. . . ."

Barbara peered across at her.

"Like Liddy?" she said.

"Yes, actually." Privately, Rose found Liddy's determination to live life by her own rules nothing less than heroic, particularly given how difficult it must be. She knew many, however, shared Barbara's view that there was no end to the ways in which Liddy offended the gods of normal.

"You're too nice," muttered Barbara and she did not mean it as a compliment, but Rose was thinking about *Coriolanus* and said, "Would you have me/False to my nature? Rather say, I play/The man I am . . ." She trailed off, realizing she must have gone too far, because at the sink Barbara was standing very still in what looked like some kind of shock.

"Are you okay?" said Rose, and then remembering where she was, "Am *I* okay?"

"Yeah. You're fine. You're pregnant."

Barbara expected a big reaction, but the word on its own would not do it. After all, it had let Rose down three times before.

"How pregnant?"

"Properly pregnant. I'd say nearly ten weeks."

Rose stayed silent.

"It's a miracle," said Barbara.

Rose would never again cajole Matty to remember every detail of his day, for after Barbara had packed her off in a cab to a clinic uptown where she was comprehensively ultrasounded and injected with progesterone in her right buttock, she remembered that morning only in a blurry haze through which the repetitive thump of her unborn baby's heartbeat sounded like a tiny hammer pounding the inside of her skull. She suspected this was the manifestation of her contradictory emotions about the news. It was true, as Barbara kept saying, that she had never gotten this far along before, but Rose could not control her fear. A Polaroid in her slightly shaking hand, she stood at the reception desk, staring at a framed photograph of a redwood forest at dawn, the light pouring like columns through the leaves. She knew she was supposed to feel moved by the new light and new life, but instead she wanted to disappear beneath the dark mossy undergrowth. It was only when she was handed the bill, and felt such a surge of gratitude for Liddy and the comprehensive health insurance coverage provided by Oates and Associates, that she actually cried. The kindly nurses seemed relieved. One put her arm around Rose's shoulders.

"I don't know how to tell my . . . partner," Rose said, sobbing.

"He'll be delighted," the young woman replied, squeezing her arm, but she didn't understand. Rose's first instinct was to protect Peter from another loss.

Outside, the sun had bleached into a gray sky. Rose tripped carefully down the subway stairs and held her bag across her belly as the train rattled downtown. The familiar walk to the college calmed her. She bought a cup of coffee and drank half. Then she worried whether it was acceptable or not in pregnancy these days and tipped the rest down a drain, to the squawking rage of a couple of dirty pigeons who flapped away from the brown puddle and toward her booted feet. When she reached the campus, she started to run, and even though two of her favorite students waved at her from a bench beside a wall of graffiti art, she did not stop. She glanced at her watch and hoped she would catch Peter before his undergraduate seminar.

Striding along the tiled corridor toward the lecture theater, she was conscious that her footsteps made an unfamiliar noise, a sort of hollow, higher-pitched clip on every second step, which she ignored in her haste. As she turned the corner, however, she saw a large black backpack disappear inside the double doors, the student's body bent in preparation to creep to a seat as near the side as possible, and she knew she was too late. She thud-clipped over to the doors anyway and peered in, knowing that sometimes if Peter caught sight of her, he would come out. Not today. He was already in full flow, his noble profile animated as he spoke, his right hand gesticulating like an orator in a Roman amphitheater. She looked at the line of female students in the front row staring at him, rapt, and then she caught sight of herself in the glass pane of the door and noticed she had the same expression on her face.

Peter had three well-regarded academic books to his name, and he was a rigorous and exacting teacher (when he controlled his tendency toward impatience and sarcasm), but lecturing was his greatest talent. Rose, by contrast, excelled one on one; every year she found three or four students to whom she knew she could make a difference, and she did.

She turned and, before heading to her office, lifted her left foot to see that the heel of her boot had come off, leaving a hole in which a piece of well-chewed gum nestled.

Annoyed, she dropped to her knees and scanned the floor behind in a futile search for the lost piece. At this moment, a pair of expensive Italian leather shoes approached. She looked up to see the department chair, Professor Sophia Lesnar (pronounced *Laynah*, as Sophia instructed), a woman of both style and substance.

"My heel came off," said Rose.

"I hate that," said Sophia. "Do you need some help?"

"No," replied Rose, and hauled herself back on her feet.

"How are you?" asked Sophia. Rose answered economically with a murmured "Good" and smiled. Sophia's fanfared arrival from Oxford University as head of literature three years ago had been greeted with almost universal horror from her colleagues, and particular resentment from Peter, who had assumed the job would be his. But although Rose had tried to dislike her out of collegial solidarity, she could not. Sophia had proved supportive and trustworthy.

"Do you have a minute?" said Sophia briskly, and as it was not really a question, Rose nodded and followed her into the spacious corner office, avoiding the large glass wall, as the vertiginous view made her feel nauseous.

"Sit down," said Sophia, and Rose did, wincing audibly as her recently injected right buttock met the chair.

"They just sent me the cover of my new book. What do you think?"

She pushed a glossy sheet of paper across the desk and Rose lifted her glasses from the chain around her neck and examined it. It was an unmistakably derivative dark gray cover with silver beads winding around the words *Bad Boys in Books*: *From Lucifer to Christian Gray*. Rose peered closer and saw that within each bead was a picture of a hero from a novel.

"That's Heathcliff? And Mr. Rochester?" she said, and Sophia nodded. "It's brilliant, Sophia. How interesting. The development of an archetype . . . of course . . . Lucifer is by far the most interesting and romanticized character in *Paradise Lost*, the fallen angel, the devil who brings his own hell with him. And to go from there to *Fifty Shades*!"

Sophia grinned happily. "Yes, well, I thought there might be some interest in a literary investigation of why sadism is quite so sexy to some women. Not to me, I hasten to add."

"Nor me," said Rose quickly, sitting up straight, and in the process feeling the stab from her buttock again. She suppressed her whimper in case Sophia thought she had been spanked, but Sophia did not seem to have noticed.

"I mean, dominant women often have to choose a man for . . . *practical* . . . reasons," she said. (At this moment, Rose remembered seeing Sophia with her husband in Whole Foods. Her husband had been following her with the shopping cart, a baby in a papoose strapped across him, as Sophia instructed him to ensure the papayas were ripe.) "But the fantasy is always Rhett Butler, right?"

"Mmm," replied Rose noncommittally.

"It's not exactly groundbreaking," Sophia continued. "But I'm on PBS tomorrow to discuss why type-A females enjoy submission, and that'll be good for the department."

Sophia glanced out the window for a moment, and then moved seamlessly to a not entirely unrelated topic. "I read the interview with Peter's ex"—*Here we go*, thought Rose—"she sounds terrifying. But we all know with her schedule she must be on the edge of a nervous breakdown."

Now she glanced at the photo of her three small children pinned on a corkboard next to a printout of her Outlook Express calendar detailing a comprehensive program of after-school activities, revision schedules, and meal planning.

"I don't know why I said that. All of us with kids and a job are hovering on the edge of a nervous breakdown, right?"

Rose was unsure how to respond to this, so she changed the subject. "Well done on the book. I'm sure it will do really well."

"Rose, you are without doubt one of the nicest women I have ever met." Sophia stopped as there was a sudden awkward catch in her throat. "And one of the best teachers . . ."

Rose looked away, as was her custom when complimented, and waited for Sophia to finish. She didn't, and when Rose looked back there was an expression on Sophia's face that Rose had never seen before.

"This is a nightmare, so I'm going to say it quickly. You've met the new provost, haven't you?"

Rose nodded yes. He had seemed a charming, avuncular man who had made a great fuss of Peter at the champagne welcome reception.

"He's instructed the faculty promotions committee to make the process of renewing senior lectureships and off-ladder faculty more rigorous. Your contract is up at the end of next semester, Rose, and they are going to expect a publishing record." She pulled open her desk and withdrew a tatty brown file with Rose's name scribbled across the top. "You've been here twenty years, I know, and you have one of the consistently highest student ratings in the entire college, but tell me you're working on something right now, because the last article you wrote was seven years ago. Why?"

Because I got together with Peter, and he was writing his book, and then Matty came to live with us and the whirl of meals and homework and playdates began and I didn't want him to go to camp every vacation and the next time I looked up five years had gone by and it's always past ten o'clock by the time I've nagged him into bed at night and I'm too tired and it's as much as I can do to keep up with the course work and in six months I could be dealing with something bigger than all of this put together and I don't want to be like you, hovering on the edge of a nervous breakdown every day, or like Liddy with her fleet of staff and no personal life, and I'm happy with everything as it is . . . or was . . . or . . .

Rose said nothing. Sophia reached over and patted her hand and Rose noticed that Sophia's fingers were slender and elegant and she wore a beautiful ring of pewter and amber on her right forefinger.

"This is what we're going to do. You're going to write a few thousand words of something before the end of the summer and I will pull every string I have to get it in print. I don't want to lose you and I'm sure you don't want to lose your job. Okay?"

"Thank you," said Rose, relieved finally to stand up.

"You know what my father used to say to me. Don't let the bastards get you down."

And with that Sophia started checking her e-mails and Rose walked to her own office, wondering as to which bastards Sophia was referring.

Finally safe among her own things, Rose knew she must consider the numerous "ifs" and "buts" of her current situation but found it almost impossible to concentrate. Thinking it might be her disproportionate irritation at the loss of her heel, she took her boots off, stuffed them in the bottom of a cupboard, and put on the pair of unworn sneakers that still nestled beside the filing cabinet from the year she had foolishly attempted to take up cross training.

This did not work. The strands of her thoughts ricocheted from subject to subject and knotted themselves around the unknown. Of course she should write the article for Sophia—drink Red Bull, stay up late—and keep her job, but what if the pregnancy actually went to term?

Suddenly her heart leapt. She would have two children!

She went over to her shelves and ran her hands along the spines of the books that had always been as close as friends to her. She greeted *Little Women* and *Little House on the Prairie* and thought how those stories had shaped her ideal of what a family could be: a group of loving, energetic kids, doting Marmee, and wise and reliable Pa. She felt euphoric. But she would be a forty-six-year-old new mother with a teenage stepson and a nearly sixty-year-old partner. It was time to get real. How could she keep working outside the home? Even *thinking* it made her feel exhausted.

"You were looking for me, my love. What's up?" Peter had come into the office without knocking. He looked pale and weak, as he always did after his classes, and Rose remembered with a jolt that he could hardly fix a door hinge in a brownstone in Carroll Gardens, let alone build a log cabin in Minnesota.

"Sophia says my position won't be renewed unless I publish something this year."

Peter flinched and Rose knew she had made a mistake. In her excitement, she had said the wrong thing first. He turned his back to her and stared out the tiny window at the staff parking lot.

"I've been warning you about this for ages, Rose. For God's sake, when I met you I told you to start writing something or you'd never get on tenure track. They need to make cuts and this place is full of young adjuncts who teach *and* publish. I don't trust that awful woman, with her media-friendly theses straight out of popular fiction masquerading as scholarship. And neither should you."

"I do trust her, actually," said Rose. "She says it'll be all right if I deliver something in the summer, but—"

"That's good," he said quickly. "And of course she'll want to keep you."

"I hope so. Listen, there's something else I have to tell you."

She smiled and took his hand. She linked her fingers through his.

"We're pregnant."

"*What?*"

"I know," she said, "it's insane, isn't it? I don't even know how to feel about it. How do you feel about it?"

"Surprised," said Peter, before smiling, "but delighted," and he stepped forward and took her in his arms. He said nothing more, however, and a tiny muscle in his cheek twitched as she pressed her face against his.

Henry James would have written a sentence two pages in

length describing how the reverberations of Peter's physiognomy reflected his feelings about her announcement, but Rose was conscious only of his silence.

Matty took the news of the impending arrival of another half-sibling like a man. He even agreed to be sworn to secrecy, but one month later, after positive blood and nuchal tests, he overheard Rose telling her brother on the phone and so let it slip to Liddy when she called him that night to check he had done his homework. Liddy's immediate response was to be glad for Rose. She knew well what the desperate longing for a child felt like, and she welcomed the advent of a new life. But then came the irrational sob from deep within her of *I will never be pregnant again*, which she silenced first with vague annoyance that she was not considered important enough to have been part of the subterfuge, and next with specific annoyance at Peter. Liddy asked Matty to hand the phone over to his father, on the pretext of congratulations, and then asked Peter outright how long he and Rose had been trying for a baby.

Although Peter wanted to tell her to mind her own business—*entente* between them had not recovered to anything like *cordiale*—he decided to tell her the truth, which was that the baby was a surprise (to others he said "a shock," although never to anyone who might repeat it to Rose), and Liddy certainly was surprised. Afterward, Peter wished he had lied, told Liddy that in his advancing years he had become desperate to have another child, because he still wanted to hurt her if he could and he knew she would find that upsetting for reasons he had never told Rose. He would have been gratified to learn that, even with no lying, Liddy was hurt *and* upset, despite having no right to be.

The following Wednesday, as had become the custom, Liddy arrived at Carroll Gardens with Cal for a "family" dinner. One evening, a couple of years before, Liddy had appeared at the door to pick Matty up so giddy with multitasking that Rose feared she would faint and so invited her in to share yesterday's leftover meat loaf. This evolved into Rose cooking for all of them once a week, and the two women found they enjoyed it. Peter found reasons to schedule seminars, interdepartmental working groups, and additional office hours on Wednesday nights from then on.

In fact, his absence allowed an ease to their interaction; there were no off-limit subjects, no phrases of Liddy's that Rose felt put his teeth on edge (at the beginning whenever Liddy smiled Peter winced like he had been pinched), and while they could not allow themselves to be proper friends, something Liddy was extremely out of practice at anyway, they had found a way of coexisting that was genuinely good for the children. Liddy always made an ostentatious display of switching off her phone, the signal for quality time, and they would sit together chatting companionably at the kitchen table.

This evening, as Liddy and Rose picked bits of skin off a chicken carcass, Cal dozed on some cushions clutching his threadbare cuddly kangaroo and Matty sat at the computer in the library researching his project on the Civil War. Because she was now nearly four months gone, Rose allowed Liddy to clean up, although it was clear that Liddy had only offered to be polite. It had been a long time since Liddy had wiped down a greasy sink, and Rose had to mask her irritation at the flicking of bleach wipes over the stainless steel by moving to the enormous couch and collapsing onto it.

"*Mom!*" called Matty from the library, and although Rose started, it was Liddy, of course, who headed toward the pocket doors.

"Did you know that seven and a half percent of the soldiers in the Civil War were Irish?"

"I didn't know the exact number," said Liddy from the doorway, "but I did know that one-third of the soldiers in the Union Army were immigrants, more Germans than Irish, in fact, and one in ten . . . I think . . . were African Americans."

"I'll check that," he said, to Liddy's approval, and she watched him admiringly as he typed quickly on the keyboard. She did not walk into the room, however. It was the one room in the house she still could not bear to go into.

Every time Liddy walked through the front door, she marveled at how comfortable Rose seemed to be living among the evidence of Peter's former life. Tonight, in the hallway, Liddy had tripped over the vintage Tony Hawk skateboard she had given Peter one Christmas; opened a drawer in the kitchen and found a couple of Post-it notes in her own handwriting; and now she was looking at a photograph of herself in the hospital with newborn Matty, still on a bookcase in a silver frame her secretary had given them as a wedding present.

Liddy would have dumped all these things into the garbage.

"How do you spell *secession*, Mom?" asked Matty.

"One *c*, two *s*'s," said Liddy, glancing over at Rose, who nodded. Then she came back to the kitchen, to discuss her plans for her second, potentially best-selling, book.

"So this is the outline," she was saying, gingerly scraping bits of potato out of the sink and peering into the drain as if unsure what might lie beneath. "It's called *How to Break Up without F**king Them Up: A Divorce Lawyer's Guide to Successful Co-Parenting*. What do you think?" Liddy genuinely wanted to know. She intended to take advantage of Rose's considerable editing skills.

"Sounds good," replied Rose carefully. "It's memorable and witty." *And Peter's gonna go CRAZY!* she thought, but decided to keep quiet and listen as this promised to be a particularly fascinating conversation, especially if this book followed the format of the first and juxtaposed practical advice with personal experiences.

"I've got all the headings for the chapters. The first one is 'Family Is Still Family'—have dinner together once a week, like we do—"

The expression on Rose's face stopped her.

"What?" Liddy's right foot was tapping impatiently on the stone tiles.

"That wouldn't work for everyone," Rose said, unconvinced.

"Okay, I'll put *month*, right? Family dinner once a month—"

"As long as no one starts shouting . . ." said Rose firmly, turning to tuck a blanket around Cal. He stirred awake.

"What did you do at school today?" she said.

"We had a field trip to the Museum of Natural History. I dissected a frog."

"Gross!" came Matty's voice from the other room.

"I didn't mind," said Cal calmly. "I liked to see where all the bits went."

"Surgeon!" whispered Liddy happily. Then she scribbled a note on the page. "I've said meet at a restaurant."

Rose smiled. She leaned over and kissed Cal on the forehead and he wrapped his skinny arms around her neck. The touch of his soft skin reminded her of a dream she had once had in which Liddy was killed in a car crash and she and Peter had adopted Cal. When she had juddered awake, she had been aware only of a feeling of pure maternal love, and because Rose did do guilt, she had then been appalled by the workings of her subconscious.

Meanwhile, Liddy had remembered something. "I went on a date last week."

This was not unusual. For the last two years, Liddy had gone on the occasional first date, but as they never progressed to a second, Rose had a suspicion Liddy only did it to keep up appearances.

"That's great, Liddy. Who is he?"

"He bought the apartment below me last year. Lloyd Fosco. He's an actor on television. Pretty successful, I think, judging from the financial statement he gave the co-op. He's big, and hairy, and a bit younger than me . . . but he is attractive."

This was unusual. Normally Liddy was set up by work colleagues. Meeting newly single people was a perk of their job.

"What's he in?" she asked. Rose had never heard of him, but that meant nothing. Peter did not believe in watching television, so her viewing opportunities were severely curtailed.

"I can't remember the name," replied Liddy. "It's some huge series set in a hospital. I really must catch up with it if we go out again. I can't tell him I only watch PBS, the E! network, and Rachel Maddow."

"I love Rachel Maddow," said Rose.

"So do I," said Liddy. "In fact, Rachel is my imaginary friend. Sometimes when she's on, I close my eyes and I pretend she's sitting in the chair beside me making me laugh."

Rose quickly returned to the subject of Lloyd Fosco and the date. "How did it go?"

"Okay, I think. We had drinks and he wants to see me again. He's booking dinner. He says he wants to talk."

"He wants to get to know you. That's good," said Rose. "Just be careful, because if it all goes wrong you can't hide from him. He lives in the building."

"Oh, I've thought about that," said Liddy seriously. "I persuaded the doorman to give me a key to the service elevator. Now . . . chapter two. Remember to enjoy the time you have with your kids, i.e., don't waste it droning on about table manners or homework. Ask them questions. How was *your* day? What do *you* think about climate change?"

Liddy continued in her positive pitching tone, while ineffectually lifting things in the kitchen and moving them from one place to another, which she called tidying.

"Liddy. I think table manners and homework are quite important."

"*Pfft* . . ." said Liddy, the distinctive noise she made when questioned. "You know what I mean. No child wants to come through the door after a long day and be harangued about music practice. It's dull and a surefire way to make them resent you. It goes for adults too. I honestly believe that at least half the divorces I do are because someone got bored."

Rose closed her eyes as an unexpected wave of nausea overwhelmed her. If Liddy was right, it was clear her own relationship was doomed. She had had a conversation with Peter the previous week about childproofing the house, during which he had fallen asleep.

"Three. Discuss money, politics, and/or religion with your children, but do not denigrate your ex's point of view. Even if it's why you separated."

Thank goodness, thought Rose, *Peter and I never argue about those things.* And it was true. As career academics in liberal arts living in New York City, they both shared the same measured, careful (or "penny-pinching," as Liddy had once referred to it) outlook and were committed to recycling, the Democrats, and godlessness.

"Then for tip number four I have to do something about 'communication,' but I've got my own twist on that. Sometimes decisions have to be unilateral. You can't hide behind the other parent once you've split. Or even if you haven't, frankly. Parenting can be a lonely business whatever your situation.There are things you just have to get on with."

Rose was not sure now how helpful this book would be to anyone. It seemed to be turning into a Vindication of the Rights of Liddy. Rose lifted her right hand and examined her nails. Pregnancy had made them weak and split-y.

"Rose, I'm feeling good," Liddy said, smiling happily. "This stuff is beginning to write itself."

"Lucky you," said Rose, and when Liddy asked her what she meant, she told her about Professor Sophia Lesnar and the situation at work, and that even thinking about it made her feel queasy.

"Don't worry," Liddy replied briskly. "It's good timing, actually. You'll have to go to bed early every night, so you can put your laptop on a tray and bash the article out over your bump."

Rose, suddenly ill, felt unable to take on Liddy one on one, exactly like Corinthia Jordan in the Style section. Of course Liddy would find a way to fit extra work in during pregnancy, in the same way that she viewed a colonoscopy as an opportunity for weight loss.

"Would you make me a cup of tea, Liddy? I'm not feeling well."

She shivered, and Liddy stopped being sententious and became solicitous.

"Do you need a doctor?" she said calmly, pulling her cardigan off and wrapping it around Rose's shoulders.

"No," said Rose, shaking her head vigorously, and motioning

for Liddy to carry on and fill the kettle, but a sudden pain in her belly overtook her and her hands clenched white over it and she cried out to Liddy, who knew the time for keeping calm was over.

Liddy immediately called Vince, her driver, and got Rose and the boys into the car. Within ten minutes they were at University Hospital, where Barbara, too tense for tears, ran over to them and took Rose down a corridor on a trolley, but not before Rose clutched Liddy's hand and said, "Pray for a miracle, Liddy, I used all mine up," and Liddy kissed her forehead and did.

For He said, Liddy whispered, *I tell you the truth, if you have faith as small as a mustard seed, you can say to this mountain, "Move from there to here," and it will move. Nothing will be impossible for you.*

And then Liddy became aware of a high-pitched sniveling beside her and she turned to see Cal sobbing and crying out for Mr. Oz, the cuddly kangaroo he had left at Carroll Gardens, and Matty juddering with the force of his emotions, repeating, "What's happening? What's happening? Is the baby going to die?" and when Liddy did not say anything, just reached her hand out to touch his face to calm him, he told her to get OFF and hit her arm away so hard she yelped, *"Matty! Don't do that!"* and shook her hand, which hurt, but he looked up straight into her face, fearless.

"I'll do as I please," he said, and walked over to the drinks machine, truculently scrabbling for change in his pockets as Liddy stood still, impotent, frozen first by the look on her elder son's face and then by embarrassment, as at least six people, including two health professionals, had witnessed the exchange.

At this moment, Peter burst through the glass doors and ran toward her.

"Where's Rose?" he asked.

"They took her off down there. Barbara's with her," she said, and without thinking they embraced, and for a long moment all the enmity between them disappeared and they dissolved into each other's bodies in the way that only once-lovers can do. Peter pulled away first.

"Thank you, Liddy, thank you for getting her here."

"I'm so sorry, Peter . . ." she began, but he had walked away as Matty silently linked his arm in his father's and the two of them headed up the corridor, searching.

Left behind, Liddy felt Cal's body wrapped around her leg, and grateful for his compliance, she lifted him into her arms and they sat down together, her promising to send Vince back for Mr. Oz. There were still tears on Cal's face, so she stuck her hand into the bottom of her purse searching for a tissue and pulled out the yellowing linen handkerchief Sebastian Stackallan had handed her almost three months ago and that she had not thrown away, though now she wished she had. It was a vivid and unpleasant reminder of another scene that had not played out according to Liddy's approved script, and a sudden and unwanted vision of Stackallan appeared in front of her now—his arrogant smile, the way he tilted his head as he prepared to make an argument, the fact that you could never tell from his tone of voice whether he was about to be nice or nasty. She shuddered and stuffed the handkerchief back beneath a stale and squashed York Pepppermint Pattie, and wiped Cal's face with her sweater instead.

She looked up. Barbara had reappeared, smiling thinly, but it was a real smile, and the news was good. It had all been very frightening and there had been some bleeding, but the baby was fine—so far. And the two women felt an urge to embrace, yet made the same decision to quell it. So instead they walked into the side ward together, Cal between them, Barbara unable to resist having a quick look at Liddy to see if she showed any evidence of the Vampire Facial around her cheekbones.

Peter and Matty were lying on either side of Rose, Peter on the right, his face buried in her hair, and Matty on the left, his arms wrapped tightly around hers, his head against her shoulder, eyes closed, smiling, so content that for a moment Liddy did not recognize him. Barbara sat down on the end of the bed and told them that Rose had gestational hypertension and that she must stay in the hospital for at least a week. Then, if her condition stabilized, the obstetric team would allow her home for bed rest for the next five months.

"Bed rest?" said Rose weakly. "That's like something out of *Gone With the Wind*. What does it mean?"

"It means bed rest, my love," replied Peter, "where you lie in bed, day and night."

"But I have to go to work," said Rose, gripping his forearm. "My job's on the line."

"For God's sake, forget about that!"

"What about income protection?" asked Liddy.

"It doesn't cover pregnancy," said Peter, in the weary voice of someone who had waged innumerable unsuccessful wars against the university's Human Resources Department.

"Bullshit! This isn't about normal pregnancy. Look at the state of her," said Liddy, typically straightforward. "I want her contract couriered to my office tomorrow. In the meantime, I'll call them first thing and tell them I'm her lawyer."

"Thank you, Liddy," said Rose.

Liddy leaned over to her and stroked Rose's hair from her forehead. "If there's any trouble they can get ready for one of my *special* letters," she whispered.

Barbara grinned and turned to Peter.

"Rose really mustn't leave the house. You'll have to look after her."

"I'll look after her," said Matty bravely, but Peter shook his head and stood up.

"No, son." And then he looked at Liddy, who nodded.

"Matty, you're going to move in with me for a while," she said.

There was a long silence.

Barbara got up and kissed everyone good night, including Liddy by accident, and those left around the bed all looked at each other as the clip of her heels disappeared down the corridor.

Liddy made an awkward stretching movement with her arms.

"I guess we'll head off then. Cal. Matty." She looked at Peter. "I'll get Vince to drop over tomorrow for Matty's stuff."

"But I want Mr. Oz *now!*" said Cal.

"Don't bother," said Matty. "I'm not going."

"Matty . . ." warned Peter.

"You can't make me, Dad. I'm staying with you and Rose."

"No, you're not," said Liddy, her tone beginning to take on an adversarial note. "Your father and I have joint custody of you and we worked out an arrangement in your best interests. Now that's going to change—"

"Don't be so smug!" the boy shouted furiously. *"You think you can make everyone do what you want but you can't. I have rights!"*

Liddy felt a white-hot wave of rage engulf her now, and a dismaying urge to lift the hand he had bruised and strike him pulsed through her. She managed to take a breath.

"I am going to the car now. Peter, I expect you to tell our son to join me."

And she looked away, as she could see Peter was about to cry.

"Matty, sweetheart," said Rose softly, "I love you so much, but you must see that your dad and I can't look after you properly for a little while. So you have to do this for me, so I won't be worried about you."

Rose gestured for him to come close and she hugged him and stroked his hair. And now a kindly nurse appeared to check on Rose and, smiling at Matty who was lying in Rose's arms, turned to everyone and said, "Now there's a boy who loves his mother."

Peter gently helped Matty away from Rose, and Rose was grateful that the nurse bustled around her, sticking a thermometer in her mouth, pouring her more water, as she did not wish to dwell upon the expression she had just glimpsed on Liddy's face. She was suddenly gripped by an uncomfortable feeling that Barbara was right and the cruel fates were just getting started with Liddy.

And Liddy, the real Liddy, felt something, too, the funny feeling again that brought tears to her eyes and made her vulnerable and careless. She took a deep breath and counted to five. She lifted her phone to summon assistance.

Matty refused to get out of the car and the only person he would talk to was Vince, so Liddy left them together in earnest debate about WWE, as she and Cal ran back into the house in Carroll Gardens in search of Mr. Oz. They found him under the cushion with the red wine stain from the faculty party Liddy had hosted in 2006, and this made Liddy shudder. Tonight she had learned that the house haunted her, not Rose, and the reason Rose had never changed the furniture or painted the walls in a different color, Rose Garden Pink as Liddy had suggested, was because she did not care about such things.

Everything in it that mattered had become hers.

Quality time is as important as quantity time, the child psychologist had said, and whenever Liddy parroted that to her clients (often when arguing for Skype access or, as she preferred to say, "virtual visitation"), she was emboldened by the fact that no one could accuse her of not practicing what she preached.

Up to now, she had even believed it.

But as she looked at Matty's back, hunched over, his shoulder blades jutting out of his black hoodie, rigid with an emotion that she knew would have unpleasant repercussions for her, it dawned on her that *she* had become Mom2, and her role in his life was to enjoy the compliments from waiting staff about his good behavior in restaurants, work ceaselessly to provide the lifestyle he had grown accustomed to, and nag him occasionally about his math results. *How had that happened?* She had sacrificed so much for him.

Liddy closed her eyes. She was well aware what military organization, no social life, and working late had brought her. She was a grown-up. She had made choices. And she was allergic to the whining of the privileged, or any form of self-pitying introspection, particularly her own. No, she could not think about anything now, it would drive her crazy. She decided she would think about it tomorrow.

As they turned onto Hudson Street, she finally remembered to switch on her phone and was greeted by a fanfare of pinging messages. She scrolled through quickly, ignoring all but the four from Curtis Oates, as the car pulled up outside her building. Mark the doorman came out, greeting Matty enthusiastically. But Matty ignored him and Liddy's humiliation continued. She hurried into the lobby—she had noticed Lloyd Fosco, languid in black, in front of the furniture shop opposite and did not want to discuss a dinner date in front of an audience—and Mark lifted a sleeping Cal out of the backseat and carried him inside. In the elevator, Matty started singing a song too loudly, rocking backward and forward and thumping his forehead against the steel wall every two beats, so Liddy made strained small talk about the weather until the doors opened at her apartment. She overtipped Mark so he might still like her, despite the rude, not to mention disturbing, behavior of her elder child.

Liddy hurried the boys into the perfectly proportioned white living space and escaped out of the darkness with relief. She turned and locked the apartment door behind them and for the first time in several hours felt safe. The irreplaceable Lucia was waiting in the kitchen, a plate of sandwiches, mugs of hot chocolate, and a large glass of merlot reassuringly at the ready. Cal sleepwalked into Lucia's open arms and they headed into his bedroom. Matty sat and ate with morose intent. Liddy took a large gulp of wine and checked her e-mails. Then Lucia returned and, with an affectionate pat on Matty's back, chivied him toward the shower. Liddy looked for the dog. She saw a small puddle of liquid on the stripped oak floor.

Oh, no, Coco! She cursed silently but said nothing. She had left a note for Lucia reminding her to take the dog out at least four times a day, but Lucia was unsentimental about animal welfare and strongly disapproved of keeping animals in the city, so Liddy knew this was some sort of statement.

She grabbed a roll of paper towels and scurried over, but as she knelt down, she felt a sudden splash on the back of her neck. She looked up. A drip fell onto her face. She picked up a vase of yellow roses and stuck it under the slow stream, but before she could even ponder the implications of water leaking through the walls or ceiling or an exposed pipe, which the architect had left as an interior feature, she heard a displeased shriek from Cal.

She ran into the bedroom where Cal was standing on the bed pointing at the floor. Her nose wrinkled at the sweet, acrid smell that greeted her. She knew it could mean only one thing. Her shoe sunk into a yellow-green turd that the dog had deposited beside the door. This time her curse was not silent.

She seized the canister of instant pet trainer, a device that shoots compressed air in the direction of an errant animal in order to discipline it, and one of which she had placed in every room in order to house-train this four-legged impulse purchase she had bought on Christopher Street when Cal pleaded. Liddy sprayed it vigorously, the loud hissing causing Cal to cry out but Coco only to yap cutely and scrabble away. She took off her shoe gingerly and took another handful of paper towels to clean up the mess from shoe and floor. She vowed that if the animal ever crapped on the cream carpet at the foot of her bed, she would pay someone to make it disappear and tell Cal it was run over. She suspected he would not even notice.

She tucked Cal into bed and came out to find Matty, the dog clutched in his arms, hot chocolate splattered around his mouth, standing in the doorway of his room staring at her. For one moment she thought, *Maybe this is conciliatory? Maybe he's decided he wants to be here?*

"What about my lunch tomorrow?" he said.

"You're on the meal plan," said Liddy.

He rolled his eyes contemptuously, put the dog down, and pointed to his chin.

"I don't eat processed foods anymore. Doctor Barbara said it might help my skin."

"What?"

"Look at my face! It's repulsive."

Liddy peered. Yes, there was a cluster of tiny pimples.

"Oh, I can hardly see them, but, okay, we'll stop at Subway on the way to school and buy something."

"I told you I'm not eating processed foods. Rose makes me a salad every night. I like quinoa—"

"That's enough. Don't wake Cal. Go to bed."

"Of course. *Don't wake Cal!*"

He turned and slammed his door behind him.

"And brush your teeth!" shouted Liddy, although by now she didn't care whether he did or not. She took a breath.

"Good night. I love you," she said.

"Good night to you, too!" he shouted back and Liddy fired off another *hiss* of pet trainer, although she knew that it had no effect whatsoever on a teenage boy.

She turned to see Lucia silently wrapping the untouched sandwiches in foil. Lucia held views about everything, from the Affordable Care Act to Beyoncé, and always shared them. But not tonight.

"I'm sorry, Lucia," said Liddy. "Thank you for coming over. I know it's very late."

Lucia nodded but did not reply. Liddy knew well that the emphatic manner in which she moved from fridge to kitchen counter was another sort of statement, in the same way as the quiet refusal to walk the dog.

"I'd be lost without you, you know," said Liddy. She could not bear Lucia's disapproval.

Lucia nodded. "You need to go to bed, Liddy. Two boys and a dirty dog. It's a lot."

Suddenly Liddy's phone rang. It was Curtis, with the admonishing tone he always took when he could not get hold of her exactly when he wanted. He asked her where she'd been, and when she said the hospital he ignored this and told her he was summoning the partners for a breakfast meeting at seven a.m. the following morning.

Liddy looked over at Lucia, who was packing up her bag in time to the steady metronome-like plopping of the water into the vase on the floor.

She braced herself to start begging.

Rose, finally alone but kept awake in the dark by the various snores and snuffles and soft footsteps of the ward, closed her eyes and imagined herself back home, where she longed to be and where, from her bedroom window, she would admire the blue and white ceramic tiles she had plastered onto the garden wall and inspect the fig tree.

When Liddy and Peter had bought the house, one of their neighbors was an elderly Sicilian man named Giovanni Matisi, who had three fig trees, and at night, lying in each others arms by candlelight, they would listen to him singing to the trees in Italian. Charmed by Liddy, whose beauty in those days could inspire poetry, Giovanni presented them with one of the trees in an earthenware pot tied with a red ribbon, and every year after that they enjoyed the late summer bounty of fresh figs and the sight of Matty toddling around on chubby legs and stuffing the plump, juicy fruit in his mouth and laughing.

Liddy loved the tree and Giovanni, and whenever Rose looked at it she was reminded that Liddy was a romantic at heart; Peter might choose not to remember now, but he had once told her the whole story and added that when Giovanni died Liddy had wept inconsolably, and every year sent a present to each one of his grandchildren now scattered along the East Coast.

When Liddy left, Peter ignored the fig tree (although he had refused to let her take it, likely because it was the only thing she had wanted), and when Rose moved in it looked shriveled and dark and almost certainly dead. But that winter Rose wrapped it in an old quilt, and even sung arias to it when she was alone in the little garden tending her lavender and rosemary, and that spring it bloomed, and then bloomed again, more than ever before.

Every summer from then on, Rose secretly sent Liddy a small basket of figs.

Neither of them ever mentioned it.

ANCIENT, AND SECRET, HISTORY

Lydia Mary Murphy met Peter James at a storytelling salon in the Cornelia Street Café when she was twenty-five years old and impatient for the next chapter of her life to begin.

She had arrived in the city in triumph six months earlier, her choice to study law in graduate school vindicated by the competing bids to employ her from every firm to which she had applied. "Rosedale and Seldon is lucky to have you," said Marisa Seldon, managing partner, who became, if not exactly a role model, at least a mentor for Liddy, and encouraged her to pursue her career goals in her own way. For, after all, Liddy had achieved all this with no family connections, an undergraduate degree in art history, and summers spent working not in unpaid resumé-enhancing internships but on the production line of a plastics factory.

In her interview, Marisa had asked Liddy why she had chosen the noble profession. Liddy had looked her straight in the eye and said, "Because of the money." When Marisa grinned, Liddy had added, "And because I want to be like Grace Van Owen in *L.A. Law.*"

Then she told Marisa about Miss Gwendolyn Harris, the teacher in eighth grade who had changed her life. Marisa listened, but she was not surprised. She knew from experience that for people like Liddy, there was always a teacher.

Miss Harris was in her midthirties, wore long suede skirts over her boots, tribal jewelry around her neck, and had long snaky blond hair like a benign Medusa. She had a boyfriend who was a musician, and occasionally he arrived on his motorbike, his guitar case strapped to the back, to pick her up after school. She would hike up her suede skirt, pull her helmet over her tresses, and clamber on behind him as he roared away.

This was an extraordinary sight outside the Sacred Heart High School.

Liddy's mother, Breda Murphy, who was also in her midthirties, wore tan hosiery, used hairspray, and sat in the front seat of her father Patrick's rusty Chevy. Breda disliked and distrusted Gwendolyn Harris, but it made no difference. Miss Harris showed fourteen-year-old Lydia Mary that there was more than one way of being a woman.

Lydia Mary followed Miss Harris around the school whenever she could and sometimes, at recess, Miss Harris would talk to her.

It doesn't matter who you are, Liddy, Miss Harris would announce (for it was she who had first called Lydia Mary by that name), *you are allowed to be successful*. Then she would add, *As long as you work ten times harder than any man in the same job!* (This was one of Miss Harris's favorite statements. The other was *A woman needs a man like a fish needs a bicycle*, which Liddy laughed at on cue, although she didn't understand it.)

That year was the year Liddy discovered that working harder than anyone else was one of her *things*.

At night in bed, she would pull the blankets over her head and practice her signature, which seemed an important part of her future, although she never found a way of writing *Murphy* that she liked. She fantasized that one day Miss Harris might invite her to live with her. They would read books about art together, and visit the museums in New York City, which Miss Harris said was the most wonderful place in the world. Miss Harris told Liddy that artists did not choose their subjects, their subjects chose them. She taught Liddy to see the stories hidden within pictures.

(Later in life, when family law had chosen Liddy, this skill served her well; she would find trust funds for illegitimate children concealed in the elaborate footnotes of prenuptial agreements, she soon knew more than most people should about off-shore accounts in Antigua, and she could sniff a bigamous marriage like napalm in the morning.)

But all this she kept a secret from her parents. She had to. Patrick and Breda Murphy had used all their courage to get themselves across the ocean and there was none left over for her. And how do you tell the two people who made you that your only dream as a child is for a different life than the one you have been born into?

"They must be very proud of you, though," said Marisa, but Liddy had said nothing, because she had not known what to say.

She had not yet learned how to make a complicated situation look simple.

Liddy had taken to her profession like a swan to water. Her formidable memory and physical stamina got her through the study and the seventy-hour weeks as an associate (for years she had worked night shifts mopping floors with disinfectant so strong it make her gag; hours spent fact checking in an air-conditioned office felt like a vacation). She took her first month's paycheck to Soho and, in the window of a gallery, saw a limited-edition print of an industrial landscape by Alfred Stieglitz, a framed black-and-white photograph of New York in 1910, the new skyscrapers rising over choppy gray water and smoke rising into the clouds. She paid too much for it, but she didn't care. It was called *City of Ambition* and it seemed the perfect image with which to start her new life.

No one had told Liddy that *nice women* never use the A-word.

Marisa's primary piece of advice to Liddy was to avoid the distractions and dramas of dating, particularly the dreaded office romances that had derailed far too many young women in her employ, and to focus on one partnership only.

"Don't marry another lawyer," she commanded Liddy, with a confidence born of the fact that she had herself married late, to a retired and wealthy entrepreneur, efficiently producing twins nine months later. "They'll always put their cases first, and if you have kids, you'll be the one doing the school run."

That night in Cornelia Street Liddy arrived with a man known as Intense Rafe, a part-time artist and full-time waiter, with whom she had been set up the previous month by her roommate.

A story about ginseng picking in Appalachia, told by an enthusiastic woman with black corkscrew curls and a Hole T-shirt, was ending to considerable applause and the woman bowed happily, lifting her hand and pointing it in Liddy's direction. As Liddy had the anterior vision of a flying spider, she sensed the movement early, and with no tale to tell, she hid behind Intense Rafe, ensuring that it was another man directly in front of her who was summoned to the little space in front of the microphone. Liddy, her chin perched on Rafe's intensely bony shoulder, watched the man saunter up and tap on the microphone.

"My name is Peter James," he said.

"Professor Peter James!" called out the very pretty young woman who had accompanied him.

Peter smiled and began to speak. His story was fluent and involving, but Liddy did not really listen. She looked at him instead.

With his messy, sandy-blond hair, his threadbare cords, and frayed Ralph Lauren shirt, Professor Peter James was shabby chic before anyone had ever thought of it; he combined this agreeably masculine disregard for grooming with the self-confidence and self-deprecation of a man who had achieved his career goals with ease.

This interested her.

Liddy guessed he was in his late thirties. He had no wedding ring on his finger, though she imagined he might be the kind of man who would not wear one, and as she looked around the room she knew she was not the only female to find him attractive. The very pretty young woman was hanging on his every word, and when he had finished she led the applause. But Peter did not hurry back to her, allowing himself to be waylaid at the bar by a tall and glamorous Slavic model in a fur hat.

Liddy spotted an opportunity. She headed over, introduced herself to both of them, and participated in their sparkling dialogue, even making a couple of jokes that caused Peter to laugh out loud. When the fur-hatted model turned away to order more drinks, Liddy looked right into Peter's eyes and handed him her business card, suggesting he call her for a date. It was the first time in her life she had ever done such a thing, she announced, confident that he would be as thrilled at her chutzpah and sophistication as she was, and that he would find her irresistible.

He didn't.

She asked around and discovered he was a well-respected professor of literature at a prestigious university downtown. She started reading *War and Peace*. Every time the phone in her office buzzed for the next two weeks, Liddy expected it to be him.

It wasn't.

She was forced to accept that Peter James had not felt the same inciting pulse of attraction as she had, and had chucked out her card with a scrunched-up tissue from the bottom of his jacket pocket. Or he had forgotten about it and the dry cleaners had done so. (Later on, Liddy would learn that Peter was content with a life that was not plot driven. He was a bit lazy about most things apart from work, but because he was good-looking and quite brilliant, people found it charming. Except for women who dated him, that is.)

This did not suit her version of the narrative at all.

It took one phone call to a private detective on retainer at Rosedale and Seldon to get his address (the Village), marital status (single!), and criminal record (none), and despite the intoxicating feeling of self-loathing this induced, Liddy began walking down his street at every opportunity, even if it meant taking detours on the crosstown train. But still she did not "bump into" him.

And then . . .

Exactly two months later, on a sublime Saturday morning Liddy, soggy with sweat, was walking home to Murray Hill from her early step class on Sixth Avenue. She had a large cup of coffee in one hand and an enormous almond croissant in the other, and for no other reason than the sun was shining and she was young and exhilarated from exercise and life, she decided to throw the dice once more and headed toward Bedford Street. She paused for the umpteenth time outside the narrow house, number 75½, and pretended to read the red plaque about Edna St. Vincent Millay. And this day the door of the town house beside it opened.

"Hello," said the man who emerged. In those days, Peter always said hello when he chanced upon a young woman in tight clothing.

Liddy turned around. They stared at each other.

"I know you. You're the girl from the other . . ." he said. Then he paused. "Are you stalking me?" he asked.

Liddy snorted in a "that's the most ridiculous thing I ever heard" way. She was convincing, just as she had practiced. "*Huh*. Don't kid yourself, Professor James. You must have read enough novels to believe in coincidence."

She turned quickly and walked away, her heart seeming to thump louder than her footsteps on the pavement. She accelerated as she approached the corner, but she did not run, as she did not want to spill her coffee over herself and ruin the nonchalant effect.

"*Hey!*"

She was stopped abruptly by the pressure of a hand on her right shoulder. The coffee spilled down her front anyway.

"*Shit!*" she howled and, embarrassed, she did not move, so Peter James walked around in front of her.

"The readers of Victorian novels viewed coincidence as meaningful providence," he said, smiling. "What you or I would call destiny."

"I don't believe in that," said Liddy, wiping her chest with her sleeve. "I believe we make our lives through force of will."

She did not smile. She was thrilled but wary. She did not know if she would be found resistible again.

"How old are you?" he said, staring hard into her face.

"Twenty-five. How old are you?"

"I will be thirty-eight next week."

"Is that why you didn't call me? You think I'm too young for you?"

"No," he said, and now she smiled, remembering the very young woman she had seen with him. "I think you're too . . . *much* for me."

"How can anyone have too much of a good thing?" she said, doing her best to affect allure despite the sogginess, sweat, and stains, and trying hard to convince him that she'd had more than three sexual encounters in her life so far, and that two out of three of them weren't bad. She suspected, however, that he had guessed this.

He laughed out loud. He rested his hand on her arm. "It must be great to be you," he said softly.

"Are you having a birthday party?" she said. "Maybe I'll come."

"Sure," he replied. "Eight o'clock next Thursday. You know the address." He pointed to the white door a little way down the street.

She nodded. She tried to think of a parting line that a professor of English literature might appreciate. She couldn't. She had spent all her time working on the introductory one.

"I'll get you a present," she said.

That fall, Liddy said good-bye to Murray Hill and moved into the loft on Bedford Street that Peter's aunt owned. Peter was on sabbatical, writing a book on moral aestheticism, and they were happy. Most weekdays they met for a sandwich in an unprepossessing deli on Forty-third Street, equidistant from her office and the New York Public Library, and they discussed disastrous romantic adventures, although his tales were from the pages of novels and hers were from depositions. In the evenings, when they weren't both working, they went to new restaurants they'd read about in the *New Yorker*, and plays and concerts and galleries, although Liddy always made the reservations. She took a photography course at the New School and was invited to display her work in a respected gallery downtown; she enjoyed this but did not pursue it. (The impoverished life of the struggling artist held no romance for her. She had eaten nothing but apples and baked potatoes during her time in college. Her hair and nails had never fully recovered.) Occasionally they would visit Peter's parents, and stay in the large house upstate Peter had grown up in, where there was Bach on the stereo, a library full of well-thumbed books, and a large pond full of shimmering red koi next to a tennis court. Peter's mother always urged Liddy to play doubles, but Liddy did not know how, and she did not have the time to learn. Instead, she learned about red wine, and sushi, and the opera.

When Peter went back to work, and her salary doubled and then tripled, they enjoyed numerous winter vacations in Europe and during the long, hot summers took a rental in the same cottage on the water in Amagansett. Often Peter traveled up alone on a Thursday to read and had the takeout ordered when Liddy emerged from the train late on a Friday night, desperate to see him. Sometimes it felt like they had started a conversation the night of that fateful birthday that had never ended. They always had something to talk about. They were "so good together," everybody said, "still crazy" after so many years, and most of the time they were—until five years later, and the Labor Day weekend that Peter's parents came to visit and marveled at how Liddy had finally "domesticated" their boy, the "boy" who was now well into his forties, and Mrs. James got a bit tipsy and embarrassed everyone by asking when Peter intended to make "an honest woman of Liddy." He laughed and then got petulant when she wouldn't stop asking and said she wanted to be a grandmother, and it was very awkward and Mr. James had to escort her up to bed, saying she can't take three glasses of wine anymore, and when Liddy asked Peter about it afterward—what *was* wrong with the idea of getting married or having a child anyway?—he flew into a furious tantrum and headed back to the city, leaving Liddy to cook a bleary breakfast for his parents.

Peter's outburst left Liddy hurt and confused. She had assumed that they had boarded the train of life together, that it was chugging along in an orderly and predictable fashion, and would eventually stop at the station of family. But she suddenly realized that while she sat enjoying the ride in peace and safety, Peter might be about to pull the emergency brake. Now that she thought about it, he positively recoiled at the idea of procreation, and while getting pregnant had never been anywhere near the top of Liddy's to-do list, the more something might elude her, the more she wanted it; what had been true of a pet when she was ten years old was true of a baby now that she was thirty.

The uncomfortable jolt had shown her she was ready for the next stage; clearly Peter was not. When he refused to apologize, or even discuss it, she spent a miserable forty-eight hours in a fog of distress. She recognized that a life lived by force of will can destroy as much as it can conquer. Clearly she had been an idiot to interfere with meaningful providence, or destiny, or whatever you wanted to call it.

She packed her bags. She moved back to Murray Hill. She took photographs again. She reconnected with her few friends (she went to Intense Rafe's exhibition of sound sculptures in Chelsea), and she refused to pick up the telephone for Peter, even when he sang embarrassingly plaintive songs into her answering machine. She had endured adversity but not tragedy, and so her personality was still bright, if brittle.

She decided to let her true fate reveal itself.

Liddy had heard rumors about the new and apparently quite devilishly handsome senior associate at Gillespie and Ross but had not come across him until one morning, three weeks later, in a side courtroom in 60 Centre Street. It was Marisa Seldon's case, but Marisa had called her at 7:30 a.m. to say that both the twins and the nanny had come down with chickenpox, and that Liddy would have to handle the court appearance until she got there. It was a formality, Marisa assured her, and as she hastily read the brief in the cab, Liddy agreed.

Marisa's client, Natalia P., was a former aerobics instructor of mysterious origin and indeterminate age, who had taken a job as personal trainer to sixty-five-year-old multimillionaire Dwight P. and married him swiftly afterward. There were no marital assets and no kids, but the case had gone on for two acrimonious years because of yoga. Natalia P. had crushed two vertebrae in her neck after a supported headstand went wrong; her ongoing symptoms included sensitivity to loud noises, numbness in her little toes, and occasional loss of bladder control, which made her unfit for work indefinitely, according to the statements made by three doctors, including an expert on Qigong medicine. Natalia P. looked certain to get a one-off settlement payment, enormous by anyone's standards.

Liddy hurried along the tiled corridor in her signature work uniform, navy pantsuit, white shirt, and ballet pumps (on days she was feeling fashion forward she wore a black metallic shirt and pinned a Sarah Jessica Parker–inspired flower corsage onto her jacket), her schoolbag briefcase slung across her chest. Natalia P. was sitting on a wooden bench, waiting. Conspicuously pale, she made an agonizingly slow trip to the bathroom just as Judge Carson arrived.

Liddy was conscious that the opposing counsel, Sebastian Stackallan, was dark-haired and extremely tall, but she kept her eyes on her notes and the judge, and so the first thing she really noticed about him was his voice. It was a deep, melodious Irish lilt that caused Natalia P. to look over and appear to swoon visibly. It had no effect on Liddy whatsoever. She had spent too many summers in her youth trapped on the rear seats of small cars in Ireland, listening to the similarly deep and melodious voices of local radio hosts and feeling despair that her childhood would never end.

"And so," she concluded earnestly, "my client has not only compromised and delayed her career potential by her marriage, she is now stricken with a debilitating medical condition that prevents her, literally, from exercising that potential. Her future is painful and lonely, with medical expenses that could last a life-time. Surely the whole point of the marriage contract is to protect the parties involved from that?"

Her rhetorical flourish was rather diminished by the gruff, dismissive laugh from Dwight P. that punctuated the end, but Liddy didn't care one bit. Judge Carson was clearly unamused by the interruption; moreover, Marisa had heard through the grape-vine that he had suffered a similar neck injury while changing a lightbulb. Liddy allowed herself a small, satisfied smile. Then she began to think through her appointments for the rest of the day. At that moment, the back door of the courtroom opened and a very young nervous-looking woman scurried in carrying a brown envelope.

"Excuse me, Your Honor," said Stackallan. "There's some new evidence that has just come to my attention."

Liddy jolted out of her reverie on whether to have a Caesar salad or club sandwich for lunch. She leapt to her feet.

"Objection. No prior disclosure," she said.

"Indeed, Ms. Murphy," said Judge Carson. "Mr. Stackallan, explain?"

Stackallan ripped open the envelope, sending fragments of white padding flying, and pulled out a VHS cassette.

"It appears there has been a substantial positive change to Mrs. P.'s health, which goes to the very heart of the settlement negotiation, Your Honor."

Liddy had a bad feeling. Stackallan had a serious voice on, but she could tell from the jaunty flourish of the ripping that he was enjoying this.

"Secret filming is not permissible under the precedent established in *Smyth v. Smyth*," she said.

"This recording was not obtained illicitly. It's from a security camera in the . . ." He paused and peered at the white strip of tape on the side of the VHS, on which a name had been scrawled in black felt tip. "Disco Go-Go, South Beach, Miami."

He enjoyed that even more.

Liddy watched in amazement as Stackallan fixed Judge Carson in a piercing blue-gray gaze, not unlike Obi Wan Kenobi in *Star Wars*, and suddenly, as if overcome by the force, Judge Carson nodded.

"I'll allow."

Stackallan handed the tape to the clerk, who switched on the VHS player and pressed play.

Liddy turned to Natalia P. Natalia P. did the worst impression of looking innocent Liddy had ever seen; then she gave up, stood, swore extravagantly in the general direction of her soon-to-be ex-husband, and hurried out of the courtroom as it reverberated to a tinny recording of Britney Spears. Judge Carson stared with interest at the grainy but unmistakeable figure of Natalia high kicking and shimmying under the flashing lights, accompanied by two Latino dancers in snakeskin trousers. *Case dismissed*.

Liddy packed her briefcase. When she looked up, Stackallan was in front of her, his hand outstretched. She took it and shook it. And now, although she hated losing any case so much it was all something of a blur, she registered that his gaze was oddly mesmerizing in its intensity and his palm was strong and warm. Yes, he was, in fact, quite devilishly handsome.

"Mr. Stackallan."

"Nice to meet you, Ms. Murphy," he said. "I take it you're Irish. Were you born in the auld Emerald Isle?"

"I was," said Liddy.

"Jinx. We should get to know each other better. Dinner, tonight?"

"Pardon?"

Liddy was genuinely shocked. The *chutzpah*. The *sophistication*. The assumption she would find him *irresistible*.

"Le Petit Cochon. Eight o'clock?" (His French pronunciation was perfect.)

"But how will you get a table?" she said, skipping straight to what seemed most improbable about the scenario to her.

He scoffed and said, "Be there, wear a skirt. I'm sure your legs are fabulous." Then he walked off, cologne and testosterone trailing behind him, pausing only to hold the room door open for Marisa, who had arrived, exhausted-looking and slightly out of breath, clutching a large bottle of calamine lotion.

Liddy was affronted, and thrilled, and in a disorienting state of erotic excitement.

"Was that Sebastian Stackallan?" asked Marisa.

"It was," Liddy replied. "Did you see the footage?"

"No, but I heard! You win some, you lose some." Marisa shrugged. "He's good, that young man. And very . . . *alluring.*"

Liddy turned to her in surprise.

"*Why?*"

"Good old-fashioned masculine appeal, perhaps? The way he talks? Those impeccable manners?" Marisa paused. "No, I tell you what it is. You look at him and you *know* he's brilliant in the sack. In fact, I do know, because Judge Killane told me he was."

"What?" said Liddy. Susan Killane was a glamorous, but notoriously uptight, fifty-year-old recently appointed to the appellate court.

"They're in some sort of open relationship."

Liddy grimaced. She had never seen the point of open relationships. The idea seemed the ultimate oxymoron.

"He just asked me out for dinner."

"You should definitely go," said Marisa. "It'll be good for you after all this business with Peter. You could even try having sex just for fun!"

Liddy had never attempted a one-night stand, but she trusted Marisa's advice in most things, so at lunchtime, instead of drafting a template document about custody of wedding presents, she went out and bought herself a new dress and tried on a pair of glittery Louboutins she could hardly walk in. The saleswoman warned her to descend stairs sideways and never to wear the shoes in the rain, as the red soles were notoriously slippery, but even after this Liddy bought them, teetering cautiously into the restaurant that night, feeling fantastically feminine and ready to have "fun."

Sebastian had not changed, which immediately made her feel at a disadvantage, but he seemed to appreciate her outfit, loosened his tie with his left hand, and ordered champagne, which she took as a positive sign. Liddy asked polite questions and made amusing comments and he seemed to find her charming and even brushed his hand against hers a couple of times, so she drank two glasses straight down in order to facilitate flirtation, which did not come easily to her. She stared at his mouth and wondered what would happen if she leaned across the table and kissed him. But she had been brought up a Catholic so she didn't. Instead, the bubbles went straight to her head and, unfortunately, when the conversation meandered into the byways of another country, her unadulterated personality belched out of her mouth in words that were slurred.

"I haven't been to Ireland for years. I hated going back there when I was young. I had to sleep in my cousin Roisin's bed, in her unwashed sheets, with her dolls staring down at me. She used to keep a pile of nail clippings under her pillow!"

Sebastian did not seem to share her outrage (or interest in cousin Roisin's cuticles).

"Where is your family from?" he asked, suddenly glancing around the restaurant in the hope he might see someone, anyone, he knew.

"Suburbs of Dublin. Elderly aunties in corporation houses, you know, picture of the pope next to JFK. And of course, once during the trip, there'd be the obligatory trudge round Glendalough in County Wicklow."

Sebastian perked up. "That's where I grew up. My family home is near there."

"Interesting," said Liddy, although she wasn't interested at all. "All I remember about it is that it always rained. You know, people say that it always rains in Ireland and you think they're making it up, but they're not, because when I was there it always did. Shall we order?"

"I don't mind the weather," he said. "I go back home every summer. I miss it. I miss the house and I miss the land. Don't you feel any connection to the place you were born?"

He began to sing.

"Oh Danny Boy, the pipes, the pipes are calling . . ."

His singing voice was as attractive as his speaking one. The couple at the next table stared admiringly.

Liddy thought for a moment. Then she shook her head. (This made her feel a bit sick.)

"Can we order some wine?" she said.

"Are you even Irish at all?" said Sebastian, and there was a sudden edge to his voice that Liddy didn't like. She picked up the bottle of champagne and poured the last glass out of it.

"Look, Sebastian," she said, propping her elbow on the table and resting her chin in her palm in what she hoped was a coquettish manner, "we're different sorts of Irish. I mean, your great-great-great-uncle Stackallan was no doubt herding my great-great-great-uncle Murphy onto some godforsaken coffin ship. *Right?* You're the 'it's not a home, it's my history' type and I'm the 'survival of the fittest, make a new life in the New World' type."

At this moment, the waiter materialized and launched into a description of the specials in a French accent that sounded like he had learned it at drama school.

"I'm just having one course. Dover sole," said Sebastian quickly.

"Really?" said Liddy, who was starving as well as inebriated. "I thought the calamari special sounded good." She ordered it as a main.

Sebastian did not ask for the wine list.

"And a glass of the house red," he said.

"Make that a bottle," said Liddy defiantly.

There was a long pause. Liddy was aware that the date was not going well. Sebastian was tapping his knife against his fork in an extremely irritating manner. Because of starvation and inebriation, when she looked at his face it moved in and out of focus, but, even fuzzy, she could tell he was bored. She attempted to get the evening back on track.

"My boyfriend and I are on a break," she announced somewhat primly. Then she hiccupped.

Sebastian put the knife down. "Let me guess," he said meaningfully. "He doesn't know if he wants to marry you, right?"

Liddy said yes, then thought she sounded pathetic. "I don't know if I like him anymore," she added. "He's older than me."

"Five years either way is the max age difference, if you ask me. It's unnatural to want to go to bed with Granddad. Or Baby, if you look at it the other way round."

"Peter's forty-three. He's not *Granddad*. He's mature."

"Really?" said Sebastian in the withering tone she had heard earlier in the day. "Then why doesn't he know what he wants?"

The waiter delivered their food. Liddy took her first mouthful before her plate was on the table.

"What does he do?"

"He's an academic."

Sebastian rolled his eyes. "Of course. Don't marry him."

"Why?"

"You and I, we work fifteen hours most days. In your case,

that's partly because the professor doesn't, but what'll happen when you have kids? How will you ever get off the treadmill?"

"I'm not going to give up work when I have kids."

"Why not?" said Sebastian. "I hear that raising a family can make a person very happy," and Liddy actually groaned, and put her head in both hands, and had a vision of a different life, a life of privilege and comfort, a life that several of her contemporaries were starting to choose (which she had previously dismissed as acts of desperation but now saw could be love). These women married men, often inferior to them in qualifications or career prospects, who were devoted husbands and gave them good-looking children and shared years with them that were as full and busy as they wanted them to be, before embarking on late-blooming second careers, frequently in nonprofit organizations.

Liddy gripped her hands tight around her face and she felt a silent scream. "I can't," she whispered. "Is that what you'd want your wife to do?"

She went back to eating.

"I'm not a marrying man," Sebastian announced, "but if I were, I'd be a provider. I would not like my children brought up by some nanny while my workaholic wife ran round with a brief-case in one hand and a baby bottle in the other!"

Liddy spluttered, sending fragments of calamari over the ta-blecloth. "You are a . . . *Neanderthal* . . ." she said, coughing.

Sebastian wiped his cutlery with his napkin. "Yeah. Right. You know the problem with women like you? You have some . . . *thing* about all this going on in your head, but, guess what, Ms. Murphy, it's okay to let someone take care of you."

As that someone was clearly never going to be Sebastian Stackallan, Liddy knew that "sex for fun" was most definitely off the menu. But still she found it difficult not to take it personally.

It took them precisely seven minutes to eat their food in silence, split the bill, and head out of the restaurant. Sebastian made some attempt at chivalrously waving down a cab, but when she asked him if he wanted to share it, he refused before she had finished speaking. She clambered into the backseat, but the heel of her right Louboutin caught in a grate and came off her foot just as Sebastian slammed the door firmly and banged on the cab window. The driver roared off and Liddy did not ask him to turn back. She looked down at her naked foot and sighed. *Oh, Cinderella*, she thought, *you've got a lot to answer for.* The appalling vista of endless unsatisfactory evenings like this opened up before her, and she decided to keep the remaining shoe on a prominent shelf in her apartment as a reminder that she must wait for the One. In the meantime, she would forget everything about the experience (the art of forgetting was something Liddy had found easy to master), forswear all men for a while, especially handsome princes, and if anyone mentioned Sebastian Stackallan she would say she was immune to his Celtic charms because of their shared DNA.

The cab pulled up on Third Avenue and she got out, barefoot, and began to weave her way unsteadily along the sidewalk. She was already dreading tomorrow's hangover, which would not even be leavened by the memory of a night of gymnastic sexual excess. *"Liddy!"* called a voice ahead of her, and she saw Peter sitting on her steps. He rose to his feet and pulled a small box out of his pocket and she knew what was going to happen next, so she stopped, and her first instinct was to shout *no*, but then she looked at the solitary shoe in her hand.

"I can't live without you," he said, so to stop him begging she said yes before any question had been asked, but she did not move toward him until she had put some conditions in place. They would get married before the end of the year, somewhere exotic, on their own, they would have a baby, and they would buy a place in Brooklyn, for she had noticed that was what her friends who had babies often did.

"Yes, yes, I like Brooklyn," he said. Then she threw the shoe in the trash. Years later, she would remember that Peter had never actually asked her to marry him and expressed more enthusiasm for Brooklyn than the baby, and she would regret that she had not exploited her advantage by defining a minimum number of off-spring. But that day, she let him into the apartment, ran him a bath, and ripped up her repeat prescription for the pill. Only then did she open the small box and see the exquisite belle epoque ring with a sapphire cluster setting he had chosen with his mother the previous weekend; it was perfect, and she allowed him to kiss her perfectly too.

In late September, Liddy and Peter flew to a resort in the Flor-ida Keys, where they got married on a beach of white sand with two witnesses they lured from the bar of the hotel. Peter was tanned, and in his mirror aviator shades looked so like Robert Redford in *The Way We Were* that Liddy's enthusiasm for making a baby quadrupled, and when the hotel manager announced that a hurricane was on its way and offered them a bus ride to the safety of Miami, they elected to stay on the island and helped the staff board up the windows and chop down the coconuts, which the storm could turn into deadly missiles. As darkness fell, they drank three rum punches each and snuggled into their cottage as the wind howled around them, bending the palm trees into horseshoe shapes.

That night the hurricane blew away all Liddy's lingering doubts and she decided that (a) no one would ever know her better than Peter James, and (b) all the evidence pointed to him being the love of her life. She would take his name, protect and provide for him (and the baby that was coming), and they would make their own little kingdom of three and live in it happily ever after.

Liddy had expected that motherhood would change her, but she had no idea of the joy that Matty would bring. The moment she held him in her arms, red-faced and screaming his way into life, she was overwhelmed by the sense that this was the only human being she would willingly die for. She directed her youthful constitution and indefatigable commitment to the project of his nurturing, and refused to be separated from him as much as was humanly possible for an ambitious associate in a top New York legal firm.

Unsurprisingly, Marisa Seldon proved an enlightened employer, giving generous maternity benefits and two-tier pay grades to allow flexible hours for the working parents. There was even a small nursery set up in an unused basement room and sometimes Liddy brought Matty into her office, where she sat her son on her lap. He would grab the curly phone cord in his chubby fists as she barked instructions at rival firms—to Peter's horror, Matty's first sentence was *"I don't think so!"* When he started school, Liddy tailored her hours to suit.

Their sleep and travel were the two casualties of their new life and Peter missed these things, and sometimes sighed meaningfully when he tripped over one of Matty's toys, even though it was Liddy who did the night feeds and early-morning risings. Peter missed Liddy, too, and felt that the conversation between them had come to an abrupt full stop. But as Liddy never complained if he stayed late at work, or had dinner alone with his parents, or went to see a new play with his students or his colleague Rose Donato, whom Liddy liked, although she was clearly a bit of a sad case, he never told her. Which rather proved his point.

Liddy had turned the destruction of her sleep pattern to her advantage (she bought a running machine to work out between 5:30 and 6:15 most mornings), and found that the constraints on her time actually increased her efficiency in the office. She accepted that she would never read Proust, and spent her Sunday hours lying on the beanbags in Amagansett watching "Bob the Builder," Matty draped across her like a hot-water bottle, allowing her mind to drift. She would often surface from the theme music with an unexpected solution to a thorny problem (sometimes writing entire briefs on Monday mornings), and although Marisa worried about her workload, Liddy did not.

Being a mother made Liddy a better, tougher professional and a better, softer person because she learned to distinguish between the two. There were moments, often by Matty's crib as he slept, when she experienced an intense sense of gratitude to the universe, or even God, that she had managed the elusive balance of work and home life that her female colleagues aspired to. Even she had noticed that this was a frequent topic of conversation, particularly late at holiday parties, among slightly drunk women who bombarded her with questions. She knew better than to attempt any reply other than *Peter helps all the time* (false), and *I only have one child* (true), but, secretly, she rejoiced in the superiority of her marriage. The love between her and Peter was special, different, invincible—

—until Matty turned five, and the desire for a second child overwhelmed her.

At first, Liddy was annoyed with herself. No one had to tell her this would turn her life upside down, so, ever practical, she kept quiet and embarked on some aversion therapy. First she volunteered with Matty's school and spent a day shepherding screaming children around a farm in Connecticut, where one student had a dramatic allergic reaction to a donkey and another threw up all over her. Then she packed up Matty's baby clothes and brought them to her legal secretary, who was on maternity leave. But as she ran back up three flights of stairs to retrieve a pair of tiny blue knitted booties and afterward sat slumped in tears on a filthy trash can in Hell's Kitchen, she knew it was not a temporary whim. So when that December she was in the little garden behind the house with Matty, dusting snow off the fig tree, and he said he wanted a puppy or a brother, she made her mind up. She told Peter that what she wanted for Christmas was for them to have another baby. She smiled as she said this, and cuddled her arms around his waist. He said nothing and withdrew from her embrace.

That weekend, when Peter bought Matty an enormous stuffed dalmatian toy and Liddy an enormous bunch of white lilies, she brought up the subject again. Peter was unsettled; over the years he had come to expect that his needs always trumped hers. She had noticed that a small muscle in the right side of his face twitched in irritation whenever she became truthful and vulnerable, and it did so now. She continued to plead, because she believed that on the big issues he would support her even if he could not do it gladly.

But again he said no, not twice but three times, adding, "I don't want another child, Liddy. I love you and I love the beautiful, healthy boy I have. I'm nearly fifty years old. I've got a book to write. I'm done with the diapers and no sleep."

"It's not just about what we want. It would be good for Matty to have a sibling."

Peter shook his head. "*Really?* This is *totally* about you. You think you would have been less lonely with a brother or sister, but you're wrong, Liddy. I never talk to my brother because he's deranged—"

"I have a vision of a family, two kids, maybe a dog, walking in the park."

"We are a family! And how on earth could you look after a dog?"

He tried a laugh here, but Liddy just stared at him.

"It would make me happy," she said, "and I'm prepared to provide for it all."

Peter did not appreciate this specificity; he liked his reality a little blurred. He had never seen her like this before, intense and energized with the desire for something only he had the power to give her.

"It's not about money," he said sadly. "It's about what we want from our lives. Why can't you be happy with what you have? Why is nothing ever enough?"

And then he walked away.

So Liddy took a pause; she had learned from practicing the law never to argue unless she could win, and for several months she was distracted. She won a landmark victory at work against the formidable Curtis Oates of Oates and Associates, who was so impressed by her that he began to besiege her with offers of employment and informed her matter-of-factly that he would not take no for an answer. One day, Marisa Seldon commanded her into the conference room and, her face tight with annoyance, announced that Oates had contacted her to ask what it would take to get Liddy to leave.

"*Are* you leaving us?" asked Marisa. Liddy did not answer this question but instead told Marisa her marital troubles.

Marisa said two words, *guile* and *lingerie*, assuring Liddy that women had used these things from the dawn of time and the world was populated by second and third children who were so-called oops! babies. Liddy replied that she had considered this, but it turned out she was guileless (and had no lingerie); moreover, Peter was tenacious in his refusal and vigilant. When she'd caught a stomach bug, he had slept in the spare room, and now she rarely bothered to take her pills, as he was either pajama'd and snoring ostentatiously by the time she went to bed or had invited Matty in with them "in case of a night terror."

"Sometimes I think he's just gonna sit it out until after my menopause."

"I'm sorry, Liddy," said Marisa kindly. "It sounds like Peter's pretty determined."

"He says he's too old," said Liddy.

"He's not that old!"

"And he's worried it'll affect his career."

Marisa looked bemused. "How? It's not like he stopped work to look after Matty."

Liddy shrugged. She had no answers.

Marisa looked at her. "Is he jealous of you?" she said.

"No! Of course not," said Liddy, shocked. "Look, he won't even talk about it anymore. He's in a bad mood all the time."

"Well, of course he's having some sort of midlife crisis," said Marisa knowingly, "but, unfortunately, that's not much help to you. You can't force this one, Liddy. If he won't, he won't. The question is, do you want to end your marriage over it?"

Hot tears of anger and injustice arose in Liddy's eyes. She shook her head.

But that night, as she imagined a new baby lying in her arms, Liddy remembered Miss Gwendolyn Harris and the fish and bicycle business and finally understood.

The following summer, Peter and Liddy were once again in the back of a plane heading to the Florida Keys, but this time Matty was wedged between them. Liddy had promised Peter the trip for his birthday, but with her ever-increasing workload and the mood he had been in, it had been delayed for nearly six months, becoming another source of argument between them. Finally Liddy had snapped and insisted they go during the summer vacation, even though Peter churlishly suggested that the July weather would be too humid. He had ostentatiously packed several aerosol cans of industrial-strength mosquito repellent.

She had not booked first-class seats, although she had wanted to, because Peter had moral objections to such extravagance and she was determined to do her part to resolve the tension between them and draw a line in the white sand.

Four thousand miles above North Carolina, the stewardess came rattling down with the trolley, and Peter surprised Liddy by buying some wine. He handed her a glass and they clinked plastic over Matty's oblivious, headphone-wearing head.

Peter's spirits seemed to lift. He talked to Liddy like a friend about his frustrations with the arts faculty, the increasing bureaucracy at the university, and how he feared he would never write his third career-defining book. And Liddy felt relief that these were things she could solve; if she billed even more hours he could hire an assistant to do research or take another unpaid sabbatical to write, and her experience at conflict resolution between warring couples could certainly help him navigate the toxic political maneuvers of his colleagues. (She was aware of the irony of this.)

"I'm sorry I've been so awful lately," he concluded, about to surprise her even more. "I think I'm having a midlife crisis."

She started because it was so unlike him. *Marisa was right*, she thought.

"Couldn't you just have bought a motorbike . . . or had an affair?" she said, and he laughed and reached across for her hand to kiss it.

"I don't want to have an affair," he said.

Then, in front of them, a six-month-old baby in pink started screaming, and the mother frantically lifted it over her shoulder and jiggled it around. Peter played peekaboo, saying, "Who's a pretty girl," and the baby smiled and giggled with delight. Afterward, he turned to Liddy.

"I know things have been difficult, my love, but . . . I want to put everything behind us and move on."

Liddy grinned and felt euphoric; she raised her hand as if to take a luxurious swig of wine, but in fact took only the tiniest sip, for at that moment she felt an unexpected, desperate hope that she might come home pregnant again.

She had booked herself and Matty a series of activities to do together. It annoyed her if he disappeared into a children's club and played video games while the sun blazed down outside. Peter had a small suitcase marked HEAVY full of books to read, and so on the first day he settled himself down on a lounger on the beach with his bug spray and a biography of Simone Weil as she and Matty lined up on the shore with a few other parents and children.

After a brief lecture on water safety and the tao of the surfer, Liddy prepared to face her true self in the waves. From a distance, the instructor, whose name she did not register, was unusually tall and carried himself as if unusually handsome; close up, with his shaggy blond hair and his mirrored aviator shades, he really was alarmingly attractive. He reminded her of a younger version of someone she knew, though at first she wasn't sure who. As he wrapped one muscular arm around her legs and they paddled out over the baby waves, she remembered. It was Peter. The tingling sensation in her groin reminded her she had not had sex for over a year.

Suddenly Liddy felt the pull of water beneath her as the ocean current moved.

"Trust me. You'll be fine," the instructor said, putting a hand on her back, the imprint burning warm through the rubber wetsuit and into her skin. She felt the rush as the big wave gathered momentum and he pushed her hard onto it. She heard him shouting, "One . . . two . . . three!" and to her own amazement she popped up onto the board, knees bent, arms outstretched to steady herself, and she rode the wave to the shore, running onto the sand triumphantly. Peter and Matty ran over, Peter shaking his head and saying ruefully, "When your mother sets her mind to something, she always gets it."

Not always, thought Liddy, as the waves had indeed made her confront her true self.

"You are awesome, Mom," said Matty, and she held him tightly, and in that moment made two decisions. Enough love had leaked from her marriage already. She was sick of thrashing around underwater; she was *going to ride the wave*.

That evening Peter and Liddy and Matty had more fun than they'd had in months: they played pool together and ate grilled fish and fries and laughed and enjoyed the resentful stares of other couples who had traveled to the hotel alone, as they could not bear to be trapped on an island with their whining children. And later, as Matty snored heavily on the inflatable mattress in the bathroom, Liddy brought two rum punches back from the bar and told Peter how much she loved him. She had more to say, but before she could continue, he kissed her forehead and said yes, they should get on the same page now, pardon the expression, as he had a book to write, and he needed an end to discord and door slamming. And he said all this in a measured, kindly way, as if he was repeating back to her something she had said rather than finishing a discussion that had not even been properly begun.

She looked at him.

"I'm going to take the job with Curtis Oates," she said.

Peter lifted up his book and opened it. He pretended to read. In the past this would have made her smile, but recently the things she used to find adorable about him had become annoying. She suspected he felt the same way about her.

"That's not a decision you can make on your own," he said at last. "We don't see enough of you as it is." Now he closed the book with a firm clip. "What about Matty?"

"He's a well-adjusted six-year-old with loads of friends who's happy in school. I'll pay for him to do hobbies and you can pick him up at five thirty every night."

Peter sighed. Liddy continued.

"I want it. It's the next step for me. Senior partner in a boutique firm dedicated to my area of expertise."

"And that's what really matters, isn't it? The relentless *Liddy Express* pulls away. . . . *All aboard.*"

Liddy was unsure whether he was making a joke, but his next comment clarified his tone. It was belligerent. "How on earth could we have another child?"

"The reason we're not having another child is not my career but because you don't want one."

"*Of course.*"

Liddy gulped in disbelief. "I am good at my job. I enjoy it. This is my time."

She knew such directness made him feel uncomfortable, but she did not stop. She was not afraid of upsetting him anymore.

"I have never hidden what I am from you," she said, for although he had not known her when she was a child, he'd said he understood when she had shown him *City of Ambition.*

"Maybe you should have."

"The salary's a lot bigger," she said.

He nodded meaningfully, like this was the only thing that mattered to her. "What's a lot?"

"A second home. A place for weekends, summers, somewhere for you to write."

"Stop negotiating, Liddy. You've told me many times Oates is a scumbag."

"He is. That's why I'll insist the firm commit to five percent of billable hours on pro bono work. And I've told him I'll do my cases my way. No leaking to the tabloids, no Page Six shenanigans."

"Yeah, yeah. . . . You're selling your soul to the devil and you know it."

Liddy flinched as his disdain hit her hard, like a shot in the chest. She turned away. He picked up his book again, pausing only to deliver his second rhetorical aside.

"You've come a long way, baby. . . ."

This time he was trying to make a joke.

He yawned ostentatiously and asked her to get into bed with him, but Liddy, wide awake, quivering with the injustice of it all, shook her head. "I'm going to read here," she said, grabbing a women's magazine from the side table. Peter snorted dismissively, and when she turned to him, he gave her an exasperated look and said, "That's not *reading*."

She was suddenly aware that the reason he often made her feel unloved and unwanted was because he felt superior to her, and maybe even thought that she was lucky to have him. On a bad day, he viewed the material comforts she provided—no mortgage, private school, five-star vacations—as a sort of compensation for his philistine wife, a woman who had turned her back on the higher verities, to swim in the filthy but lucrative cesspool of commerce. She knew, of course, that only those born into wealth can afford such thoughts. He had never hidden from her what he was. This knowledge did not temper her rage.

He lay down and she picked up her magazine, flicking the pages loudly, which always drove him crazy, but he fell into a deep sleep and she could not even niggle at him. She sat very still and tried to breathe slowly, but the pain that had entered her chest seemed to ripple through her whole body. She told herself to calm down. She knew better than most people how random hurts fuel the fires of discontent, and the most dramatic marital conflagrations can start over laundry or the school run. But she also knew there was a fundamental problem at the heart of her relationship.

Peter didn't love her anymore.

This was a quiet and bloody realization in the stillness of a starlit Caribbean night.

She walked out onto the balcony. It was impossible not to remember when they had stood together in the same place, arms around each other, full of hope and love, staring into the black sky and searching for the Milky Way.

Oh the disappointment!

"It's over," she said out loud, but quickly bit back the words in case saying it might make it happen, like in a novel of magic realism, although in such a novel there would be external drama too, another hurricane, certainly a flying coconut or two.

Reassuringly, the weather was balmy and the waves lapped rhythmically, on and on. Liddy relaxed. They would go on too, she would make sure of it; she did not believe in divorce, particularly where children were involved, and she had sat through enough mediation sessions to absorb the message that if you want to change something, the only person you can change is yourself. She had no doubt she had become blinkered and boring. What she needed was to have some fun.

In the hotel a band had started playing and she found herself swaying in time with the irrepressible reggae beat. She wondered what it would be like to hang out barefoot in the bar with people who were young and stayed up late. And she wanted another drink, not a glass of wine that tasted metallic in the heat, but a large cocktail with a straw, one that she could gulp down.

She stuck her head back into the cottage.

"I'm going for a walk," she said.

Half-asleep, Peter rolled onto his side.

"Don't be too late, my love."

She strolled along the beach. She felt an intoxicating sense of freedom and she actually broke into a run, kicking the water as it slid over her feet. When she stopped and threw herself onto the sand to rest, she became aware of a gentle splashing in the distance. A ghostly figure was swimming in the black sea. She craned her head forward, peering into the darkness, and then the figure emerged and walked toward her waving hi.

It was the alarmingly attractive surf instructor, six foot five with muscles in perfect proportion, his wetsuit rolled down over his impressive torso, glistening with sea salt. Liddy stared. She could not help herself. Across his entire chest crawled a vivid tattoo of a serpent, an image of biblical horror, its jaws wide, its tail snaking up around his right shoulder.

He said nothing as he held out his hand to her. He whistled very softly.

ADVENTURES OF THE
GUILT-FREE WOMAN: PART I

It was a Saturday, the third in April, but from force of habit, Liddy blinked blearily awake at 5:30 a.m. *Where am I? What's happening?* The habitual moment of disorientation in the darkness before she located herself. Liddy always woke up raw. She lifted up her eye mask, glanced at her watch. *Noooo!!!!* She collapsed back into her pillows in frustration.

She stretched her fingers and wiggled her toes. She gave thanks she had made it through another week. Then she propped herself up on her elbows to search for Cal. As usual, he had left his room and crawled into the bottom of her bed during the night, where he now lay, snoring softly, a leg and an arm flung luxuriously over the edge.

Liddy knew she should have stopped this years ago. Matty had been put in his "big boy" room by his father at an appropriate five months of age, but there was no point even pretending that her two sons were treated the same way. Cal was six years old today. *Incredible.* Six years that had sometimes crawled and sometimes sprinted by, but enough time for her to have forgotten what life was like without him. Sometimes when she woke in the mornings, she would find that he had wriggled up close to her, curling himself against her belly in a fetal position as if they had never been separated.

Liddy closed her eyes. Her current morning meditation was to take a mental inventory of her whole body, encouraging her every muscle to liquefy; instead, she saw herself as a skeleton in a biology lab that had fallen off its hook into a crumpled heap of bones on the floor. She did not think this was a very positive image, but she was prevented from doing better by a plaintive canine yap in the distance. She swung one leg over the side of the bed, then the other. She pushed her weight onto her feet and pulled herself up to her full height. She turned slowly and precisely and walked like an automaton toward her marble and steel kitchen, straight past the exercise equipment she had dutifully left out the previous night (following the plasticized weekly planner meticulously dotted with a rainbow of differently colored symbols). She switched on the coffee machine Lucia had left prepared and glanced around at the huge picture windows, the white walls, and the rows of white shelves and cupboards. Six years ago, Liddy had used all the spare time she had for swatches and sample paint pots and silk rugs to create her new office; all she had wanted from her new home was a place in which to hang her print of *City of Ambition*, and acres of storage space in anticipation of the new life that would fill it.

The cupboards and shelves were still empty.

She clipped the dog's lead onto its collar and, with the boys still fast asleep, hurried into the elevator. In the lobby the night doorman, an elderly Lithuanian with a literary bent, was sitting behind the desk reading *Doctor Zhivago* in the original. Liddy smiled as she passed.

"It's quiet out there," he said.

And indeed, Hudson Street at six a.m. was deserted, apart from the odd jogger or comatose body wrapped in a filthy sleeping bag in a doorway. This early Liddy always felt she was walking into the opening scene of a disaster movie, the morning after a nuclear explosion or an alien attack, but it was at these times that she loved the city best. She sniffed the early-morning smell of coffee grinds and damp spring air. She heard the distant chugging of the tugboats on the river, watched a stray cat chase a small bird behind a scrubby tree, and remembered that, once, Manhattan had been a place of fields and farms. *This is my New York*, she thought, for at that moment it seemed as if it had been created as a location for her alone. Meanwhile, the dog obligingly delivered a fulsome crap on the sidewalk just as a high-pitched whine signaled the slow progress of a garbage truck trailing broken cardboard boxes like tumbleweeds. Liddy hurled the plastic baggy into its back with devastating aim. She felt disproportionately pleased because she had not excelled at sports in her youth. But as she looked skyward and saw the looming clouds her spirits sank. There was a green tinge to their grayness that even someone ignorant of freakish weather could tell looked bad. She turned back to the apartment as a few slow, heavy drips of rain began to fall. She thought of Cal's birthday at the Central Park Zoo that afternoon and hoped umbrellas were provided in the party package. She sighed. The capricious late-spring weather was just one of the phenomena that refused to accommodate the demands of her new schedule.

Liddy had longed for Matty's return for a very long time, but she had anticipated that it would create challenges. Her mistake was that she had imagined these challenges would be concentrated in the area of time management. One of the first things she had done after he moved back in was to pay for an hour-long consultation with her life coach. As instructed, she had printed the data off her customized Jawbone and organized her day planner for a "typical" weekday in some detail. Afterward, the life coach sent his bill and three suggestions (although not one of these suggestions was an alchemical formula for creating more hours in a day). Liddy dutifully put Matty into homework club, cajoled Lucia into extra hours on a Saturday, and went from three to two blowouts at the salon every week. She also canceled her personal trainer's visits to the apartment at 5:45 a.m. in favor of online sessions, but the life coach had warned against this. To assuage him, Liddy promised to have a massage once a month.

But, unfortunately for Liddy, a planning and prioritizing ses-

THE REAL LIDDY JAMES

sion with a life coach does not of itself calm a resentful and disoriented adolescent, particularly one determined to make the point that he would rather be *anywhere* but here. For example, she discovered almost immediately that, contrary to Chapter 1 of her new book, she did care about homework and table manners. Matty, however, did not, something he communicated with an eloquence and vigor that was never to be found in his Mandarin compositions. When he was not arguing, he did not speak, and while this should have been a respite, the monosyllabic grunting drove Liddy so crazy that she would command him to address her in proper sentences. There would follow a day or so of elaborate responses to simple requests involving exaggerated syntax and referring to her as Mommy Dearest. Inevitably, Liddy would lose her temper and shout at Matty until he stopped. The first few times this made Cal cry. After that, he would sigh, put his hands over his ears, and disappear into his bedroom.

Liddy's superproductive existence was based on a foundation of micromanagement and monastic order—green smoothies, exercise, and rest. When home alone with Cal they both went to bed at eight o'clock, and as he snored softly in his room, she answered e-mails and caught up on paperwork. Now she was lucky if a cacophony of discord and door slamming resulted in Matty's lights off at eleven, at which point, on too many nights, she poured herself a second glass of wine to face an hour or two of writing her book, and then poured a third to wash down the Ambien that might give her five hours' sleep. And on stormy mornings like this one, due to traffic snarling in the rain-soaked streets, Liddy had to send Matty off in the car with Vince at 7:20 a.m., walk Cal to school, and then, after trying and failing to hail a cab, race to the subway. There was no audiobook together, no chatting about the day ahead, no quality time whatsoever. Just nerves jangling, organization in shreds, a bundle of unread briefs, and a large cup of coffee with three shots.

Liddy's capsule wardrobe had become exclusively black. She could not risk a catastrophic spillage on a white silk shirt somewhere between Grand Central and Fifty-ninth Street.

She lifted Coco up and ran back into the building. They took the elevator up to the apartment. On a sunlit morning, the effect was of walking into a perfect series of illuminated squares across the length of the dark wood floorboards, like a chessboard or an eighties disco, but today the windows were dark and streaked almost black with grimy running water. It was like being stuck inside an armored vehicle in a car wash, an insistent percussive sound track playing too loudly.

In desperation one morning Liddy had called Rose, on the pretext of confirming the time of a music lesson, and made a couple of oblique references to Matty's "mood swings" in the hope of eliciting some information on how best to deal with him. Rose had appeared bemused and, while conceding that he was sometimes a bit grumpy in the mornings, told Liddy that this was all to do with the shifts in the prefrontal cortex of the teenage brain and it was *not his fault at all*. There was even a hint of a sob in her voice as she reminisced about washing his filthy soccer shirts, so Liddy quickly backtracked and told her everything was fine. But Rose was not quite finished.

"Have you thought about the summer?" she said. "What are you going to do?"

The thought of Matty's long summer vacation with no school, no structure, and no plan to cover it was something Liddy had been uncharacteristically avoiding. For the last few years it had not been an issue; Rose had taken over apart from the two weeks in August when Liddy took the boys to a cabana with a personal butler in a luxurious, all-inclusive hotel somewhere. (She always paid for Lucia to come too. But when Liddy tried to insist that Lucia visit the hotel spa or treat herself in the lobby shops, Lucia demurred, preferring to roast lobster red by the pool, eating the croissants she had saved from the buffet breakfast. This reminded Liddy of her parents, until she remembered that Lucia was two months younger than she was.)

"I don't know yet," Liddy muttered. "What *do* people do?"

"Well, a lot of his friends go to camp," said Rose disapprovingly. "And to be honest, last year he was begging to go, but . . ."

Camp? Begging? Brilliant! thought Liddy, and as she had indeed heard gruff mutterings about a "totally sick" place in Vermont the previous night, she had ended the conversation abruptly, as if it had been Rose who had called in desperation and disturbed her.

Now she emptied the large bucket collecting water from the roof leak and sat down at her desk. She pulled out her desk drawer, only to be greeted by a pile of brown bills, the letters marked URGENT from the bank, and three pairs of pajamas she had bought online that didn't fit and she'd never had the time to return. She pushed it back in again. She reached forward to switch on her laptop, but her carpal tunnel flared as she moved her arm, and so, although she should have used this time for the tasks itemized on her laminated weekend to-do list (*call building repair company about roof* being at number one), she sat quite still and stared at the corkboard hung at her eye level.

On it were pinned two photographs: a black-and-white snap of her parents, young and excited, standing proudly behind a large old-fashioned stroller in front of a small terraced house on a street in Dublin, Ireland, and a school photograph of Liddy aged about twelve, grinning, a broad stripe of pink gum across her oversized front teeth, above the hideous uniform of her Catholic middle school in Silver Lake. There was also a faded announcement card of Matty's birth, a Polaroid of Cal's twelve-week ultrasound scan, and a copy of the poem *Desiderata* by Max Ehrmann. She started to read, but suddenly the words became blurry, and Liddy's head jerked forward at "sham, drudgery, and broken dreams." She blinked herself awake, narrowly missing a collision with her keyboard. She considered how tired it was possible for a person to be and still be alive.

She stood up. She went to the fridge and peered at the bowl of millet porridge the nutritionist had recommended and which she ate most mornings as punishment for abandoning her dawn exercise regime. Not this morning. She decided she'd rather be starving. She inflated six red balloons with 6 TODAY! on them and tied them to an exposed pipe. Then she sent herself back to bed. Two hours later she was awoken by Cal, singing lustily in a pure choirboy soprano.

"Happy birthday, baby!" she said as she rested her forehead against his. She watched him dress and then marveled at the advanced development of his motor skills as he climbed up onto a kitchen stool, poured himself some juice, glugged it down, and washed out the glass before putting it in the dishwasher.

Liddy would never fully understand what had fired her desire to have unprotected sex with a stranger on the floor of the scuba shack (although the disappointment with Peter, the drunkenness, and the lure of the serpent tattoo counted for a lot). She had only discovered his name by calling the hotel six weeks after her return. The manager had sniggered and told her that the Surfing Guy had been dismissed the previous week for professional misconduct and left no forwarding address. "Several angry ladies are looking for him, so if you have any information . . ." he enjoyed announcing before Liddy hung up. It was the single moment of comedy in the high tragedy that followed.

But from the moment she learned they had procreated, she knew it must be for a reason. She watched Cal, his blond hair framing his angelic face like a halo, and was reminded of how Rose, one of the few people who knew the truth, had talked of him as a golden child in a myth, like Helen of Troy or Hercules, born of an encounter between a mortal woman and a god (who had appeared as a force of nature). Liddy deflected all questions about his paternity, apart from clarifying that Peter was not his father, and although she had resolved to tell Cal in an age-appropriate manner whenever he asked, so far he had not. In the meantime, she felt curiously comforted by Rose's poetic explanation; Cal had somehow been conceived out of her own passion and energy by an event she could not control. And who could say his unorthodox entrance into the world had disadvantaged him? Cal was advanced intellectually as well as physically, and coursed through with Liddy's genes. His first question on being shown a new game was always "How do you win?"

"Where's Matty?" he said now.

Liddy tripped jauntily to the door of Matty's room and tapped on the door, calling his name with an enthusiasm that even she felt was unconvincing.

"Go away!" was the response.

"He must have been up late on his computer," said Liddy to Cal and the dog.

"Huh," said Cal wearily. "He's *add-ict-ed.*"

He trotted over to her, opened the door, and went straight in, clambering on top of his brother and staring into his face.

"Wake up!" Cal said. "It's my birthday!"

Matty's eyes opened and Cal leaned forward and kissed him before exploding into giggles. Matty growled in mock horror, then threw his arms around him and they rolled across the bed together.

A pulse of love rose within Liddy. The sight of her sons at play never failed to move her, and it was not just that they were adorable together (although they were). Rose's point during the "golden child" conversation was to suggest that having such a half-divine younger sibling might be hard on Matty (in fact, in a world where a child who wasn't "gifted and talented" felt like a parental failure, Rose worried that Matty's contented ordinariness and resolutely average grades bothered his extraordinary mother), but Liddy had retorted that it was an immeasurable gift to the two boys to have each other.

"Get up now, Matty!" called Liddy, as Cal picked up a pair of Matty's smelly socks and threw them at him. "We're opening Cal's presents! And put your dirty clothes in the hamper! It's not fair to Lucia to leave them lying around!"

Exclamations over, she grabbed Cal's hand and they exited before Matty could respond. In truth, Liddy had little hope of a change in Matty's slovenly behavior. Despite her constant reiteration that Lucia was a *valued member of the family* and should be treated as such, Matty treated Lucia like his servant. As Liddy scrabbled around every morning, retrieving underpants and scrunched-up tissues from his bedroom floor and wiping blue globs of inexpertly sprayed shaving foam off the bathroom walls, it was small consolation that he treated her in exactly the same way.

"Shall we start?" she said, and Cal and the dog yelped with excitement. Liddy handed Cal a large box, glamorously wrapped by Lucia, which contained a wooden construction set with mini-lathe. Cal examined it curiously; he was genuinely intrigued, it seemed, at the prospect of making a decorative candle holder.

Matty then sloped out of his room with a brown paper bag, a packet of Starburst stuck to it with duct tape, which he handed ceremoniously to Cal. Inside was a slightly tatty wrestling magazine, but Cal's eyes lit up.

"It's your best one," he said, and Matty nodded and replied, "That's why I want you to have it," and the two brothers hugged before chasing after Coco, who had stolen the Starburst.

At this moment, Liddy's phone beeped. She looked down at the text and then over at Matty.

"It's your father," she said slowly, crossing to the doorway to buzz Peter into the lobby. "Do you know why he's here?"

Matty's jaw suddenly set and a complicated expression of anger and guilt rippled across his face. Liddy's heart sank. She knew he had done something he regretted.

The elevator doors opened and Peter appeared. He started when he saw Liddy in her bathrobe. It had fallen off one shoulder and she was conscious that his eyes were drawn to the line of her slender neck.

"How's Rose?" she asked. Peter replied, somewhat distractedly, that Rose was doing well, but she had already watched every Turner Classic Movie and there were still four months to go. Then he looked back at Liddy and this time he kept his eyes fixed on hers.

"What's going on?" he said.

"I don't know," she replied simply. "Did Matty make an arrangement with you?"

"Yes. He told me he was spending today with me."

They both turned and looked at Matty, who was curled up on the sofa with his eyes closed, as if that would make him invisible. Cal grabbed his new lathe and scurried into his bedroom.

"It's Cal's birthday," said Liddy.

"Of course," said Peter, looking at the balloons.

"We're having a party at the zoo this afternoon. Cal chose the jungle adventure package."

"I don't want to go," called Matty, though haltingly.

"So you sneaked behind your mother's back and lied to me? Get over here, *now*," commanded Peter. Matty, unused to this tone from his father, shuffled over and stood close to Liddy, although it had been her he wanted to hurt.

She rested her hand on his shoulder.

"I thought you'd enjoy it, son. Remember the times we went to the zoo? You used to love it. We collected a jar full of flattened pennies."

Outside, the rain was sputtering to a halt.

"But I can't force you to go, if you really don't want to," she said, resigned, and she looked old all of a sudden. While in the gray light Rose would have been all Dutch Masters softness and curly gray-blond hair, Liddy, with her pale skin and her angular grace, was a woman painted by Modigliani.

"I'm sorry, Liddy," Peter said. "I had no idea. I should have remembered."

Matty suppressed a triumphant grin as he knelt down and started putting on his shoes. Peter turned toward the door—

But then he turned back.

"Matthew, you're going to your brother's birthday party, and that's it."

"*What?*"

What? thought Liddy, thrilled to glimpse once more Peter's quiet authority, his blithe confidence, his shabby chic, in fact all the things she had been attracted to, and which had disappeared the day she had left him.

"I'm coming too. If that's all right with you, Liddy."

"Of course!"

"And you can keep those shoes on, my boy, because we're taking that dog out for a long walk first."

Matty's face narrowed into an arrow of fury. He fired it.

"Mom's fed up with me already. She wants to send me away to camp for the summer," he hissed.

"You've been begging me to go!" said Liddy, her composure finally faltering. "And last year you begged Rose to go. I'm sorry, Peter, with everything that's been going on, I made a . . . unilateral decision."

Peter fell silent for a moment. Up to this point, he had not even considered the impending summer vacation, although he dimly recalled Rose having mentioned it. After a rapid analysis of the different variables, however, he found Liddy's solution to be the correct one.

"You're a lucky boy. I loved camp when I was a kid. Knowing your mom, she'll have found the best for you. I'm sure it's very expensive. Have you said thank you?"

"It's only if it's okay with you and Rose," said Liddy. "We can visit on the family days."

Matty was confused. He had anticipated a vociferous and lengthy disagreement, but had forgotten that without Rose to offer an alternative view, his father's default parenting setting was "hands-off."

"It's okay," Peter said. "Go and get your coat."

Matty pulled away from them slouchily.

"Huh," he muttered. "I'd go anywhere to get away from all this shit."

"Matty—" said Peter, his temper suddenly rising.

"Leave it," whispered Liddy, resting her hand on Peter's arm. He nodded.

"Right. *Heel!"* he called to both boy and dog, and Liddy smiled.

The elevator doors closed behind them, and in the reflection, Liddy saw that the clouds outside had disappeared and she was suddenly suffused with sunlight and serenity. Inspired, she seized a pen and ran over to her desk to find the pretty cloth-bound notebook Rose had given her. She jotted down a few more thoughts on successful co-parenting for the introduction of her book. Then she brought Cal with her into her bedroom, where they walked into her wardrobe and considered what might be a suitable outfit to wear (skinny jeans + Armani blazer = work/life balance) in the photograph she planned to have taken this afternoon under the Delacorte clock, with Cal in a piggyback and Lucia beside her. She'd print this with a cheery caption just before the acknowledgments in her new book.

It suddenly occurred to her that Peter and Matty might join them. Her publisher had been asking for a happy family image to put in the promotional package. *We broke up without f**king him up!*

She caught sight of herself reflected in the mirror. Instead of wrinkles or rosacea, she saw her green eyes bright and her face in a wide grin. *Still some time to go before Botox*, she thought cheerfully.

Today was going to be a good day.

"Mommy, look!" shouted Cal. "Everyone's coming!"

Liddy and Lucia, who had been waiting at the entrance to the zoo, turned and waved.

It was easy to spot the kids from Cal's class, as several of the mothers had been doing boot camp together in Washington Market Park and they could hardly walk. But they were laughing happily in the sunshine, teasing each other about their various infirmities, and Liddy, seeing how much they enjoyed their easy camaraderie, felt a pang of something that was not quite regret, more like wistfulness. On Liddy's infrequent appearances in the school hall a crowd gathered, and she had to be interesting and amusing at its center, all the while wishing she could sit companionably in a corner with some nice, friendly woman talking about head lice or the Tracy Anderson method.

"Anything juicy at work at the moment, Liddy?" said one such nice, friendly mother, depositing a child next to Cal and a large book-shaped present into the black plastic sack Lucia was carrying for the purpose. "No names, of course, just details."

Liddy nodded obediently. "I'm doing a major sporting star who accuses his ex of trying to poison him with the Thanksgiving turkey."

"*Really?* Did she?"

"Her lawyer says she was using Nigella's cookbook and didn't know how to convert pounds to kilos."

The clock struck two and played "Twinkle, Twinkle, Little Star," and the jungle adventure party leaders, Dwayne and Leona, appeared on cue, resplendent in khaki shorts and pith helmets.

Dwayne clapped his hands and lifted up one end of a long, large rope with multicolored cords hanging off it, shouting, "Tie yourselves on, jungle adventurers, and don't get lost!" The little boys and girls obeyed eagerly. Peter and Matty appeared from the café, Peter's arm around Matty's shoulders, and Liddy gestured for them to tie themselves on too. But Peter dallied and so Louisa Tilney, class mom and former captain of her college tug-of-war team, helped him, wrapping her muscular arms around his waist and leaning her head into his chest. Peter looked over and caught Liddy's eye. His expression of bemused horror was priceless, and she began to giggle.

"First stop!" called Leona. "The red panda exhibit!"

She blew a whistle and the procession moved off.

"Look! Up there!" said Cal, pointing, as they reached the exhibit, and several phones were raised to capture the bundles of red fur curled up asleep in the branches. Liddy lifted her phone too and captured Lucia and Cal, in perfect profile, smiling into the distance. She zoomed in to take another picture, but the expression on Lucia's face was suddenly so pensive that Liddy recoiled.

"Red pandas are mainly nocturnal. What does that mean?" asked Dwayne.

Cal shot his hand up. "They move around at night," he said.

Lucia bent down and kissed Cal on the top of his head. Then he took her hand and kissed it. Suddenly Lucia burst into tears.

Liddy dropped the rope to head toward them, but at that moment her phone rang. She held it to her ear without checking who was calling. She regretted having done so.

"I'm in the lobby of the St. Regis with a new client and you need to meet us here now."

"Curtis. I can't." Behind her a mynah bird started squawking.

"Where the hell are you?"

Liddy did not reply. She never mentioned her kids in front of Curtis, as he liked to pretend she didn't have any. Curtis was of the old school on the issue of working parents, except that in his view, children should be neither seen *nor* heard. He dismissed all talk of flexible working hours, paternity leave, or, worst of all, working from home as "too Scandinavian."

"Get in the car. I need ten minutes. This is a big one."

Liddy guessed it must be a celebrity. Curtis had a particular tone to indicate "famous" as well as "rich," and this often meant Liddy would find herself climbing up fire escapes to "secret" meetings, only to leave through front doors into paparazzi that the celebrities' publicists had called themselves.

"If it's a big one, I'm too busy. I have too many ongoing cases as it is."

"You'll make time for this, believe me."

Liddy thought of the check for several thousand dollars she was about to write for Matty's summer camp. She glanced at her watch: 2:40. At three o'clock the kids would be in the cinema watching a short animated film about lemurs.

"I'll be there at five past three, and I'm yours for strictly ten minutes," she said. She hung up, texted Vince to stand by, and ran back to the party to find Lucia. Lucia was simultaneously follow- ing the bobbing pith helmets and conducting an animated con- versation with her only daughter, twenty-five-year-old Rosita, who had just arrived. The torrent of excitable Spanish made Liddy smile, but as she approached them they both fell silent.

"I'm glad you came, Rosita," said Liddy, kissing the young woman on both cheeks as Lucia walked on.

Rosita said nothing. She was the image of a young Lucia, only wearing more expensive clothing, her face set determinedly to nonexpression. Liddy continued.

"I heard about your new job in the bank. Congratulations. Lucia is so proud."

Liddy noticed that Rosita's eyes, always ringed blue-gray, were particularly baggy and strained today. *She works too hard*, Liddy thought, but said nothing, as she knew from experience that Rosita bristled whenever she tried to be nice to her. Rosita was too young and too driven to tell the difference between a concerned tone and a patronizing one and Liddy understood. At twenty-five, Liddy had been exactly the same.

"What color is the polar bear's skin?" asked Dwayne of the children, desperately trying to avoid eye contact with Cal.

"Black!" Cal shouted anyway, and Liddy was delighted that she had rejected Dwayne's suggestion that a prize be awarded for the child who got the most answers right. Louisa Tilney, whose daughter was now licking the information board, disliked her enough already.

"Your mom seems a bit tired, Rosita," she said.

"Of course she is," snapped Rosita. "She was up late doing the party bags."

She walked off before Liddy could reply, which was good because Liddy didn't know what to say. At that moment, an enormous polar bear, a magnificent adult male, swam downward, paddled, and then stopped in front of them, hanging spread-eagled, suspended like a puppet, staring out with his beady black eyes and resting his black-skinned paw on the glass. The party gasped, transfixed, and Liddy was transfixed too, mesmerized by this awesome moment of confrontation.

Matty appeared and pushed her onward, saying, "Strange things are afoot at the Circle-K!" (a private joke from the one time they had watched *Bill and Ted's Excellent Adventure* together), but then Peter saw Liddy's face, sent Matty on ahead, and asked, "What's going on?"

"I'm worried about Lucia. She's not herself today."

"Maybe she's sick?" he said.

Liddy turned to him, her mouth agape with revelation. *Of course*, Lucia was *sick*, that must be it.

"I hope it's not serious," he continued.

"God, yes," said Liddy, and she followed him into the darkness of the Polar Seabirds Exhibit, only to be greeted by the astonishing sight of Rosita shouting, "You have to tell her, Mama!"

as Lucia ran away from her, both figures silhouetted against a diorama of the Antarctic landscape.

Peter and Liddy looked at each other in dismay.

"Can you get everyone to the cinema?" she pleaded. She looked at her watch: 2:50. *SHIT!*

And to her amazement he did, grabbing a pith helmet and ramming it on top of his head, announcing that he would give the child that got outside first a can of cola.

Meanwhile, Liddy ran out into the sunlight and there, blinking, she found Lucia sitting mournfully on a bench in front of the sea lions.

Liddy approached tentatively. She sat down beside her and reached over and took Lucia's hand. "Lucia, what is it?"

Lucia turned to look at her, her eyes watery and an expression on her face so anguished that a sob rose in Liddy's throat. Liddy swallowed it back down.

"Are you ill?"

Lucia shook her head. "No. But my papa is," she said slowly. "I have to go back to Colombia."

Rosita came out and sat down on Lucia's other side. She put an arm around her mother, and Lucia leaned against her.

"We've been arguing," said Rosita. "Mama thinks you won't cope without her. She says you are late most nights and your phone is always ringing. She is sad to leave you on your own."

"Oh, Lucia," said Liddy. "We'll be fine. Of course you must go. When are you leaving? How long will you be?"

"She's flying out next Friday." Rosita paused and glanced at

Lucia, who squished her lips together in an urgent attempt not to cry again. "And she won't be coming back. I've bought her a house near my granddaddy's. All our family live there. I have twenty-three cousins."

Liddy looked at Rosita, who folded her arms and leaned back onto the bench. She considered asking Rosita to leave for a few minutes so she and Lucia could talk together. Lucia, however, fearing Liddy's renowned powers of persuasion and problem solving, obviously did not want that.

"I came to America for Rosita. She has been a good girl. She has everything. And now I am done and my papa needs me, Miss Liddy. You have been so kind and generous to me always. But I have to go home."

Liddy knew the conversation was over. Only six months ago she had finally made Lucia promise to call her "Liddy" and, most of the time, Lucia had complied. Liddy's right foot started to tap uncontrollably. This would take more than an hour with the life coach to sort out. Lucia had patrolled the hospital corridors as Liddy gave birth to Cal. She had barred the door to Curtis Oates during Liddy's two-week maternity leave. Liddy had assumed she would be accompanying her to Cal's high school graduation. *How could she replace the irreplaceable?*

"Why didn't you say anything?" she said.

"I didn't want to spoil my little Cal's beautiful party," Lucia said finally.

Liddy stood up and the two women embraced. Then Lucia took Liddy's face in her two hands and kissed her forehead.

"I would like to tell him myself tonight so he understands.

Okay? Can I bring him home with me after the cake for a sleepover?"

Liddy nodded slowly, and Lucia turned to leave. Then she stopped.

"Give that dirty dog away, Mama," she said.

She returned to the party. Liddy turned to Rosita.

"I'll pay for your mother's flight."

"No, no, you don't need to. I got it."

"You're a very good daughter."

"My mama did everything for me," Rosita replied.

"Yes."

Behind them, the sea lions barked in what now seemed to Liddy like a mournful ululation.

"Oh, Rosita, we'll miss her not being around. Poor Cal."

The Delacorte clock chimed three.

"He'll get used to it," said Rosita, and she stared right into Liddy's eyes. "I did."

Hurrying into the lobby of the St. Regis, she located Curtis immediately by his low, sulphurous cackle. But as she ran over to the fireplace, she realized he was talking on his phone, the chair opposite him empty. When he saw her he hung up with an excited flourish.

"Where's the mystery client?" asked Liddy.

"In the powder room. I told her I'd fill you in."

"What've we got?"

"Three years married, they lived in the husband's apartment on the Upper East Side, some stocks, shares, all his, and a summer place they bought after the wedding."

"Does she work?" asked Liddy. "I mean, outside the home?" she added quickly.

"Fashion PR. But she gave it up when they married to start a family."

"Did they?"

"No. No kids."

"Curtis, this is a straight down the line no-fault. There's nothing in this for us, unless the husband's a miserly multimillionaire with a lot of hidden assets. Is he?"

"No. He's like you and me. Look, she wants you."

Irritation rose within Liddy.

"I'm off," she said scratchily. "You can explain what I was doing here tomorrow. Give her the number of that woman on Riverside Drive who does mediation. It'll be done in a few days—"

"You don't understand, Liddy. Her great-aunt is Lisbeth Dawe Bartlett."

Liddy sat down in the empty chair. Lisbeth Dawe Bartlett, a billionaire nonagenarian heiress who refused to die, was Curtis's most valued client (he often said that his relationship with her was the longest and happiest of his entire life). Providing a legal service for any member of her family, however distant, was compulsory.

"Then she's loaded. What about her assets? Did you do the prenup?"

"Let's just say she's benefited from the estate-planning services of Oates and Associates. Of course Lisbeth won't let her starve, but the real cash goes to her kids—when she has them."

He looked around and lowered his voice.

"She's a bit . . . *bitter* . . . to be honest. She wants the apartment, a chunk of the shares . . . as much as we can get her, basically. I need you to run it all up the flagpole and see what flies. And by the way, Lisbeth has a particular interest in her so I promised you would be available—don't tell her she should get a therapist, whatever you do. If she wants to talk to you about *anything*, you listen. It's on Lisbeth's clock."

"Who's the husband's attorney?"

"Sebastian Stackallan."

Liddy burst out laughing.

"You're dreaming, Curtis. We don't have a hope."

But Curtis grinned maniacally.

"Oh, yes, we do," he said, standing up to greet the returning client. "This is the fun bit!"

Liddy turned.

A slender woman in a cream trench coat, a perfect sheet of blond hair over her shoulders, approached them daintily on her four-inch heels. She was holding a small leather purse in her hands and Liddy's attention was drawn to her tiny wrists, where the white skin stretched translucent, revealing the patterning of blue veins beneath like the branches of a fragile tree.

Liddy stared at her. She was sure she recognized her from somewhere.

"Hi, Liddy," said the woman. "I'm Chloe Stackallan."

Chloe Stackallan in the flesh was proof of the failure of mechanical reproduction to reflect the aura of a work of art. The photograph Sydney had shown Liddy of Chloe as the perfect bride had still utterly failed to convey the reality of Chloe's extraordinary beauty. Liddy was momentarily transfixed by her patrician perfection. Then she pulled herself together.

"Hi, Chloe," said Liddy. "It's good to meet you, although I'm sorry for the circumstances."

"Thank you, Liddy."

It took only a graceful wave of Chloe's manicured hand for two liveried doormen to appear with a chaise longue onto which she reclined. Liddy wondered what it must be like to have that as a superpower.

"Tell me why you want to end your marriage," said Liddy.

Chloe bristled. She considered such straight talking a little vulgar.

"We've been arguing for months and I can't go on anymore," she said.

She waved her hand again. This time a waiter arrived with jasmine tea.

"Sebastian blames me, you see. But it's not like you can get pregnant to order, is it? I mean, God knows I want a baby. I've been a vegetarian since I was thirteen years old and yet I've had to eat mackerel every week for two years to improve my fertility."

Curtis was not sure what expression to adopt here so he went for "avuncular sympathy."

"He's like that English king who kept chopping off his wives' heads because they didn't produce an heir."

"Henry the Eighth?" suggested Liddy.

"*Exactly*. He's not the person I thought he was. I should never have married him. He doesn't value me like he should."

She paused and lifted the cup to her lips, the slight tremor in her fingers betraying her outrage, and in that moment Liddy understood the story of their marriage. Chloe was a woman reared to be a holy grail of womankind, a reward for a handsome, wealthy bachelor who had spent years playing the field in search of it. The idea that a man might hand back such a prize was incomprehensible to her.

"Okay," said Liddy. "Any drugs, alcohol, cruel or inhumane treatment?"

"Apart from the mackerel eating . . ." said Curtis to lighten the tone, but Chloe's lips pursed so tightly they almost disappeared.

"Abandonment? Imprisonment?"

Chloe shook her head.

"Infidelity?"

Chloe looked surreptitiously side to side.

"Only once," she said, "but I promise he'll never find out." She looked at Curtis. "I was *desperate*," she said. Curtis looked back and tried to convey the unspoken message that in similar circumstances she could always give him a call.

"So," she continued. "What can you get for me? Ballpark, of course."

Liddy glanced at Curtis, who nodded at her to speak. He and Liddy were a practiced double act. They knew the steps to this dance of expectation management.

"I'm sure Curtis has told you what a fair settlement for a childless three-year marriage looks like under New York State law."

Chloe raised a hand to indicate that Liddy should stop talking. Liddy did not like this, but she stopped anyway.

"Sebastian keeps telling me he will be 'fair,' too. I don't want what's fair." She paused. "I want what I deserve."

She leaned forward to make her point.

"Before Sebastian met me, he never went out, he had no taste, he didn't know where to go on vacation and every night he used to sit on his own at home listening to music and smoking cigars. Yes, of course there were women, lots and lots of women, and people said he couldn't be tamed, but I did it! It took me a while, but I did it! I gave him a *life*!"

At this moment, Liddy found herself wondering how on earth the marriage had lasted as long as three years. She had enough sense of Sebastian's personality to know that he would not stay happy in a cage, however tasteful, for very long. It also worried her that, like any wild animal, he might chew off one of his own limbs to escape. He was a relentless adversary on the best of days; what he might do under this kind of provocation would be lengthy, expensive, and bloody.

"Your best chance of a decent lump sum will be for lost income," said Liddy.

Chloe looked confused.

"You need to send me a very detailed breakdown of your earnings before you were married."

"When I worked for Manolo he paid me in shoes!" Chloe shrieked, quivering.

She turned to Curtis. "I've got no job and nowhere to live. I'm older than I look, you know. Six of the best years of my life! *Wasted!* On *him!*"

"I understand," said Liddy with practiced calm. "You gave him the priceless gift of your childbearing years, but in law it counts for nothing. I'm sorry. If we're lucky, we'll get you half a million dollars all in."

"*That's it?* That's not near enough!"

And with that, she burst into tears.

"Dear Chloe, try not to get so emotional, it won't help you," said Curtis.

Liddy looked at him. "I disagree. Emotion may be the only thing we have to help us."

She handed Chloe a napkin.

"Let's forget judicial reasoning and equitable division for a moment. Put yourself in Sebastian's *heart*, Chloe. What does he care most about in the whole world?"

"His mother," said Chloe quickly. "He's devoted to her. She used to be an actress, Roberta Stackallan, but you won't have heard of her, she never made it in America. All she does now is the odd voice-over for things like bladder support underwear, cash Sebastian's checks, and get married—five times so far, and counting. When we first met, she was living in a druidic community. I had to watch her go through the cauldron of rebirth. Honestly, it's no wonder he's the way he is. When I rang her to say how he treated me, she wouldn't listen. She said he was her son and she could see no wrong in him, so perhaps I should reconsider my own behavior. And she wasn't so polite about it, let me tell you—"

"She's not an asset, she's a liability," said Curtis, trying another joke, and this time Chloe rewarded him with a chuckle, fixing him in the full beam of her white teeth.

"Indeed," said Liddy. "What I'm looking for is an *emotional asset*. Is there something, *anything*, that he would sacrifice everything else to keep?"

A tiny, catlike smile played on Chloe's lips.

"The house in Ireland," she said.

"Ireland?" said Liddy. "Is it valuable?"

She had a vague recollection of Sebastian mentioning a family home during their date from hell. She remembered, ruefully, that he had also announced that he was "not a marrying man." *Too right*, she thought, then she stopped; it had also turned out that she was "not a marrying woman."

Chloe shook her head. "No. It's tiny and there's never enough hot water, but it's the gate lodge on the land of the house he grew up in, where Roberta still lives. She sold it once when she was broke, in between husbands two and three, and he waited years to buy it back. He'll never give it up." She paused. She raised her hand to her mouth and her fingers trembled slightly. "He told me it was his dream to walk those fields with his children."

"Excellent," said Liddy. "We'll say you want it and use it as leverage to get you an enhanced settlement."

"How will it help?" asked Chloe, looking at Curtis.

"It's joint marital property," said Liddy. "If we went to court, the disparity of your assets would have to be taken into account. Sebastian owns the Manhattan apartment outright, and if we were *convincing* enough, the judge might award the house in Ireland to you. Sebastian can't take that risk. Start thinking of reasons you might want to live there."

Liddy glanced at her watch: 3:35.

"I have to go," she said.

Chloe leapt to her feet and hugged Liddy like an excited child. "I want this behind me. I want to get married again. Get it done, Liddy! You know Sebastian's your number one fan. He says you're the best divorce lawyer in town—he used to be cross if he saw your name on court papers. Honestly, when we first met I thought he had a bit of a . . . *thing* . . . for you!"

"No danger of that," said Curtis, chuckling.

Liddy extricated herself with a firm good-bye and headed toward the car. Curtis hurried after her.

"Don't be so sulky. Everyone knows you hate Stackallan."

She stopped. She turned. Her performance over, she could not conceal her weariness.

"I don't hate Mr. Stackallan. I hate this case. I wrote a book called *Equality Means in* Everything, remember, where I spent a whole chapter arguing why stuff like this should never happen. 'Marriage is not a meal ticket, *et cetera, et cetera*. . . .' She's already looking for husband number two. Doesn't seem to occur to her that she could get a job!"

Vince was standing outside holding the car door open.

"And by the way, Curtis, she definitely needs a therapist. She can't always have been as demented as this. She's got a strange glint in her eye. She's either medicated or she's been watching too many episodes of *The Good Wife*. She wants her moment in court."

Curtis shrugged.

"If people were mentally healthy, we'd be out of business."

Liddy growled as she climbed in.

"You're losing your sense of humor, Liddy," he called as Vince closed the door firmly behind her.

Back at the party zone, trestle tables were covered with green plastic tablecloths, and speakers in the corner played the sounds of the Amazon rain forest, although the real roar was not from cockatoos or distant howler monkeys but from overexcited and screeching children, their faces painted like frogs and lions. When Liddy entered, Cal was sitting on Lucia's lap while she smothered him in kisses. Peter was hiding beside a tissue paper collage, comfort eating chips off a paper plate.

"Where've you been? You missed all the games," Peter said.

"I don't get to do everything I'd like to," she replied briskly. She was not in the mood.

"I'm sure Lucia was filming it all."

Matty lumbered toward them, an enormous birthday cake perilously resting in his arms.

"Did you remember matches, Mom? For the candles," he said.

The cake was decorated with a banana and six monkeys, a candle stuck unceremoniously into each of their heads. Matty set it on the plastic tablecloth.

"I did," she replied, pulling a red Zippo lighter out of her pocket and lighting them. Dwayne and Leona started to sing as the kids gathered around. Peter and Liddy stood side by side as Matty helped Cal blow out the flames.

Liddy turned to Peter.

"Lucia's leaving us."

"*What?* What on earth are you going to do?" he said.

"Handle it, of course." She paused. "Peter, I want to thank you for your help today. I really appreciate it."

He nodded.

"And now you should go. You've done enough," she said. He did not disagree. Liddy called Matty and Cal over.

"*Cal.* Say good-bye to Matty. He's off with his dad now."

Cal had an icing sugar monkey in his mouth, so they waited patiently as the brown legs disappeared down his throat and he chewed up the authentic pink soles of the feet. He tapped his head against Matty's arm, waved at Peter, and then looked up at Liddy plaintively.

"*Where's MY dad, Mama?*"

Words failed Liddy.

She looked at Peter for help, but the small muscle on the right side of his face tightened as he shook his head and walked slowly toward the door. His shoulders had slumped once more under the heavy weight of his bitterness.

She knelt down and held Cal very tight.

"Your dad lives a long way away," she said. Cal thought about this for a moment, and then nodded. It seemed to satisfy him, temporarily at least, and he hurried off to look for Lucia and another slice of cake.

Liddy looked up. Matty was shaking his head.

"You're going to have to tell him more than that, Mom," he said seriously. "You don't want Cal thinking he was, like, stolen, or cloned in a lab, or bought from a surrogate."

"It's age appropriate," said Liddy, ending the discussion. She grabbed Matty's arm and led him toward Peter, who was now discussing the cake with Louisa Tilney.

"It looks amazing," Louisa was saying. "But they always taste disappointing. You'd think for all that money they'd use butter."

"It doesn't matter," he replied grumpily. "It's just a prop."

Liddy waited for Louisa to leave.

"What does that mean, Peter?" she demanded.

"It means what I said." And with that, he walked away from her again, his voice getting louder as he went farther, which was disconcerting.

"You think my life is fake?" she snarled, her tone so sharp it made Matty look frightened.

"It doesn't matter what I think," said Peter. "You went to work in the middle of this party, didn't you?"

"So what if I did?" She looked around. "The 'props' cost a lot."

He looked around. His gaze alighted on Cal. "They certainly did," he said, more cruelly than he meant. Then he looked at the ground in shame.

"*Mom! Dad!* Stop it!" said Matty.

Liddy stopped, chagrined.

She moved slowly toward Peter. She put her hand on his shoulder. She whispered in his ear. *"Forgive me."* She pulled back, but their faces were still very close.

"Why did you call him Cal James, Liddy?"

She paused. It was another question she had not expected today.

"For the same reason I took your name. I think everyone in a family should be called the same."

She smiled weakly. "And I didn't know what else to do."

There was a pause.

Then he kissed her, very gently, on the lips. For a moment she felt that his mouth parted and he seemed to yearn for her to reciprocate. She did not.

"Please, forgive me," she said again. And then she backed away.

"I'm trying," he said. "Matty—let's go."

And without another word, they did.

Liddy looked around the room: overtired children being carried off in their parents' arms, food and deflated balloons strewn over the floor, the icing banana crushed on a chair. She took a deep breath and counted to five.

At that moment, a text came through. It was the photographer waiting under the Delacorte clock. He said the light was perfect.

Portrait taken, Liddy hauled herself and the black sack full of presents up the path toward Columbus Circle like a disconsolate Santa. Before the photographer could ask her why she had not brought the others with her as agreed, she had put on her right-side-of-rictus grin and answered, "I'm alone."

Now, she realized that she was.

She made a quick plan: Bikram yoga (extreme!) at six, then into that place on Crosby Street that could do a facial, a massage, and an eyebrow threading in ninety minutes, detox drink for dinner, two pills, and ten hours' sleep. She sat on a black bench and took out her phone. There was an e-mail from Lloyd Fosco to his five fellow residents in the building, asking for a meeting to discuss the urgent need for roof repairs. She decided to ignore this. Then the phone rang. She checked the screen and to her surprise it was not Curtis but her father, Patrick, calling from the condominium in Orlando she had bought for her parents. She smiled. Although they had never quite got over how Cal came about, it was better late than never for the birthday greetings.

"Hi, Dad."

"I'm in the bathroom so your mother can't hear. She's always tellin' me I'm not to disturb you when you're so busy, but I can't take it anymore."

"What?" said Liddy, momentarily disoriented. Then she hoped fervently he was not about to describe anything anatomical he might be examining in the mirror.

"Listen," he said, his voice echoing off the tiles. "I've got the hot tap turned full clockwise now. Nothing." And he placed the receiver into his tub, under the nonrunning hot faucet, and shouted into it, *"You need to call the management company today!"*

"Yes, Dad," she said obediently. "How is everything else?"

"The woman next door's gone gaga," he replied. "She was always away with the fairies, but she's off the bleedin' charts now. She arrived at the door yesterday morning tellin' me I'd messed with her bush. I told her, Missus, I wouldn't touch your feckin' bush without safety goggles and a plunge in the sheep dip afterward." He cackled delightedly. "Won't be long now before they cart her off to the looney bin. It's that early-onset Alzheimer's."

"What a shame," said Liddy.

"Ah, she's as well off. When I think of all the things in my life I'd like to forget—"

Fortunately for Liddy, Patrick's descent into mournful rumination was halted by the arrival of his brother, Frankie, who had also retired nearby. Frankie had been a plumber, so there were the three obligatory minutes as he hit the pipes with a wrench, Patrick providing a running commentary, before once again instructing Liddy to sort his hot water out.

"Is Mum there?" asked Liddy, but he had hung up. He did not ask Liddy how she was. He did not ask how his grandchildren were. He had forgotten Cal's birthday. *At least early-onset Alzheimer's would be an excuse*, thought Liddy, but her father suffered only from late-onset selfishness.

She slumped backward and the bars of the bench dug into her back.

Mmm, she thought. *Fuck the Bikram!*

She answered Lloyd's e-mail, saying she was free that evening.

She did not press reply all.

ADVENTURES OF THE GUILT-FREE WOMAN: PART II

It turned out that all the books were right to say pregnancy was a real game changer, physically and emotionally. Particularly if you had a lot of time on your hands.

Rose spent her days in solitary confinement, marking dots in her diary as the weeks went by (although Peter suggested she finally read Proust, counting hours had become one of her main occupations), and imagined herself like Edmond Dantès chained in the Château d'If in *The Count of Monte Cristo,* scratching lines on the limestone walls of his prison cell. She was awakened every morning by her own anxiety, something she could not fumble for in the dark and switch off, her only task for the next twelve hours to lie prostrate on her bed trying to contain the unborn being who was her jailer, frequently drinking glasses of ice water, eating chocolate, or watching violent films to agitate it if she could not feel it punching her from within.

In this unusual and hypersensitive state, it was unsurprising that the dramas of the lives of others had become her obsession.

Four weeks had passed since the unfortunate events at Cal's birthday party, but although anyone else would be lying on the bathroom floor sobbing with the stress of it all, Liddy was not. Within twenty-four hours, she had found three people to replace Lucia: a daily housekeeper, a dog walker, and a temporary nanny, or rather, "manny," who was a qualified elementary teacher and strapping ex-athlete named Josh. And it was all going to be "fine," even "fabulous," Liddy said, as she had spoken to a parenting expert who told her that the boys should have a male around the house. As to what Liddy would tell Cal about his parentage, Rose could only wait and see.

One thing was for sure. Liddy was not an ordinary woman and therefore unlikely to deal with it in an ordinary way. After all, Rose often thought, Liddy could have seduced Peter and pretended Cal was his. She could have had an abortion and pretended nothing had happened. Instead, she had told Peter the truth, held her head up high, and had the baby on her own. *No scarlet letter for her.*

Meanwhile, Rose missed Matty so much it ached. She missed breakfast and bedtime and music practice. She missed doing his English homework, literally, writing down abstract nouns on a work sheet in a counterfeit illegible scribble on nights she was too tired to argue. She missed the packs of boys returning to the house after soccer, sniggering and punching each other, the noise and violence of the sniggering and punching directly reflecting their level of happiness. She missed the routine of her previous life, the order she, Liddy, and Peter had imposed by demarcating their roles within it. And then she missed the life she had imagined she would have if she had ever discovered she was pregnant, an imagined life that had never included the words *geriatric pregnancy* or *hypertension* or *bed rest*.

Matty, however, had settled quickly into the new manny-style regime in Tribeca—*Josh doesn't believe in more than half an hour's homework a day, Josh wants to take me to a comedy club on a weeknight, Josh says drinking protein shakes builds muscle and he'll show me how to get a six-pack*—and although Rose tried to take comfort in his apparent peace of mind, a couple of the mothers from the school had dropped by and let slip some alarming information. "His last book report was on the biography of Kurt Cobain," said one. The other reported that his grades had plummeted and he was buying at least two or three sodas from the vending machine every day. When she tried to mention this to Peter, he dismissed it as gossip, but it preyed on Rose's unoccupied mind.

Rose became at first concerned, then consumed, with the idea that she was sacrificing one child to save the other growing within her.

She checked her watch. Matty had mentioned that Liddy was to be featured in a news item on NY1 that morning, and so Rose switched on the TV. Liddy, positively petite next to the enormous and clearly famous football player walking beside her, was making triumphant progress down the steps outside the courts downtown, through a posse of clacking cameras and clamoring journalists seeking a comment on yet another victory. Liddy, radiating confidence and poise, cruised toward her car, smiling broadly and ignoring most of the shouted interrogation, apart from a question from a showbiz correspondent about the "bling-tastic" gold chain wrapped around her collar.

"Is it real?" the young woman demanded, thrusting the microphone so hard toward Liddy that it almost grazed her nose.

"It certainly is," Liddy replied, unfazed. "It was a thank-you gift from one of my clients."

At this, the enormous football player leaned over, booming, "And I'll be buying her another one!"

"I love my job!" trilled Liddy. Then she waved good-bye to the cameras, and with a happy "Thank you, guys!" allowed Vince to guide her into the backseat, crossing her legs with the practiced air of a woman used to entering and exiting limos in front of the national press.

Of course Rose knew that this Liddy James was a *brand*—the Superlawyer! Supermother! Barbara had described—and her success was based on this image of Supercompetence! that allowed her to dispense advice on chat shows, represent celebrity clients, and write best-selling books. Liddy had once confessed to her that as a law student she had taken acting classes for this very purpose; she had learned to hide weaknesses, anything from bad skin to emotional upset or, in the case of women, age. But still, Rose had an irrational dislike of people who said, "I'm fine," when meaning the opposite (this came from her father, who viewed politeness as a sign of mental illness and therefore took pride in "plain speaking," despite the fact that he was regularly asked to leave family events). Intensive therapy in her twenties notwithstanding, trapped in bed, Rose found herself enraged by Liddy's composure.

Liddy was more . . . *Liddy-ish* than ever.

In the late afternoon Rose awoke from a doze to hear Peter bouncing up the stairs two at a time. He kissed her on her nose and announced, far too excitedly she thought, that Liddy had picked Matty up from school and they were heading over, Cal in tow. This had been happening two or three times a week since the birthday party. Liddy would find an excuse to drop by and suddenly would be ordering takeout.

"I decided to cook so I did the shopping on the way home," he said. "Chicken cacciatore. Your favorite."

"Don't you have end-term papers to grade?" she replied ungraciously.

"I want to see Matty," he said, and then, before she could say anything else, added, "It's *Wednesday*. Can I bring you some tea?"

Because Peter had no experience with the sheer monotony of years of cooking for a family (a life measured in meatballs on Monday, chops on Tuesday, pasta with jar sauce on Wednesday), he was enthusiastic about his new domestic role and set about reading recipe books, marinating, and even making homemade mayonnaise. He asked Rose whether to use canned or fresh tomatoes, but, in fact, he had already decided. He went back downstairs to start stewing, leaving Rose to do the same.

Forty minutes later, the front door double banged and she heard the sounds of Liddy's entrance, pursued by her boys. Liddy called out hello to Peter, told Matty to give him the bottle of wine she had brought and, after settling Cal on the sofa to watch cartoons on her laptop, headed up the stairs.

Liddy bustled into the bedroom carrying her briefcase and a large bunch of yellow roses. She put the flowers into a vase and opened the briefcase. Her manner was brusque and efficient. Her brain was all business.

"I saw you on TV this morning," said Rose, a little wary. Liddy was in exactly the same outfit, although she had replaced the heels with flats. "Did a client really give you that necklace?"

"Yep. Wanna try it?" said Liddy, lifting her hands behind her neck to unclip it. "How are you?" She threw the necklace on the bed between them. It was heavy and it made a dent in the quilt.

"Good," answered Rose, holding it up against her. "I mean, I'm a bit bored. How's Matty?"

"He seems fine today. Long may it last."

"I've been researching behavioral modification techniques for teenagers using positive discipline. For example, Liddy, if you catch him on the computer instead of doing his homework he has to do extra chores that evening—"

"He doesn't do any chores, any evening, Rose, and he never has. If I catch him on his computer again when he shouldn't be, I swear I'm going to throw it out the window. If I could accidentally hit his vile friend Enzo with it as well, then I'd have killed two birds with one stone."

Rose looked at her in horror.

"Metaphorically speaking, of course," said Liddy. "How's work going?"

"What do you mean?"

"I mean, my dear Rose, have you started writing your article? I was under the impression it was extremely important for your job."

Her eyes moved to the large potted plant in the corner, where an encouraging note from Professor Sophia Lesnar still nestled in the cactus-like flower.

Oh, no, thought Rose, *she's going to discuss MY problems.*

"I've been thinking I might give up work after I've had the baby," she said boldly, but when she saw the expression on Liddy's face, she wished she had tried it out on someone else first.

"What about your students?" asked Liddy.

"They seem to be managing fine without me," replied Rose sharply.

Liddy, unused to such petulance from Rose, made a little exhalation. Rose mistook her reaction.

"I know you might not approve."

"No, no," said Liddy, taking it in her stride. "One size can't fit all. That soft gold looks good on you. Borrow it." She paused. "Does Peter know?"

Rose stared at her resentfully. Sitting so close to Liddy in her current mood was like watching her performance on the TV again.

"No," said Rose finally. "I haven't discussed it with him yet."

"Then it's very good I've prepared this document for you," said Liddy. She pulled out a slim blue folder with a couple of pages inside it. The cover page read "Couple Cohabitation Agreement."

"What's this?" asked Rose.

Liddy put on her glasses.

"It's a couple cohabitation agreement," she said, patiently. "New York State doesn't recognize common-law marriages, as I'm sure you know, so unless you and Peter make an agreement, you have no legal protection."

"*Sorry?*"

"Rose, your name isn't on the deed of this house, you don't have a joint bank account, and you're on my health insurance policy, not Peter's."

"How do you know all this?"

Despite Rose's insistent tone, Liddy ignored the question. She and Peter had always maintained what amounted to a compulsory gag order on the financial aspects of their separation.

"It wasn't my business to interfere up to now, but you have a child to think about. *If* you give up your career, and you and Peter split up, you'll be homeless and incomeless."

"Hang on a minute, Liddy. It's not that I want to give up my career, it's that I don't know how I can do what I have to do and do everything else." (Anger always made Rose inarticulate.) "And Peter and I are not going to split up!"

Rose stabbed at the document with her finger and pushed it away.

Liddy was unmoved. "You have no rights. *Nada.* Nothing. If

you were a new client in my office and described your current situation I would not let you out of the door without this agreement."

"*No!*" said Rose. "I am not your client, and it isn't your business."

Liddy took off her glasses. "Rose, I don't mean to upset you. Please. Listen to me. What about Matty? A stepparent has a tenuous legal relationship with stepchildren in the event of a divorce anyway, but you . . ." She raised her hands upward, palms aloft, and shrugged.

Rose stared at her in disbelief.

"At the moment, your role in Matty's upbringing relies on Peter's *goodwill*. So sign, or get married. It's not like Peter doesn't know all this. He was with me for a long time and believe me *we* discussed it. It's not personal, it's the law."

"*Liddy!* Of course it's personal. I'm *me*. And Peter is *Peter*. He's your ex-husband! You know him. How could you question his goodwill?"

Liddy paused. "Can you honestly tell me that none of your friends have said this to you?" she said.

Rose folded her arms. "My mother has." (Rose winced at this memory. The ensuing argument had ended with her mother calling her a doormat.)

"That's because she loves you. Only a person that cares would bring this stuff up. I mean, it's not easy . . . you look as if you want to bite my head off."

Liddy patted Rose's legs under the bedclothes reassuringly,

but Rose did not feel cared for, she felt patronized. She imagined how, later, Liddy would congratulate herself for raising an issue that others less plain-speaking would avoid.

"If you're nervous, let me talk to him," continued Liddy, oblivious.

"I'm not *nervous*!" spluttered Rose, looking extremely nervous. "How dare you say these things!"

"I loved Peter very much. He's the father of my child. But I'd say this if he was standing in front of me. I do know him. That's the truth."

"What? He's got some dark side that you're warning me about?" Rose rolled her eyes at the absurdity of this suggestion.

Liddy did not answer. She had seen plenty of people demonize their partner's ex-spouse, calling them everything from "unreasonable" to "lunatic" rather than acknowledge any deficiency in said partner's behavior. One thing was clear about Rose. She might teach a course in the micro-examination of a text, but she was useless at reading between the lines.

The two women looked at each other, both daring the other to be more honest. Rose backed down first. She had had quite enough of the "truth" for one evening.

"Okay. I'll read it," she said.

"Good," said Liddy. She put her glasses back on and opened the document to page one.

"*Not now!*" hissed Rose.

"Sure," said Liddy. Rose watched as she put the papers into a brown envelope and put it in the drawer on Rose's side of the bed, carefully hiding it underneath the hot-water bottle.

"How are you, anyway?" said Rose coldly. "You've got a lot on your plate at the moment."

Liddy looked confused by such a suggestion. "I'm *fine*," she said firmly and exited the room, leaving Rose to fume.

Rose picked up her book of baby names, but without Peter to discuss whether something like Shayna sounded like a made-up name, she put it down. She switched on an episode of *The Affair*. Through the floorboards she heard a cork popping out of a bottle of wine and Liddy laughing. She stabbed at the remote to turn up the volume. She could not settle.

Rose rued the times she had lamented Peter's refusal to forgive Liddy. Now she realized she had been threatened by his burning hatred; she was not enough to make him forget Liddy. This, not the unselfish motives others attributed, had always been a leading factor in her insistence on rapprochement. But now Rose found herself wishing fervently for the previous hostility between them. She thought of *Wuthering Heights* and imagined Peter and Liddy as the Heathcliff and Cathy of Carroll Gardens, capable of extraordinary acts of emotional violence, unable to live with or without each other, and herself as poor Isabella Linton, a watery substitute for her husband's true love.

She heaved out of bed and locked herself in the bathroom to practice ordering Liddy out of her home (whether it was legally her home or not), which was a temporary release.

But what if the problem with Liddy and Peter was not that they hated each other, but that they still loved each other?

Downstairs, Peter was playing Scrabble with Matty and Cal in the kitchen.

"LI!" said Cal triumphantly.

"That's not a word," said Matty.

"It's a Chinese unit of measurement," Cal replied. "Mom told me."

"So it is," said Peter, and he glanced over at Liddy. "And I told her."

Liddy grinned and settled herself down on the couch. She opened her briefcase again and took out the net-worth statements of Chloe and Sebastian Stackallan. She picked up his and scanned it. He was forty-six years old, had graduated from Trinity College, Dublin, and Harvard Law, was a member of the English, Irish, and New York bars and a fellow of the International Academy of Trial Lawyers. In his midthirties he had spent five years working in Nicaragua and had received an honorary doctorate from Managua University (this explained why she had no recollection of him during the time when Matty was a small child). She was delighted to see that his salary and bonus package were marginally lower than hers, but irritated that his share portfolio was performing much better. (She flipped to the end to see the details of his financial advisors, which were listed in the package.) For religious affiliation he had typed in "Jedi," which, though childish, she found rather amusing. He owned a first edition of *Ulysses* by James Joyce and a number of drawings by the artist William Orpen, whose work Liddy had heard of but never seen. She saw from the dates he had stopped collecting after his marriage. She suspected this was not for fear of any joint marital property, but because he had to spend all his spare cash on Chloe.

Under real estate was listed, first, his apartment on East

Eighty-fourth, and second, the gate lodge Chloe had described with such disdain. Liddy saw from the attached title deed that it had originally been part of something called Stackallan Demesne, County Wicklow, but even allowing for the inflated purchase price Sebastian had paid to secure it, with the vagaries of the Irish economy it was worth next to nothing.

She picked up her laptop and typed the address into the search engine. Within seconds she was looking at a photograph of two stone pillars on a narrow country road, and could just glimpse a slate roof and the edge of a silver lake in the distance. It had been taken on an overcast day and there wasn't much to see beyond the trees, tall grasses, and far fields of the rolling Irish countryside. She thought of the interminable drives she had taken as a child with her parents, in the drizzle, through places with names like the Sally Gap. She could only imagine what this property might be like, with the lack of upkeep and the endless rainy weather and the damp erupting from the walls—no wonder Chloe hadn't been able to think of any reasons she wanted to spend time there. Nevertheless, Liddy composed a creative e-mail to Sebastian explaining Chloe's need for a home of her own, and that, if denied the Eighty-fourth Street apartment, she would seek sole ownership of the property in Ireland, which was of incalculable sentimental, if not financial, value to her. Liddy pressed send.

Peter poured her a glass of wine and brought it over. Liddy smiled her thanks and returned to the photograph. She moved the cursor around and was about to zoom in on the lake, when suddenly she glimpsed an out-of-focus image of a tall man in black trousers and a slender woman in a green dress, holding hands just outside the perimeter of the property. She paused and peered more closely, certain she was in the presence of Sebastian and Chloe, captured together forever in that place in a happier time.

Thunk!

"What the hell!"

Liddy sat up with a scream, laptop thudding to the ground, papers flying all over the rug, as a large square object hurtled past her face and hit the cushion next to her. Disorientated, but amazed that she had miraculously caught the glass of red wine, she suddenly saw Rose standing on the stairs.

Rose was shivering, barefoot in her capacious white nightgown and panting with exertion, her hand still raised from hurling the book.

"Get out of here!" Rose shouted, eyes wild, then rather ruined the effect by yelping as her right foot went into a spasm.

"Rose! Stop it!" shouted Liddy.

But Rose hobbled toward her in attack, flapping her two hands like the flippers of a performing sea lion. Liddy plunked her glass on the table and ducked behind the couch, wrapping her hands around her head for protection.

"What on earth is going on?" said Peter sternly, marching out of the kitchen.

"I don't want her around anymore," Rose replied, waving an agitated finger in Liddy's direction.

At this point, Matty and Cal appeared, Cal frightened, Matty aggressive.

"What have you done, Mom?" Matty said, in exactly the same tone as his father. "Have you upset Rosey?"

"Obviously!" hissed Liddy.

There was a moment as she stared in horror at the moonscape of dust, fluff, and dead flies that nestled on the rug at her eye level, and then she tentatively raised her head above the furniture, her eyes scanning side to side for any further missiles.

"Rose?" said Peter.

Liddy looked at Rose, who was grimacing and shaking her leg.

"I've got a cramp in my foot," Rose said plaintively.

Now Liddy looked at Peter, who was staring at Rose in disbelief.

"Try walking on it," Liddy said.

And Rose seemed to wilt in front of them, gathering her billowing nightgown around her with her arms. Then she bobbed slowly up and down, like a hot-air balloon deflating on a Stair-Master.

Liddy picked some lint off her skirt and glanced around at her jumbled papers. Cal ran over to her.

"Are you and Rosey not friends anymore?" he said.

Rose gasped and put her hand to her mouth.

"Rosey and I are always friends, baby. We had a silly argument. It's okay," Liddy said firmly, and kissed him. She looked over at Peter. "We should go."

"I have spent an hour cooking dinner," said Peter, "and it will be eaten. Boys, get back into the kitchen."

"Of course," said Rose, lifting her hands and inflating again as the boys obediently sat down at the table and started to eat.

Liddy picked up her glass.

"I'll follow you in," she said, and she patted Peter on the arm, which meant "try not to make too much out of this in front of the boys," something both women understood because of mindful parenting. He shook his head and she knew he was formulating some explanation for this madwoman-descending-from-the-attic performance, which would inevitably involve the overemotional-ism of pregnant women. (Peter had always been reluctant to re-inforce such gender stereotyping, but then, he had previously considered the idea of two women catfighting the sole preserve of daytime soap operas.)

"Oh, dear, Peter, I'm so sorry," said Rose. Peter nodded, still bewildered, and closed the kitchen doors behind him.

Rose sat down and massaged her instep. Then she put her head in her hands and peered at Liddy through her fingers.

"Do you want Peter back?"

Liddy burst into incredulous laughter.

"No," she said. *God no*, she thought.

Rose swallowed hard. "Clearly I'm going crazy stuck up there," she said.

"No, you're not crazy. I have taken advantage of your kind-ness. And I should be in my own home, but . . . family is still family."

Except when it isn't, she thought.

"Is this really not my home?" said Rose.

Liddy shook her head. "Look," she said, "I was only trying to help. If nothing's broke, I guess you don't have to fix it. I'm sorry if I was too . . . straightforward. I'm always in such a hurry, you see."

This was true. Liddy was finding it harder and harder to transition between the different areas of her existence, to remember that although her life was a marathon run as a sprint, few others had the stamina to keep up.

"I do want to get married. Peter doesn't," whispered Rose.

"That's not a surprise. He wasn't convinced about marriage the first time around."

"And I don't know if he even wants this baby."

Rose's face crumpled like newspaper in the rain. Liddy moved toward her, put her arms around her, and held her as she sobbed.

"You have to talk to him," said Liddy.

"I can't. I can't think straight about anything. I know you think I'm mad to stop working, but when I try and focus, the words fly around and around in my head. I can't explain it to Peter and I don't think he'd understand anyway. Did you ever feel like that?"

She pulled her sleeve to her face and wiped her eyes.

"No," said Liddy.

Rose smiled despite herself.

"I don't know what to do. I'm scared, Liddy."

I'm scared too, thought Liddy. One of the difficult things about having a relationship with Peter was that, while he wanted to be top dog professionally, he also had a philosophical objection to being sole financial provider. Rose had so far managed this far more successfully than Liddy ever could, but she disregarded it at her peril. Liddy found herself hoping that, for all their sakes, Peter loved Rose far more than he had ever loved her.

She was aware that this could only be described as fucked up.

"Concentrate on the baby," she said. "Everything will be fine."

"I don't know how you had a baby on your own. I don't think I could do it."

There was a pause. Liddy glanced at Rose's bare feet, which were bony and calloused and rather ugly.

"You'd be amazed what you can do if you have to," Liddy said. "Not that you ever will have to, of course. Now you should get back into bed." She rested a hand on Rose's shoulder.

"I'm worried about Matty," said Rose. "One of the other mothers told me he was drinking two or three cans of soda every day. What about his skin? Is he eating enough salad?"

"I doubt it."

"Is he practicing his keyboard? I used to sit with him and sing along. He's really good, Liddy. And I'm not just saying it."

Liddy turned and clipped her briefcase shut. It was too much all of a sudden.

"I'm glad you didn't throw that necklace," she said. "You could have taken my eye out."

Rose smiled in relief.

"I'm sorry I was such a brat," she said.

"Yeah. Who'd have thought?" said Liddy. (In fact she had often thought that extreme aggression lurked beneath the sunny smiles of many "nice" women.) But she smiled too.

Then she picked up the book Rose had hurled. Rose was glad in her frenzy she had grabbed a paperback and not a weighty hardback such as *Silenced Voices: Forgotten Hungarian Plays from Transylvania*, which was at the top of the pile on her bedside table.

Rose looked at Liddy. Liddy looked at the title.

It was *Lean In*.

"You've got to be kidding me," said Liddy, and her smile disappeared.

Back at the apartment, Liddy put Cal straight to bed and then forced Matty to take the puppy down to the sidewalk in front of the building. She leaned out of a window and watched as they walked up and down between two lampposts, but although she had set the alarm on his phone for twenty minutes, the moment the dog pooped, Matty made a great grimacing show of cleaning it up for his audience of one in the balcony and raced back inside.

She filled the kettle with water, selected a suitably soothing blend of herbal tea, and reached for a mug. This made her wince. She had asked the new housekeeper not to rearrange the mugs on the mug tree, which she had alphabetized according to logo, KEEP CALM AND CALL YOUR ATTORNEY going above THIS MIGHT BE TEQUILA and so on, but had been ignored. This caused Liddy considerable distress, even though she knew part of it was displacement. It had taken her hours to master most of the kitchen appliances, and she had given up on how to work the toaster oven. It was not just Cal who cried about the absence of Lucia.

The elevator door hissed open and Matty emerged talking, although not to himself, as was usual.

"She's here," he was saying and called out, *"Mom?"* and Liddy knew he had company, as he had not grunted at her or hissed unintelligible mutterings behind her back.

"Matty, you should buzz before you—"

"It's my fault. I invited myself in."

She turned and there was Lloyd Fosco, in his signature black boots, leather pants, and scoop T-shirt revealing a little too much matted chest hair, against which hung a large silver pendant. He was carrying the dog in his arms, a purposeful look on his face that contrasted with his usual languid demeanor.

"Lloyd knows The Rock," said Matty.

"Interesting," said Liddy. Then she looked over at Lloyd.

"Are you here to talk about the roof repair?" she said, indicating with a nod of her head that this was by way of explanation to Matty.

"I am," said Lloyd convincingly. "I also wanted to see your apartment."

He walked into the center of the living room and spun around slowly.

"*Fantastic!* I like what you've done with the space. Great sight lines."

Liddy thought resentfully of the many hours of her life she had spent with the architect, measuring the exact heights of door frames and drape poles. She looked around, her gaze alighting on the silver-streaked Italian marble worktop she didn't particularly like. "Fantastic" wasn't worth it.

"Well, my iPad's not gonna watch itself," said Matty, knowing that Liddy would not say no in front of this hairy actor, and before she could answer, he dived into his room, slamming the door and then burping loudly behind it.

She turned to Lloyd, mock sighing. "*Kids!* Do you want a drink?"

"No," he said. And then he tenderly placed the dog on an armchair, walked toward Liddy, and took her into his arms. "I want you."

Liddy's mouth opened in surprise, but Lloyd took it as a cue and thrust his lips against hers. After a couple of awkward seconds, where teeth hit teeth, Liddy responded enthusiastically, although she would have preferred him not to lick upward onto her palate. Eventually, he lifted his head to draw breath, pulling her tighter toward him. He was a tall, well-built man, and this meant her nose nestled against his chest like a little thrush in a brown nest.

"We had an amazing night together. Why won't you return my calls? I think you've been using the service elevator to avoid me!"

He kissed her neck, laughing at the absurdity of this. He smelled tired, and this made Liddy like him more, which was a relief. What had ensued after Cal's birthday party had certainly taken her mind off the day's events, albeit till the next morning, but she had been unsure if she had the stamina to repeat it.

"I like your pendant," she said quickly, running her hand across his chest.

"It's kinetic. Look." He stepped back and pulled the chain up and down. The pendant moved between the masks of comedy and tragedy.

"Wow. I've never seen anything like that before," said Liddy, which was true.

"I designed it myself," he said proudly. "Do you see the words?"

"*All the world's a stage*," read Liddy.

"Yeah," he said enigmatically. So Liddy said the first thing that came into her head, which was, "It is indeed," and then, "Have a drink."

She went over and pulled open the fridge door and filled two glasses with ice.

"Thanks. Juice, please. I've got an early call tomorrow."

Liddy looked longingly at the bottle of lemon-flavored vodka in the freezer as she poured them two orange juices, but she admired Lloyd's self-discipline and work ethic, meticulous and monastic like hers. He settled down, leather pants on leather arm-chair, and cradled the dog, who licked his hands in gratitude for the attention.

"So. How've you been?" he said.

"Busy," she said. "I'm always busy."

"That's why we should date each other," he said. "We live in the same building. It's so convenient," and then he held the dog up to his face and nuzzled its wet nose. "What's her name?" he said, and Liddy replied Coco. The dog panted excitedly and Lloyd exclaimed, "*Coco! Who's a pretty girl,*" over and over again. On another evening, Liddy would have found the juxtaposition of his cynicism and sentimentality incredibly annoying, but to-night it had a completely different effect.

She walked over and sat on his lap and petted the dog too.

"Do you have any kids?" she asked.

"No. Not yet. But I have a dog. You ever seen my dog? I got joint custody of her last year, but then my ex moved to LA and dognapped it." He paused meaningfully. *"Bitch."*

Liddy guessed that Lloyd was not referring to the well-groomed pug in black booties she had once seen trotting behind him. She wanted to laugh but was glad she didn't.

"She was my emotional-support dog. I haven't been able to fly transatlantic since then. My manager wants to get me another one, but I'm not ready."

"You should have hired me. I'd have got you full custody."

She leaned over and kissed him, and they put their hands all over each other, until they fell off the sofa with a crash and woke Cal, who cried out. Liddy extracted herself and hurried into the bedroom, where she lay down beside her son for a couple of minutes until he fell asleep again. She looked up to see Lloyd in the doorway, watching. He smiled as she walked toward him.

"You can't stay," she said.

"I know," he said, "that's okay."

Lloyd put his arm around her shoulders, and they went over to the window. Through the triple glazing the city was silent, the skyline black against the dark blue sky, the buildings patterned with golden squares of light, windows that looked like cutouts.

"Your view is better than mine," he said, congratulatory.

Liddy gazed into the distance.

Then she moved closer to him.

"Just so you know. I couldn't fully commit to someone who already had children," he said.

"I'm not looking for full commitment," said Liddy. "I told you. I'm always busy."

He grinned. From another woman, this statement could have been game playing, defensiveness, or a straightforward lie, but from Liddy it had the ring of absolute truth. He felt disorientated. It made him like her more.

"Good. I'm always busy too. Is that water damage from the leak?"

Liddy nodded. One wooden window frame was cracking, the paint blistering and the surrounding wall stained with damp.

"It's a mess. The sooner we get that fixed the better."

"I know," said Liddy. "I just can't face the bill at the moment."

He stroked her hair. "And your roots need doing. My friend Pedro's opened a new salon on Beach Street. I'll hook you up. You should think about a lighter shade. Less aging."

Her right foot started tapping insistently on the floor. She pressed her thigh against his to stop it.

Peter went night walking for two hours in an attempt to work off his confusion. When he finally returned, Rose was still huddled on the couch feeling sorry for everything (and for herself). It had been one thing to shout her paranoid orders into the mirror in the bathroom, but quite another to let it rip at Liddy in front of Peter and the two boys. Worst of all, Liddy had reacted with such exemplary consideration and calm that Rose found herself in the difficult position of having to explain her behavior, without telling Peter the real reasons for it.

"I don't know what happened to me," she said, holding out her arms toward him. "I'm embarrassed for myself. Poor Liddy."

"Oh, believe me, there've been several times I could have murdered her. What happened? What did she do?"

Rose looked away. She wanted to talk about the "Couple Cohabitation Agreement" and giving up work, but Liddy had been right, she was nervous. She feared she would seem distrustful and feeble, and thus unworthy of Peter, whose moral certitude she venerated. So she told Peter of being awoken every morning by terror, and described more palatable fears: of giving birth, of parenting, of menopause with a toddler. Liddy had said the wrong thing at the wrong time, Rose said, and the Liddy-ishness had driven her crazy.

Peter understood. He chuckled. He sat on the couch beside her and held her hand.

"Yes," he said, "that really is the only word to describe her. She has always seemed to me to be utterly sui generis, unique in her own characteristics."

Rose relaxed. They appeared to have moved remarkably quickly from the subject of her bad behavior to Liddy's.

"And Liddy does appear to live in her own self-created reality. We all do it, of course, we all justify our particular *choices* to a greater or lesser extent; it's just for her it seems to be a matter of survival. That's why it was shocking when Cal asked her who his father was. It was a moment of pure truth. She will have to deal with the consequences of her actions, and she may not like the outcome."

"Why is she like this?" said Rose, anxious to continue the conversation, as she had never heard Peter be so loquacious on the subject before.

He paused for a moment to analyze the question further. When he finally spoke, his reply was considered, but unexpected, and exactly how he would speak in a student seminar.

"We were in Paris once, years ago, before we had Matty. Liddy studied Impressionist art as an undergraduate, so we wrote out a list of pictures that we wanted to see and we went around to galleries, day and night. On about the third evening, we went to the Musée d'Orsay to look at the Monets—in particular his portrait of his young wife, Camille, on her deathbed. It's an incredible image. Do you know it? She's lying there imprisoned in brushstrokes that look like a cave of ice."

Rose shook her head. Peter continued.

"I remember saying to Liddy, how could Monet do that? How could he paint the death of his wife, the mother of his two young sons, whom he loved? Liddy didn't seem to understand what I meant, she just looked at me and said, 'Because he's an artist, that's what he does.' Back at the hotel, I read the catalog and there was a quote from Monet about why he had made this picture, something about his reflexes compelling him to do it in spite of himself. That's why Liddy understood him, because *that's what she does.* When she's decided on a course of action, her reflexes compel her in spite of herself."

Rose looked at him. "I'm sorry I ruined the evening, my love."

"Hush. I quite enjoyed seeing a new side of you—it's cute."

"Cute? I'd have thought more fiery, Latin, *sexy?*"

She ran her fingers up his thigh. He rolled his eyes.

"You'll be lucky, particularly at this time of night."

"Oh, Peter," said Rose, laughing, taking his hand and resting it on her belly. "Won't it be lovely when the baby is born and everything can go back to normal?"

"Yes," agreed Peter. "Let's just get through the next few months without any more drama."

After a long afternoon in the office perfecting a complicated motion, then a speedy and acrobatic change in the bathroom, Liddy, handsome in gun-metal silk and a tousled updo, sat beside Curtis Oates, handsome in immaculate black tie and spray tan, in the back of his car as they cruised past the imperially proportioned apartment blocks of Park Avenue. A discreet card in white and gold lay on the seat between them, an invitation to the BARTLETT FOUNDATION ANNUAL BENEFIT DINNER, JUNE 15.

Normally Liddy looked forward to such events. Although in the abstract she was repelled by the idea of a life of unabashed hedonism supported by unearned riches, she enjoyed the private viewings of Lisbeth's unparalleled art collection, and was seduced by Lisbeth's irrepressible life force and her stories: the big bands flown in from Havana in the fifties, the elephants with jeweled headdresses coming up in the elevator, the elopement with a hunter she met shooting big cats in Kenya.

But this evening Liddy stared out the window, her phone clamped to her ear, preoccupied. Not only had Josh, the manny, gone missing in action with her children yet again (he had an infuriating habit of taking the boys on impromptu adventures after school), but she was also rehearsing how to tell Chloe Stackallan that she had received no counterproposal from Sebastian about the divorce settlement.

Liddy dialed her apartment for the tenth time, but there was still no answer. She dialed Matty's phone, but again, no answer. She tried not to worry. She blew breaths onto her window and made drawings with her forefinger in the condensation, as Curtis happily sipped a pomegranate juice and talked about himself.

"This is what 'Manhattan' means to me," he was saying, surveying the wide avenue. "I shoulda been born in a different time. This is where I belong."

Liddy looked up from her drawing, a Keith Haring–style heart with two halves and a jagged edge. She knew exactly what he meant. The two of them shared the same relentless, pioneering spirit that would have served them well skinning buffalo on a hostile prairie but had driven them almost mad in the suburbs. If Curtis had come of age in the early years of the twentieth century, he would have escaped his childhood poverty in a more mythical way than a school scholarship. He'd have discovered a gold mine, or built a railroad, or brokered real estate as the city rose on limestone and marble legs into the sky. With a judicious marriage to the daughter of an Astor, he would have made a substantial life in a triplex fortress of wealth and privilege, such as the one they were heading toward.

Of course, if Liddy had been born poor in the early days of the twentieth century, despite her relentless, pioneering spirit, she would have been lucky to enter such an apartment building by the servants' entrance.

"And here we are, Liddy, you and me. We made it here."

Curtis started to sing "New York, New York" softly, as he sometimes did, and Liddy always found this endearing, as she too loved a musical medley on the marvels of Manhattan. (Her particular favorite was "Put On Your Sunday Clothes" from *Hello, Dolly!*). But today she did not join in and Curtis trailed off.

"What is it?" he said.

The car changed lanes, pulling sharply to a halt outside a canopied doorway, where a liveried doorman was waiting in the frescoed lobby.

At that moment, a text from Josh saying *all g!* beeped through on her phone. Liddy wiped her window, obliterating the broken heart.

"Nothing," she said.

Like many men of his age, Curtis looked best in formal wear, the bow tie and buttons corseting and concealing the withering of muscle and gobbling of neck. From a distance, as the city turned black and white and romantic at dusk, they were a magnificent sight together. But close up, illuminated by the street lamps, Curtis was rigid and yellowing like a mummified corpse, and Liddy knew this was why, in all the time they had worked together, she had never experienced so much as an ion of sexual chemistry. When alone, they treated each other like distantly related members of the same family, a rakish uncle and his bookish niece, perhaps, meeting at a christening. This was not surprising, Liddy often thought, as she spent more time with him than any member of her own family.

A butler shepherded them into the entry hall, where the first guests were already mingling, most of whom she either knew or recognized and each of whom had paid several thousand dollars for the privilege. Mirrorlike silver trays glided around them, heaped with exotic canapés and signature cocktails, and both Curtis and Liddy had to restrain themselves from grabbing two drinks and caviar toasts, as neither had ever quite got over the impulse to take food if it was free.

Curtis headed straight into the gathering, but Liddy paused for a moment. Marisa Seldon was standing in front of a large statue of a Roman general. Liddy went over and kissed her on the cheek.

"Is that real?" Marisa whispered, looking at the marble head before them.

"Everything in here is real," said Liddy.

"Not everything," said Marisa, surveying the faces of the crowd, many of which were as smooth and immovable as the Roman general's. She nudged Liddy.

"Look!" she said, pointing toward the doorway. "Dr. Chip Hunter! You know, from that show *Cardiac Arrest!*"

"You mean the actor Lloyd Fosco?" Liddy said, enjoying the moment thoroughly. "He's my date."

"You're seeing an *actor?*" said Marisa, trying and failing to conceal her astonishment.

Liddy looked at her. "Lloyd does a lot of humanitarian work."

On the couple of occasions they had been in a public place, Lloyd, who seemed not to know how to dress incognito, would be accosted by complete strangers who wanted to talk to him or touch him. Tonight was no exception. As he made his progress toward her, Liddy watched the party divide into people who stared dumbstruck at him and people who pretended not to.

Marisa fell into the former category.

"You're early, Lloyd," said Liddy. "Curtis and I have got to talk to Lisbeth."

"I couldn't wait to see you," Lloyd replied. "You look amazing in that silk!"

"You look amazing too."

"This old thing! I just threw it together," he said theatrically, winking at Marisa, who was so overcome she turned and disappeared, off to find her husband by the El Greco. Although Lloyd had obviously been joking, Liddy steered him away from the crowd toward a red velvet banquette in a corner.

"I've got something to say," he continued, throwing himself down and pulling her beside him. "It's about you and me and your current situation."

"*Really?*" said Liddy curiously.

"Yeah." He smiled and touched her cheekbone with his forefinger. "The way I see it, Liddy, your life's too hard. When d'you get to have fun?"

"Don't we have fun?" said Liddy, with what she hoped was a twinkle in her eye.

"Sure, I guess, in the forty minutes after midnight when your kids are asleep and you can sneak downstairs before disappearing back to use your micro-dermabrasion kit."

"I did that one time," said Liddy, a little offended.

"Whatever. You need to simplify your life, that's all. So . . . my plan might sound big to you, but if you think about it, it's obvious."

Liddy was momentarily spellbound. It had to do with the soft lighting, his broad shoulders, and the perfect delivery of his lines.

"Liddy!"

From across the room, Curtis's call echoed into her reverie like a voice-over.

"Go on," she said to Lloyd. "I'm intrigued."

He took her hand and stroked her palm.

"I wanna buy your apartment," he said.

"Sorry? . . ."

She pulled away, folding her arms and crossing her legs, something not easy to do with a glass of champagne in one hand.

"I'm gonna be very straightforward, after all we're in the co-op together, right? I saw the figures from when you bought. You've got a two-million-dollar-mortgage and no savings. Man, I don't know how you convinced the others to let you buy— you're a very persuasive woman, Liddy—but I just saw the estimate for the repair work on the roof, two hundred grand at least. *Each.* If something went wrong at work, we both know you'd be fucked financially. I want to take that stress off you."

Liddy stood up, shocked but refusing to acknowledge it.

"You won't get permission to extend upward, you know," she said. "The lease forbids any internal renovations without board approval. And we stopped Hermione in the penthouse from building a sauna and plunge pool, so forget a home cinema."

"I don't want to do any of that. My ma died last year and I want to bring my pa and my brother Wayne to the city."

Liddy looked at him.

"Is that why you wanted to go out with me?"

"'Course," he replied, bemused by having to explain himself. "That's why I asked you for drinks. But then . . ."

He paused and rose to his feet. He leaned over her lasciviously. "Events took over . . ."

FLASH!

The event photographer appeared at this point to capture the magic of the moment.

"What are you doing, Liddy? Lisbeth's waiting. Come *on!*"

Liddy turned. She had never been so relieved to see Curtis. "I'm ready," she said, and they hurried off together.

"Who's that?" asked Curtis, glancing back at Lloyd. Liddy glanced back too and caught Lloyd's eye.

Lloyd looked furious, and she knew he must have heard.

They followed the butler through a spacious gallery lined with Chinese scroll paintings and into an oak-paneled library. The library had been shipped over in crates—wood, books, even the gold-leaf roses on the ceiling—from an eighteenth-century manor house in Cornwall, England.

"Curtis, my sweet," said Lisbeth Dawe Bartlett from the red-leather armchair into which she had been placed by the two male nurses on duty day and night. She raised an arm so thin it was like a claw-handled poker. Curtis, who had been flirting with her for forty years, approached her with awe, lifted her hand—its skeletal fingers hung with a selection of heavy gold rings—and raised it to his lips.

"Did Robert die?" asked Curtis, noticing the magnificent stuffed cockatoo in a glass display case on the wall.

"Yes. All my friends are falling off their perches," she replied, giggling so hard that Liddy feared she might break in two. "I miss him madly, but they're going to take him to Slane to live in the ballroom with Magda." (Liddy translated this as meaning that the deceased cockatoo would be shipped to Lisbeth's estate in Montauk, where he would sit beside the glass case containing Magda, the serval cat. In days of yore, Lisbeth had once been featured in *LIFE* magazine promenading down Madison Avenue with Magda, both in matching diamond-studded collars.)

"I'm going to follow them soon."

Curtis made an exasperated face and shot a conspiratorial comedy look at Liddy. "Lisbeth's been saying that for twenty-five years."

"My dear, believe me, my time is coming, I know it. There's something I want us to do today—*Chloe, darling?*"

Chloe Stackallan, dressed in rippling silver, materialized from a secret door carrying a matching tray with four slender flutes of champagne upon it.

"Chloe tells me you have been working tirelessly on her behalf, Liddy."

Lisbeth fixed Liddy in her most piercing of gazes.

"Yes," said Liddy. "I am confident that, with a reasonable amount of compromise, we will reach a speedy and satisfactory resolution."

"Chloe? . . ."

Chloe handed them each a glass and demurely lowered her eyes.

"I know what I want."

"Just remember, a protracted battle may keep Sebastian in your life for longer, but he's not coming back, Chloe."

Liddy looked at them. Lisbeth was one shrewd old bird.

"I know," said Chloe quietly. "I've seen his face when he looks at me now. He can hardly bear to look in my direction. But it wasn't like that at the beginning. He couldn't get enough of me."

There was a hollowness in her voice, and Liddy knew that, like so many others, the insane bravado Chloe had exhibited during their first meeting had been replaced by a deep and debilitating sense of loss.

"Why did you invite him tonight, Aunt Lisbeth?" she said.

Liddy glanced up in surprise.

"I've always been fond of him," replied Lisbeth. "And his firm donated to the auction. Dignity at all times, my dear. There are plenty more fish in the sea for you." She paused. "Now, Curtis. You are to accompany me to my private sitting room and you will choose one painting for yourself. As a gift. To remind you of me when I am gone."

"*No!*" said Curtis sharply, and Liddy looked at him concerned, as it was a sound of pure emotion, between a sob and a shriek. "No," he continued, a little more under control the second time. He looked at Chloe in appeal. "Your family will think I coerced you."

He took an ungentlemanly slug of champagne.

"That is why these two ladies are here as witnesses," said Lisbeth firmly, but her hand shook so much as she reached for her own glass that Curtis leapt to his feet to take it. He held the flute to her lips so she could sip.

"I can't," he said softly. "I don't want this."

But Lisbeth simply held out her arms to Curtis, who lifted her up with the greatest care and carried her away. And Liddy, watching them, suddenly wanted to be Fay Wray carried up the Empire State Building by King Kong, not because she felt helpless in her life, but because she wanted to be rescued from it. She knew this was absurd, but she also knew there was nothing absurd in the sight before her. She glanced at Chloe and wondered if she was thinking the same thing. *No one has ever loved me like that.*

Liddy thought of how, straight after the split from Peter, she had been endlessly reassured that "someone like her" would find a new soul mate within a year, or two, or three.

But recently the consolers had given up. She wondered if this was because she had given up too. She feared she would never again have sex with a man who truly desired her. She tried to remember what sort of love she still believed in. And right there and then, she knew the cause of the strange melancholy feeling that had overwhelmed her when she least expected it in the past months.

It was loneliness.

She was struck by a profound sense of distance from the events in her own life. It was as if they were being acted on a stage and she were trapped in the audience, watching from the wrong side of the curtain.

Liddy reentered the hall to see that the velvet banquette on which she and Lloyd had been seated was empty. She knew she should look for him, but she didn't feel like it. Instead, she decided to wander through the French bucolic landscapes in the stone loggia, and ended up in front of a Whistler drawing beside the ladies' cloakroom, so entranced she forgot she was woebegone.

"*Hello, Lydia Mary.*"

Liddy turned, shaking her head, not just in disbelief but also as a desperate attempt to see if there were any escape routes nearby.

"Your client will have my response tomorrow," said Sebastian Stackallan.

"We've been waiting," Liddy replied.

"I won't ever give her the house in Ireland, as well you know." He paused. "It was you who said 'it's not a home, it's my history.'"

She looked at him.

"Just before you told me I was a *Neanderthal*," he continued.

"When did I say that?"

And then she stopped. She knew what he was talking about.

"I truly don't remember much about that night, except that I was a total idiot," she said sincerely.

"Jinx. I was an arrogant prick."

They stared at each other. Out of the uniform of his working life, Sebastian was transformed. Liddy realized that in his tux, mismatched studs, and ill-tied bow he was still devilishly handsome, one of the most striking men in the room. She also realized that in the past years she had probably stood next to him at events like this, or brushed past him on the way to the coat check, or taken a last drink he was coveting from a tray and had not noticed him.

"It's a funny old world, isn't it?" he said.

There was something in his look that conveyed he had always noticed her.

Behind him, Liddy saw Marisa wandering aimlessly at the end of a tour group. When she saw Liddy, Marisa waved to catch her attention and mouthed *Lloyd's looking for you*.

Liddy waved back, but she did not move.

"How are you?" he said.

Liddy opened her mouth to say "Fine," but she didn't.

"My supposed boyfriend just let slip that he only dated me so he could buy my apartment. My ex-husband's new partner has complications in her pregnancy, so my teenage son, who acts like he hates me, has moved in full time. My beloved nanny left and I'm stuck with this jock I don't particularly trust and I spend every day worried he's going to lose my children," she said. "Not to mention the fact that my new book is late, my hours are too long, the roof of my apartment building is falling down, and my beautiful six-year-old boy asked me where his father is and I don't know what to tell him."

The words had tumbled out, and Liddy was startled. Sebastian, however, appeared remarkably unfazed. Liddy put it down to his being European.

"Where is he? The father."

"The private detective says possibly Brazil, but he dropped out of sight about a year ago. For all I know, he's in jail."

Liddy had never said this out loud before, but she had often wondered how it would sound. Now she knew.

"That's a joke, right?" said Sebastian, then he saw Liddy's face. "Isn't it?"

Liddy shook her head again. "It was a one-night thing. I have a file prepared with everything I know about him. I mean, he's not a psychopath or anything . . . a few petty thefts, that's all, but . . . I just wanted more time before I had to deal with it. I thought it would be like in a film, and I'd tell my son everything on his eighteenth birthday."

There was a long silence. Liddy found it excruciating. It was occurring to her that the main reason she had not confronted the possibility of Cal's interest in his paternity was because she had assumed she would have met someone else by now, and therefore found him a father figure.

"I didn't know who my father was until I was fourteen," said Sebastian. "And I found out when my housemaster at school told me he'd died."

Liddy did not suggest he was joking.

"My mother wanted to protect me, of course. The man was completely indifferent to my existence, apparently, and she was driving to the school to tell me herself. It's just some wires got crossed."

"That must have been awful for you."

"It was, but what I remember most is being given a glass of sherry. It was the seventies."

In the distance, a gong signaling the start of dinner sounded. People poured from rooms all around them and headed toward the dining room like tuxedoed trout in a stream.

"I can't let anything like that happen to Cal. What am I going to do?" said Liddy.

"I've got a brilliant ex-CIA guy who does work for me in South America. I'll give you his number."

"I wasn't asking you as a lawyer. I was asking you as a human being."

Sebastian considered this. "Liddy, most days I don't remember the difference," he said. "Look, I turned out reasonably okay, I think."

"Yes, you did," Liddy said. And she smiled a real smile.

"I don't know why I told you all that," she said. "It wasn't . . . *professional*. Now I might regret it." (Liddy did. *Not again*, she thought.)

But he reached over and touched her lips with his finger.

"I am a forty-six-year-old man exiting a crap marriage with no kids, wondering how I pissed so many good years away and at what age I'll stop being a good catch and become a tragic skirt-chasing has-been. I suppose I should blame my mother, Chloe certainly does, as I'm sure you know. Mum's personal life is like a car crash—I have a half-brother and a half-sister, four step-brothers, and at school I used to pretend I was an orphan."

Sebastian loosened his tie with his left hand, a gesture that seemed familiar to her. There were dark hairs on his chest just below his collarbone.

"My therapist thinks I married Chloe because she fit all the criteria I was looking for in a wife and that she married me because I was a 'good catch' and to her surprise she caught me. Neither of us asked ourselves if we loved each other."

"That sounds a bit harsh."

"I don't know. I liked that she was remarkably beautiful, old, but not too old, and she had a glamorous job, but not so glamorous that she wouldn't give it up when we had kids."

Liddy shook her head.

"You don't fool me, Sebastian Stackallan," she said. "I don't buy it."

"Okay, yes, I wanted the dream. I committed for better or worse. But things got worse pretty quickly. I think we both thought we'd get pregnant straightaway, and when we didn't . . . it all got ugly. Before I moved out, Chloe told me that the worst thing for her was that she hadn't had a baby. She said then, at least, she'd have got something out of it. I was glad she was so honest. I felt exactly the same way."

Liddy did not know what to say to this.

"And the thing is, all the same people who told me how *perfect* we were for each other, and how I'd never meet anyone else like her, are now sending me links to OKCupid and texts setting me up with women they consider suitable for me. Even my brother's giving me strict instructions that I should 'get back in the saddle again.' I wish I could bloody well throw my phone away. I dread which single female's going to be on the line next. The other week Chloe's *sister* called me."

"That's it. Enough information," said Liddy. "It's good you're talking to someone about it."

"Oh, yes," Sebastian replied. "I'm doing everything. Reading self-help books. Journaling."

"Is *journaling* a word?" asked Liddy.

"I wondered that too, but I fear so. Yes, apparently *journaling* can be a useful tool on the journey of self-discovery, blah di blah, you know." He adopted a stenorous tone. "'When an object breaks, the light comes in.' That's what people say, isn't it?" He paused.

"I'm very in touch with my feelings these days—a reformed character entirely."

They both looked around the loggia.

"Don't worry, Liddy. We have *omertà* between us now. Like the Mafia. We know too much about each other to break the code of silence."

"Really?" she said, and when he nodded she added, "Thank you."

He stood still for a moment, not quite sure whether he should stay or go. Now that they knew unexpected secrets, their perception of each other had changed and it was harder to walk away.

"Will it make Chloe happy if she gets my apartment, Liddy?" said Sebastian. "You see, I find I don't really care what happens to her, though I suppose I should. But if it would make her happy, I'll give her what she wants."

"Well, she does want the apartment," said Liddy.

He appeared oddly content all of a sudden. He smiled roguishly. She noticed the gray stubble on his face. *Maybe age had mellowed him? Or just exhausted him?*

"It's only money," he said.

Liddy suppressed a smile too. *So that's it*, she thought. Her reactions to Sebastian Stackallan, nice and nasty, had nothing to do with physical attraction or repulsion; they arose because she recognized the nice and nasty aspects of her own personality in him. They were not magnets but mirrors; both shrewd, both selfish, both capable of extraordinary acts of kindness and carelessness. She had told Curtis she did not hate Sebastian, and had discovered this evening it was true.

"Send me over the papers," he said. He moved to walk away.

"I hope everything works out for you, Liddy."

"Likewise," she said.

"You know, I hear your Irish accent today."

She smiled again. "I'm tired, it always comes back when I'm tired, even though I tried so hard to lose it. I spent hours watching *Dallas* to train myself out of it."

Then Liddy's phone rang and when she saw the number she answered it, tenderness in her voice.

"Hi, Mommy, Josh took us to the water park!" said Cal.

"It's my son," she whispered, and walked a little ways away.

When she hung up, Sebastian was gone.

The dinner gong sounded again, and suddenly starving, Liddy

followed its call. Lloyd was waiting for her attractively in front of the seating plan, and she decided to shelve any further conversation about real estate and concentrate on his looks, not his helpful ideas. Her stomach was growling now, and with speeches about to begin, and at least an hour to go before the whiff of a main course, Liddy scurried after a disappearing silver tray in pursuit of the rare roast beef on tiny triangles of rye. When she caught up, she stuffed three straight down. This was a mistake.

She started coughing, first delicately for a couple of exhalations, and then barking and gasping alternately as the third sliver of meat stuck in her throat. Lloyd, alarmed, ran over with a glass of water and forced it into her hand, but when Liddy raised it to her mouth, her body convulsed forward and she poured it over her face and down her dress. A few people laughed until she dropped it, and the sound of glass shattering reverberated around the room.

Liddy gripped Lloyd's outstretched hands in terror now, as the feeling of slow strangulation took hold of her. Bright white star-like specks were floating all around her and she could no longer cry or scream or breathe. Lloyd looked around frantically. Although he had played a doctor in more than fifty episodes of a TV show, he had absolutely no idea what to do.

"*Help!*" he shrieked, as the crowd froze in fear and disbelief. A waiter ran to find the chef, who was trained in CPR, and Marisa Seldon called a private ambulance, but then, from nowhere, a strong pair of male arms wrapped around Liddy's waist. She felt herself lifted into the air and a sharp, insistent pressure just below her rib cage, once, twice, three times, until the piece of meat was expelled from her mouth, fast, in a perfect parabola, ending against a minor work by Gainsborough.

There was silence, then a polite round of applause. Curtis, entering at this moment with Chloe on his arm and expecting a string quartet to be playing, instead saw Liddy, crumpled like a length of gray silk, her mouth wide, drinking in air. They ran, horrified, over to Lloyd.

"Is she drunk?" asked Curtis. Chloe gripped his shirt cuff and listened as Lloyd explained why her attorney was lying on the floor.

The chef arrived, turning Liddy gently onto her side into recovery position. Liddy, coming back to full consciousness, kept her eyes closed and wondered what on earth she was going to do now. Out of the darkness she heard a deep, melodious voice with an Irish lilt telling everyone to head into the dining room. Then she heard a woman's voice, falsely bright, almost shrill.

"*Sebastian!*" called Chloe. "That was terribly gallant of you."

Liddy knew Sebastian had saved her.

She blinked her eyes open and sat up as he knelt beside her. She saw him regard Chloe with the icy stare she had seen on several previous occasions, though then it had been directed at her. Because her throat felt like someone had rasped it with an iron file, she whispered, "Help me, please." When she was on her feet, she looked up into his face.

Without a word, he lifted her into his arms and carried her away.

And behind them, Chloe, all dignity deserting her, burst into brokenhearted tears.

Although many were concerned for Liddy after her near-death experience, even those who expressed it in ribald and unfunny jokes, there were three notable exceptions: Lloyd, who brought the curtain down on their brief relationship; Curtis, who was embarrassed for her, and therefore for his firm; and Sydney, who was jealous. In fact, Liddy had overheard Sydney on the phone, confessing to a friend that she wouldn't mind the humiliation of having the Heimlich maneuver in front of most of the senior members of the New York Bar Association if it meant she could feel Sebastian Stackallan's manly arms around her.

Liddy kept her counsel through it all. She knew she should have dropped Sebastian some form of thank-you note, but it had seemed inappropriate to include it with his draft divorce agreement, so she had not. Anyway, she could not think of what to say. He had insisted on accompanying her home after the benefit, and she had leaned against him in the back of the car, too weak to speak, his arm around her shoulders, his hot breath on her cheek.

She did not even mention it to Peter and Rose, and when she dropped Matty off at Carroll Gardens one week later, the night before Peter was taking him to Vermont, she explained away the sudden chest pain that overcame her as the result of an altercation with a revolving door. Peter, of course, invited her in, but Liddy, anxious not to be on the receiving end of another flying feminist tome, shook her head. She attempted as much of an embrace as Matty would allow.

"Be good, be safe, obey the rules, text me every night, and your dad and I will be there for the family visit in three weeks' time. Okay?"

He grunted and headed off into the kitchen in search of food.

"I love you," she said, but his head was buried inside the fridge.

Liddy and Peter looked at each other.

"Ring me and tell me what it's like," she whispered. "If it sucks bring him straight back home." She reached out her hand to him, he took it, and they both felt incredibly sad for a moment. This was something complicit between them as parents that they could not share with Rose.

"It won't, Liddy," said Peter firmly, and the next day he duly reported that the camp was freshly painted and eerily tidy, full of good-humored athletic young men running around in shorts, building campfires they clearly intended to sing songs around, and Matty had given every indication that he would, indeed, enjoy it. Liddy was glad. She said farewell to the back of the manny's muscular thighs, hired an obedient and enthusiastic young woman named Sally to look after Cal, and threw herself into work.

She had to.

Liddy did not consider herself to be a materialistic person, but when her accountant presented the total amount of her monthly expenses in accusatory black and white, she was shocked.

"Your mortgage interest payments have gone up, you've

got two sets of private-school fees, monthly child support to Peter, the service charge on the apartment, the allowance to your parents, a full-time nanny, housekeeper, dog walker, and . . . *sundries*. . . ."

At this the accountant waved a weekly bill for yellow roses.

"Shall I go on?" he said, but because he was a kindly man who had known Liddy for many years, he trailed off, as he feared he was sounding spiteful (he had not even added that he had no clue where the money for the roof repair could be found).

When she came home, she saw a large crack had emerged from the window frame and spread across her white supporting wall, like a scribbled arrow pointing toward her overdraft.

Most evenings she staggered into the apartment in time to kiss Cal good night, and then she sat alone, the dog on her lap, a glass of whiskey in her hand, and got nostalgic for the days when she was a Mistress of the Universe. She drank too much, and she slept too little, and one night in the gray twilight before dawn she awoke screaming from a dream of death. She had seen the crack on the wall spread violently across the ceiling, raining chunks of plaster down on her, the lights fizzling and sparking, and had thrown herself out of bed and crawled on all fours to escape. She shuddered into consciousness curled up in a corner of the room, her cheek resting against the cool radiator, and afterward, heart palpitating, she closed her eyes and prayed to sleep and feel nothing. When she awoke again, she did feel reassuringly numb.

The next morning, she reached the office to see a note, handwritten by Curtis, stuck on the ornamental elevator doors saying

OUT OF ORDER. She walked up the three flights of steep stairs, but when she asked Sydney if the repairmen were on their way, Sydney giggled.

"There's nothing wrong with the elevator," she said. "Curtis has got an opposing attorney coming in for a settlement meeting."

"So?" asked Liddy.

"He's very overweight," whispered Sydney. "Curtis wants to exhaust him before the negotiations begin."

"That's evil," said Liddy, though it was not the first time she had made this observation.

"I know," said Sydney.

Sydney was in fact vibrating with the aftershock of an unexpected visitor. She told Liddy she had looked up from her desk to see the newly single Sebastian Stackallan standing right in front of her, his black hair slightly curly from sweat, his bicycle clips removed, and his settlement papers in his hand.

"Did he ask if I was in?" said Liddy, trying to sound casual.

"No. He was only here for a few seconds," said Sydney. "But I managed to ask him if he was speaking at the Equitable Distribution and Maintenance conference next week, and he is, so I said I'd see him there." Sydney could hardly contain herself, and the strange honking laugh erupted out of nowhere for no discernible reason other than lust.

"Anything else," said Liddy, trying to be indulgent as well as admonishing, "*important?*"

"Curtis has some files for you to review."

"Right."

"Tea, Liddy?" said Sydney quickly, desperate to get back to her desk and call her best friend, Jenny, to talk about synchronicity.

"Coffee," said Liddy, and headed purposefully into her office to the unpleasant discovery that Curtis had moved the magazines on her ottoman to make room for three bulging file boxes. She shifted them onto the floor, then fell onto her knees and fixed the magazines, *Allure* on the top, *Vanity Fair* on the bottom, measuring the distance around them so they sat in the exact center of the upholstery. As she hauled herself up, a muscle memory of the bruises on her ribs erupted, and she collapsed down again hard. She yelped in pain.

Sydney returned with a mug and some papers. Liddy put on her glasses, scanned, and signed, as Sydney told her that she had to appear on a network daytime TV show that afternoon.

"It's an item about celebrity custody battles," said Sydney helpfully. "Mary Jane and Jolene talk 'Celeb Splitz!'"

Before Liddy could say no, Sydney explained that Mary Jane had personally called Curtis and he had accepted on Liddy's behalf.

"They're biking over some information and the researcher will call you later. You can keep your nine thirty with the summer interns, and you have to be at the company audit meeting at ten, but I've rearranged your other appointments, apart from the two you can do on video conference from the car. Curtis says it's good for business, Liddy. The show has three million viewers."

Liddy looked at the file boxes. She would not get home tonight until after eleven o'clock.

"I'll need to get hold of Sally. And I'll need my hair done. Will you call the salon for me and tell them to fit me in at noon?"

Strictly speaking, this was outside of Sydney's administrative duties, but as Liddy did not seem quite herself, Sydney let it go.

Liddy put on the tailored jacket that always hung on a hook in the corner of the room and pulled on a pair of pointed court shoes with commandingly spiky heels.

The phone on Liddy's desk beeped. Sydney picked it up and put it on hold.

"It's Cal's school, Liddy. Miss Andrews."

"I'll take it," said Liddy, gulping her coffee and nodding at Sydney to leave the room. She was trying to remember which teacher this was: the slightly stern bossy one with the khakis and the military manner, or the fluffy, smiling assistant with the gingham and the open-toed sandals?

"Steph Andrews here," the teacher said, and Liddy knew it was the slightly stern bossy one, the one who was not scared of her.

"Liddy James."

"I'm sorry to say Cal's a little upset, Liddy. It's the last-day-of-school party today and the children were asked to invite a relative for lunch. Cal says he's got no one coming."

"Oh," said Liddy, playing for time.

From the desk, her mobile phone rang. She glanced over to see a number she did not recognize that started with 802. Vermont. *It must be Matty's camp*, she thought, remembering that they had left a message the day before about an issue with a permission slip. She let it ring.

"There was a note last Thursday in his bag, it was in the

weekly newsletter and on the school website, and we sent out a text reminder yesterday," Steph continued.

Because Liddy could not bear to reopen any discussion of family with Cal, she had thrown away the weekly newsletter, hidden the note in an old shoe box in the bottom of her wardrobe, and deleted the text. Unfortunately, in this frenzy of ignoring, she had forgotten to mark the date on the wall planner and had accidentally let Cal go into school today.

"What time is the lunch?" she said to Miss Andrews, rather more feebly than she intended.

"Twelve thirty. Will we see you there?"

Liddy made the calculation. *If I move the hair appointment to 11:45, they put that colored powder on the roots instead of dye, and I get made up in the salon chair, I can make it to the school by 12:45, stay for half an hour, and still get to the TV studio with five minutes to spare.*

"Yes, I'll be there," she said.

"Anyone else you can bring? We'd love to meet a grandparent, an aunt, or a cousin?" said the teacher, glancing at Cal's file and being tactful. "We believe children are best reared in a shared, convivial environment."

"Thank you, Steph."

Liddy managed to put the receiver down without throwing it. Or throwing up. She turned to see the two new interns, one male, one female, scrubbed, suited, and earnest, standing in her office, staring at the pictures artfully pinned on her wall. She too looked at the collage of her fabulous life, which now included a framed copy of her interview in the Style section of the *New York Times* (the one in which, beaming and airbrushed, she had proclaimed her lack of guilt) that hung next to Cal's scribbled drawing saying BEST MOM IN THE WORLD. Liddy was aware that today, with her skin pallid with sleeplessness, a shade that no makeup could cover, and the stress tremors in her arms, she did not represent any *tableau vivante* of magnificent midlife. She hoped the summer interns would not find this disappointing.

"That was my son's teacher," she said brightly, motioning them to sit down. "The balls are all in the air today!"

The two interns nodded politely, but they didn't understand. *Oh to be young*, she thought, looking over and glimpsing Curtis in the lobby as he handed a glass of water to a rotund, red-faced, and very sweaty man in a navy suit, who appeared to be clutching his heart. For one desperate moment, she considered asking Curtis to pretend to be Cal's godfather.

Her mobile phone beeped that a message had been left. She switched it off.

"So—Brent and Brianna. Welcome to Oates and Associates. Where shall we start? What can I tell you?"

"How do you like your coffee?" said Brent, very pleased with himself, his egg-shaped face flushed pink. Brianna nodded, and Liddy saw that unless the girl smiled, she looked angry. She made a mental note that she must find a polite way of telling her this.

"It's Rose on line one!" said Sydney, appearing in the doorway.

"No," said Liddy, waving her finger. "I can't speak to her."

"She says it's very important," said Sydney.

"Tell her the camp has the permission slip."

Turning back to Brent and Brianna, Liddy did not miss a beat.

"You will both work with me on one complex, long-term case, but your primary duties will be writing and research."

But they were looking past her. Liddy followed their gazes to the doorway, where Sydney was hopping nervously from foot to foot.

Liddy lifted her finger for a second time, a sight calculated to strike terror in a junior associate, but Sydney just gesticulated toward the phone.

"Excuse me for a moment," Liddy muttered.

She lifted the receiver and stabbed at the red flashing button.

"Yes, Rose?" she hissed.

Rose knew she had a limited number of seconds to get the very important information across so she spoke too loudly and exaggerated the consonants in the sentence.

"They found marijuana edibles in Matty's pocket."

"I'm sorry. What are you talking about?" said Liddy. "What are marijuana edibles?"

Brent and Briana eyeballed each other and sniggered. Liddy eyeballed them.

"They're sweets made of hash," said Brent quickly.

"They can look like gummy bears," said Brianna.

"That's right," said Rose, who had overheard this. "Matty says he took them from Josh's rucksack, and he didn't know what they were, but the camp doesn't believe him. He shared them with two other kids, and they all got stoned out of their brains last night. They were running around screaming, then they threw up everywhere, and . . . look . . . he's okay, but . . . he's got to leave."

"He's got to leave?"

Liddy's mouth sagged open. She gripped the phone so hard her knuckles bleached pink and white.

"Yes," said Rose. "They've kicked him out for taking drugs."

Liddy snapped her jaws together and started to think. She looked at Brent and Brianna. "Please wait outside while I finish this call."

She stood up, scurried over to the door, opened it, waved them out, closed it, and ran back to the phone.

"Rose, we have to get Matty home," she said.

Rose lowered her voice, although the tense distress in it remained. "I know, but Peter's really angry. He says he won't go."

"He has to. I am up to my eyeballs at this moment. Is he there?"

"He's upstairs. Liddy, don't talk to him."

Liddy kicked off her shoes, exasperated. "What is the point of him getting angry with Matty?"

"He's not angry with Matty," replied Rose slowly, and at that moment Liddy heard Peter's crashing entry into the room and his voice shouting, *"Is that her?"*

Then he marched over and took the phone. "This is your fucking fault!"

"Calm down, Peter."

"How could you employ a fucking pothead?"

His voice was cold and hate-filled, but Liddy countered, regardless.

"How was I to know? Josh had impeccable references."

"My God, Matty could have choked on his own vomit. Or one of the other little fools could have. Why do you think he did this?"

"*I don't know!*" shouted Liddy, her own fear and confusion now at the same level as his.

"Do you spend *any* time with him at all, Liddy? What the fuck have you been doing?"

Liddy's leg started juddering violently, her shoe tapping insistently on the floor.

"Oh, I don't know, Peter. Earning the money to pay the mortgage, the private school fees, the child support to you, the service charge on the apartment, the allowance to my parents, not to mention the nanny, the housekeeper, and the fucking dog walker."

"I always said you could never look after a dog!"

"What has the dog got to do with this? *What do you expect me to do?*"

"*Be Matty's mother!*"

Liddy flinched and fell silent. In the background, Rose pleaded helplessly about the need for someone to go to Vermont.

There was a long pause. Peter calmed down. "It's your turn, Liddy. I took him there. Go and get him. We'll talk tonight."

Outside the door, Sydney was ushering the company auditors into the conference room.

"I can't," said Liddy quietly.

"*Why?*"

"*I have to work!*" she screamed.

There was a thud, the line went dead, and she knew he had thrown the phone onto the floor.

She sat very still for a moment.

There was a tentative knock on the door.

"Come in," she said.

She looked up to see Sydney standing in the doorway.

"Are you okay?" said Sydney.

"I'm fine," said Liddy, and she put on her fake smile.

Sydney closed the door.

Liddy started laughing because she didn't know what else to do.

And because Sydney and the summer interns, listening outside, were young and had no understanding of what heartbreak looked like, they believed Liddy really was laughing and did not understand that Liddy's fall was coming. And because Liddy was Liddy, her fall did not come in an ordinary way.

At two p.m., after successfully walking into the TV studio in her heels to the theme music from *Jaws* (the researcher had told her they were "having some fun" with her reputation), Liddy successfully navigated the discussion on some recent "Celeb Splitz!," during which she commented on such, striking an appropriate balance between perky and serious and eliciting an appropriate balance of laughter and nodding from the already excited audience. (Before Liddy's appearance they had watched a major film star learn how to stack a dishwasher, an item Liddy found very interesting because she was a Virgo.) But then, as Liddy recited two perfectly judged lines on what New York State law might mean for the children of such celeb splits, she noticed in her anterior vision that Mary Jane, the younger of the two enthusiastic presenters and the one farthest away from her on the sofa, was listening earnestly to her earpiece and glancing at the typewritten notes on the coffee table.

"Let's talk about you for a moment, Liddy," she said, leaning forward with her orthodontically perfected smile. "You've said many times that you don't believe in divorce, particularly when there are children involved, but sadly your own marriage ended. How did your experience shape your view?"

Liddy blinked a couple of times before ignoring the question and concentrating on her well-rehearsed answer.

"Well, Mary Jane, when settlement negotiations become unstable, there's a tendency for children to be used as bargaining chips by one or both parties."

(She thought of Peter, tired and sad and gray-faced, sitting alone on the train to Vermont.)

"So my new book, which will be available later this year, is about how parents should work together for the practical and emotional welfare of their children during a separation."

(She thought of Matty, his jaw set bravely but terrified inside, sitting alone in some log cabin.)

"Right. But specifically, how has your elder son coped with your divorce from his father?" asked the younger presenter, returning, insistent, to her theme.

"My sons are *fine!*"

(She thought of Cal, a mournful expression on his face, sitting alone in the corner of his classroom earlier today because, after a blowout crisis in the hair salon, she had been twenty minutes late to sit cross-legged in a circle with him as Steph Andrews banged a small drum.)

Tears spouted in Liddy's eyes. She wiped them away with a flick of her forefinger, but she felt suddenly dizzy, disoriented, and desperate to be alone. Her right leg was now tap-tapping so quickly that even the most severe smoothing of her skirt could not hide it. "I mean, there are always bumps in the road with teenagers, right?" she said.

"Tell me about it!" said Jolene, conspiratorially patting Liddy on the arm. "The day my youngest turned thirteen he started walking around looking like a Marilyn Manson tribute band! I love your message, Liddy. Keep calm and put the kids first."

And she whooped and waved her hands in the air, causing the studio audience to whoop and wave too. Liddy stuffed her right hand into her jacket pocket, formed a fist, and pressed hard into her thigh until it hurt. She picked up a glass of water from the low table in front of her. She took a sip.

"Yes, I hope my book puts me out of business," she said, praying that Curtis wasn't watching, but relieved to have gotten through the intrusive personal questions. "Honestly, I'd say to any couple contemplating separation, sit down and read it together, see if you can stay amicable and agree on what's fair, and I mean what's truly fair, not what you think you *deserve*, then download the relevant forms and fill them in. It'll cost you forty-nine dollars."

There was another enthusiastic round of applause. Liddy plastered on her smile, gave a halfhearted whoop, and nodded with a self-deprecating expression into the camera. She glanced over at the clock on the wall. Two minutes until the segment ended. She resolved never to do this sort of thing again. *Ever.* Meanwhile, Mary Jane was not to be dissuaded. "So, Liddy, you think the adversarial court system is not in the best interests of hurt and confused couples?"

Liddy looked at her. *Duh!* she thought.

"In most circumstances, yes, I believe court should be the last resort," she said, firmly, but not firmly enough. Jolene sensed the opportunity for a profile-increasing move-to-prime-time storm in the Twitter-sphere. "But the multimillion-dollar divorce industry is how celebrity attorneys, like you, make your fortunes. Are you saying you make things worse, not better?"

Liddy glanced over at the clock again. Sixty seconds to go. *Okay, Liddy, keep it together*, she thought.

"In the end, clients decide how . . . aggressively . . . a case will be fought. I don't take a moral position, I take an instruction." Liddy forgot to do her media-friendly grin. "But in dangerous waters my reflex action is always to attack."

Like now, she thought, squeezing her fist even harder.

Jolene shook her head in awe. "*Wow!* You really are a shark!"

The studio audience burst out laughing, and Liddy should have laughed too, and countered with a soothing sentence or two about the importance of counseling and collaborative law. But the sudden rush of adrenaline into her bloodstream was so intense, she could almost visualize it pulsing through her veins. It was fight, flight, or freeze time, and as her official script suddenly vanished, she froze. Words stopped in her throat and began to choke her until she saw bright white starlike specks in the air.

"You know what?" she gasped. *"I am not my fucking job!"*

She was overwhelmed by a paralyzing feeling of despair, and without missing a beat, she turned and looked into the audience to see the rows of people no longer laughing but staring at her, some shifting in their seats, some whispering to one another, all concerned. Quivering, she whispered to herself, *"It's all bullshit. I'm bullshit. I can't do this anymore,"* but when she heard this reverberating through her mic live to the studio, she recoiled from the anguish in her voice and leapt to her feet, trying to pull the mic off her shirt, and when she couldn't, shouting, *"Get it off me!"* to the considerable discomfort of the two presenters, whose enthusiasm was instantaneously replaced by abject terror. The producer immediately went to a commercial break, during which the clip was uploaded to YouTube.

The video promptly went viral under the heading "Top Lawyer Goes Nuts on Television" and was of particular interest to all those who had been on the receiving end of Liddy's bite. They gleefully sent it to everyone in their address books, apart from Gloria Jane Thompson, who found she felt sorry for Liddy, although she could not resist sending it to Sebastian Stackallan. Who, as he watched, saw the real Liddy James, and noticed, at the last second, that the handkerchief she pulled out of her pocket to dry her tears was his.

TO: Liddy James, lmjames@oatesandassociates.com

FROM: Sebastian Stackallan, Sebastian.Stackallan@gsr.com

DATE: June 30

RE: HOUSE IN IRELAND

Dear Liddy, have been thinking of how to write this for about twenty minutes, but am too busy to waste more time so will be straightforward. I am currently in my apartment, or rather my soon-to-be-ex-wife's apartment, packing up my stuff, and reading the charming notes she has left in my sock drawer (my particular favorite is that I only married her so people wouldn't think I was a homosexual). The point is that I am about to head to a remote island in Alaska for a few weeks, to fish and hike and lick my wounds, and my house in Ireland will be vacant for the summer months. Having just seen your funny turn on the telly, I think you need a break. Rest assured I don't want anything from you and, anyway, I have already saved your life so there is nothing more you can owe me. It is a beautiful place on Lough Dan in Wicklow, nothing fancy, but right on the shore between the lake and the mountain. It might just be the thing to help you get a grip.

PS Bring the kids.

PPS My mother is currently touring South America with her latest beau so you need not expect an encounter. (Just make sure you do not disturb the sacred grove behind the woodshed!)

PPPS You will no doubt bump into my sister Storm at some point. She's staying at the main house while Roberta's away. Ignore everything she says about me and do not let her drive you anywhere. Ever.

TO: Sebastian Stackallan, Sebastian.Stackallan@gsr.com
FROM: Liddy James, lmjames@oatesandassociates.com
DATE: June 30

Dear Sebastian

THANK YOU!
I wanted to escape but I didn't know where to go.
I am tired, it's true—mentally, physically, every way I can think of.
Mostly I'm tired of being me.

Liddy

THE LAND OF EXILE AND REDEMPTION

Of course Rose had heard Peter angry with Liddy before, but when she heard him shouting on the phone there was a tone in his voice that made her want to cry. After he had hurled the receiver to the floor, however, his ire defused and he was engulfed by the violent despair she had not seen for years. *"How could Matty do this to us?"* he kept saying, and at first Rose thought he was referring to her in the collective pronoun, but afterward, as he pounded around the bedroom, grabbing his coat and searching for his keys, she understood he meant himself and Liddy.

Rose soothed, "The only thing that matters is that he's safe. He needs to come back and live here right away. We'll manage.

We know it's difficult at Liddy's, with her hours. Maybe he should *never* have been sent to camp. . . ."

"I wish it was that simple, Rose. What if the problem isn't Liddy. What if it's you and me?"

"If anyone it was that idiot *manny*! I hated the sound of him."

"He's been looking after Matty for six weeks. We've had what amounts to primary custody for nearly six years!"

"Peter!"

Peter had never made any criticism, implied or otherwise, of Rose's relationship with Matty before and she felt shocked and upset. Rose had assumed he would continue to blame Liddy, allowing her to breathe the self-congratulatory air of the moral high ground. She soon saw, however, that she could not take credit for the prize for drama and the captainship of the soccer team without the reverse applying. She cast around to blame something else.

"It must be the school," she said.

"*What?* Liddy put him in private school supposedly to keep him out of trouble. She coughs up thirty-five thousand dollars a year in fees for it!"

Rose sat down on the bed, wishing he had not been so unusually *specific*. She had followed Peter's lead on the fact of Liddy's financial support, pretending it didn't exist, in the same way that she added extras and trips and music tuition onto the school bills without even thinking about it. And she had never asked him how much money Liddy gave him every month, because she avoided any evidence that their combined salaries did not cover their expenses.

"What did we do wrong?" Peter demanded, and this time he meant himself and Rose. "Where the hell are my keys?" He rifled through the drawer of her nightstand, in his frenzy ignoring the envelope containing the draft "Couple Cohabitation Agreement," which so far she had ignored too.

"Peter, please, all teenagers experiment, especially ones who live in New York City. He's probably scared himself more than us."

Rose felt quite proud of the measured way she delivered this, particularly given how hysterical she had become about the two sodas a day and lack of keyboard practice, but Peter turned to look at her as if she had slapped him.

"Rose. Matty is my flesh and blood and I cannot allow him to head further down a self-destructive path that will bring misery to all of us, including you. Do you want an out-of-control adolescent taking drugs around our small child?"

"No," said Rose helplessly.

She listened as he stomped down the creaky stairs, his exit punctuated predictably by the sharp double bang. She tried to sit up, but an excruciating pulse of pelvic pain sliced between her legs. She clutched her belly tight and felt helpless. She called Doctor Barbara.

Four hours later, however, when a call came through from Liddy's office and a young woman named Sydney told her that Liddy had "gone fucking nuts" (Curtis's words, not Sydney's) live on national television, Rose decided to be helpless no more. She was glad Peter was already on his way to Vermont, and despite the sciatica and the sleeplessness and the high blood pressure, and despite Barbara's protestations, she did what the nicest woman anyone had ever met would do. She stood up, every pain-filled step reminding her of the Little Mermaid in the original story, who gives up her tail and walks as if on knives for love, resolved to go to Liddy's apartment herself.

She did not get past the couch.

So it was an exhausted Peter who arrived there in the early hours of the next morning, with a dirty and malodorous Matty, to be greeted by Sally, the new nanny, her obedience and enthusiasm considerably diminished. Sally opened the door, pointed them in the direction of Liddy's bedroom, and promptly quit.

"My mother says I have to leave," she said, running into the elevator. "I've never seen anyone behave like this before. It's scary. Her phone rings every five minutes. She doesn't pick it up."

Peter told Rose all this when he called that afternoon. He said that he and Matty were back safe, but that Liddy was lying motionless on her bed in the stifling New York summer heat, eyes shut, body half hidden under a white lace throw (like Camille Monet in her husband's painting). He would have to stay in Tribeca for the night.

"Did she say anything to you?" asked Rose.

"Only that she wanted to know how bad her . . . *episode* . . . was. Did you google it?"

"Yes. It's bad."

"I don't like to see Liddy like this. She looks dreadful," said Peter. "I hope she's going to be okay."

"Should we call her parents?" said Rose, concerned.

"No," Peter replied. "She's wouldn't thank us for that."

"Barbara says it was probably some form of panic attack brought on by stress and she must rest. And so must you. How's Matty?"

"I've spent seven hours waiting for him to apologize and he hasn't and now he's in his bed and I don't want to see him. I shouted my head off at him all the way from Albany to Grand Central, and I've had enough. It seemed to distress me far more than him, I might add."

Rose knew this before Peter said it. She told him she loved him before hanging up.

Sleep banished for the time being, she picked up her laptop to look again at Liddy's "episode" and see if it was better on the second viewing. She pressed play, heard a few bars of the theme music of *Jaws*, winced, and automatically pressed fast forward. She reached the bit where Liddy burst into tears and started shouting, *"It's all bullshit. I'm bullshit. I can't do this anymore,"* and decided she'd had enough. However, she accidentally hit pause instead of stop, and as Rose saw the image of Liddy frozen on the screen (Liddy's face stretched wide in a savage cry, her fingers clawing at the clothes on her chest, as if a terrifying, toothy, little alien Liddy was about to burst out of her stomach), she had a vivid sense that this event was not just about the disconnect between appearance and reality in Liddy's domestic life, but also revealed a fundamental disconnect within Liddy's self.

It wasn't better the second time around (if anything it was worse), and though Rose did, of course, feel desperately concerned for Liddy and her altered mental state, her own mind raced with a series of far more ignoble preoccupations. What was the "it" that Liddy couldn't do anymore?

Rose wondered if she should read about nervous breakdowns, but feared what she would learn, so she did not. Barbara had assured her that what Liddy needed most was sleep—there was, after all, no imaginable universe in which Liddy would not be, in the end, a woman who coped—but she could not tell how long this would take. Rose shivered and lay on her back to rest, but the baby kicked in protest, so she tossed and turned around and let it sleep on her bladder again.

The next day Peter had not called by lunchtime, so after Rose had finished researching psychiatric institutions in New York State that offered rest cures, she dialed the number at Liddy's apartment. When Peter picked it up, he sounded harassed. He said he had just finished cleaning up a puddle of dog pee, after feeding the boys pizza, and was now building a LEGO starship with Cal, as the nanny had quit. *You told me that yesterday*, Rose was about to say, but she decided against it.

Peter reported that the apartment phone had rung twice that morning. The first call was from Liddy's former boss, Marisa Seldon, who had said Liddy must get in touch with her the moment she surfaced, and on no account was she to talk to Curtis Oates on her own. When Rose asked why, Peter said, "Marisa says Liddy needs a lawyer. Curtis will try and fire her."

"But she's not well," said Rose.

"Marisa says that's why."

Rose shook her head, appalled by the unpleasantness of such a working environment. Then she remembered how several of her own colleagues had waited less than forty-eight hours after her hospitalization to rush to the new dean's door waving their peer-reviewed articles and proposals for upscaling the courses she taught.

The second call had been from Liddy's literary agent, on his way to a meeting, who said that Liddy must get out of bed and finish her new book, as he was already fielding offers for serialization. "She's trending at the moment, so tell her to tweet from her bedroom!" the agent shouted as his cab went into the Holland Tunnel.

Rose and Peter allowed themselves a shared chuckle and Rose was relieved. Even if Liddy did get fired, it seemed her earning potential had not diminished. And the dramas of the previous day had proved that she could not manage on her own. *Now Liddy'll see how much she needs me,* Rose thought. She was aware this was not something a nice woman would think.

She felt ashamed. Then she felt reassured.

"Is Liddy up yet?" she said.

"No," said Peter. "But I heard her talking to herself, and Cal says she's reading e-mails, so there's definitely movement. Oh . . ." He paused for a moment. "Her shower's on. I'll call you later."

In fact, Peter did not call; he just texted the news that he was staying another night and then arrived back at the house the following morning, desperate for some peace and unwilling to face any sort of interrogation. Rose, however, desperate for information, could not control herself.

"Where's Matty?" she said.

"I left him with Liddy."

"How long for?"

He made the sort of soft groaning noise that so irritated Rose and took off his shoes, at that moment looking every minute of his fifty-seven years.

"She's going to take him and Cal to Ireland on vacation this weekend. Some friend of hers has lent her his house for a few weeks."

"*What?* What friend? A boyfriend? Will he be looking after the boys too? What about what happened with Josh?" said Rose.

Why didn't you discuss it with me? she thought.

"It'll just be her and the boys," Peter replied slowly.

He pulled off his clothes, on which Rose could detect the smell of Matty's sweat and sick, and headed into the bathroom. Rose arose from her bed and followed him.

"Liddy should be getting professional help, not leaving the country with two children," she said, before delivering a succinct précis of possible treatment options.

"She says she's fine."

Rose looked at him. If the "fine" comment wasn't annoying enough, she knew now she had wasted her time reading about how to get Liddy involuntarily committed, and, worse, it had lulled her into a false sense of security.

"Liddy doesn't cook, she doesn't clean, she doesn't do child care. How will she cope?"

Peter looked at her. Then he replied evenly, "There was a time when Liddy did all those things."

"Well, Matty *must* see the child psychologist."

Peter, naked, sat down on the toilet seat.

"We talked to the child psychologist yesterday afternoon. You were right, Rose. He said it was very regrettable behavior and a warning, but it's important not to overreact. Drugs, drink, sex. They're all out there and we have to deal with them. Liddy checked the history on his laptop and read all the messages on his phone. There's nothing scary, I'm happy to report. A few curse words and self-penned rap lyrics about the injustices of his life, but no visits to terrifying websites and no porn."

Peter shuddered.

"I thought you didn't believe in us spying on him," said Rose quickly and quietly, not wanting to admit she had no idea how to do this.

"Not anymore," said Peter.

Peter stood up wearily and turned the bath on. She saw the blue-gray ridges of the varicose vein on the back of his right leg, the legacy of a football accident at Harvard when he was nineteen and the handsomest young man on the field. She felt a pulse of lust at the image. On the days when Rose regretted the fact that she had not met him sooner, she reminded herself that if they had coincided at college he, Mr. All-American hero, would never have looked at her, bespectacled and Birkenstocked.

"What about Liddy's job?" she asked.

"She's taken a leave of absence. She needs time off." He paused for a moment. "It's the quietest time of the year, apparently. The biggest day for divorce attorneys is January second, closely followed by September fourth—just after everyone's spent a holiday weekend with their spouses."

"What about the dog?"

Peter sighed as he climbed into the tub. "The guy who's buying her apartment loves dogs. He's looking after it for her."

"She's selling her apartment?" said Rose, bemused now by the rapid fire of startling pieces of information. *"Why?"*

"She can't afford it, it seems. She says she never really could."

"My, oh, my," said Rose. "Talk about once she has decided on a course she is compelled to take action."

But he had sunk down under the water and did not seem to hear her.

Rose looked down to see Peter's clothes discarded on the floor. She lifted them gingerly to throw them into the hamper, when a piece of paper fell out of a pocket. It was an itinerary Liddy had prepared, with her address and contact numbers in Ireland. Rose stared at it as she lay back down on the bed. *Why would she go there?* Rose had never once heard Liddy talk about her childhood. *And who was this mysterious friend who had come to her rescue?* Rose had never heard Liddy mention such a person. She closed her eyes and tried to imagine Liddy in a muddy field. She felt as if there was a puzzle portrait of the real Liddy James in a box out of her reach, and she was being given random pieces to try to fit it together.

"Is that the address?" said Peter, who had reappeared wrapped in her aged pink bathrobe. Rose nodded.

"Lough Dan, County Wicklow," she read.

"We visited Ireland together once before we had Matty. It was Liddy's grandmother's funeral and then we drove around a bit. The countryside is incredible," he continued, resting his hand on the top of her head. "You can see why it inspired so many poets and playwrights."

Rose slammed the piece of paper down beside her. "How can you let Liddy do this?" she pleaded. "Maybe we should have a family therapy session together?" (By this Rose meant they would all sit in a room with a therapist who would agree with her and forbid Liddy to go.) "Why can't everything go back to the way it was?"

"Rose," Peter said calmly. "The psychologist said that six years ago Matty's life was turned upside down because Liddy had another baby. Now you're expecting and it's all happening again. No wonder he's angry. No wonder he's acting up. I know it's hard for us to let him go, but my personal view is that he should spend time with Liddy. I think he needs her."

There was a long silence, but for once Rose was glad that Peter had stopped talking. It was entirely in character for Liddy to respond to a crisis with an adventurous or reckless act; but Rose knew that Peter had agreed to this not out of the opposite qualities of caution or paralysis, but because he believed it was the right thing for his son. His words stabbed into her; they drove other words that were already under her skin deeper: *you, have, no, rights.*

He stood up and looked vacantly around the room.

"Where are my socks?" he said.

Rose pointed to the wicker basket in the corner.

"I'm exhausted," he said slowly. "I haven't had a wink of sleep in two nights with the stress of it all."

Rose nodded. She felt exhausted too.

"Peter, with everything that's going on, you know, sometimes I think I'd like to stay at home with the baby when it comes. For the first few years, at least."

"You mean give up your job?"

"Well, not necessarily. I'll take a career break first. Liddy will need more help, not less, when she recovers."

Peter held up two black socks and measured their size against each other before carefully pulling them on. It seemed like he had not heard her. But then he spoke.

"Rose, I'm sure that would be wonderful. But . . . I'm sorry, we can manage for six months or so, but more than that we can't afford. Liddy stopped Matty's child-support payments when he went to live with her. And now . . . she says she has to downsize."

His face was set in an expression of disappointed resignation.

"By the way, I bumped into Sophia Lesnar at the seminar for the doctoral students last week. We need to get the baby registered for the university day care so we have a place for when you come back. It's a wonderful center, according to her, heavily subsidized. We're extremely lucky."

He paused. "And she hasn't heard from you about your reapplication. She's been able to extend the deadline, but you need to get your article in."

Rose pulled the quilt up to her neck and seethed. Peter had no inkling of the fact that she had not written one single word, so it was irrational to think he had spoken to Sophia to sabotage her project of passive resistance. But this did not stop her. She thought for a moment about telling Sophia the truth, and imagined a couple of versions of the scene as if she had nothing to do with it. They did not go well. She struggled to explain how her slow, fermented desire to devote herself exclusively to motherhood had risen so intensely, she had become convinced it was a *right*, and more prosaically, why she had not replied to any of Sophia's e-mails.

"I fear I may have misjudged Sophia. She appears to be going out of her way to help us." Peter smiled. "What's your article about?"

He looked at her expectantly. Rose smiled back but said nothing.

"Why won't you tell me?"

Rose's smile disappeared. She braced herself. So this, finally, was the moment.

"To be honest, Peter, I haven't started."

Before he could reply she reached over and put her hand in his.

"How can Liddy not have any money?"

He snatched his hand away.

"I don't want to talk about it."

"Then I want to speak to a lawyer. She has obligations, doesn't she?" (Rose was disoriented and cross and scared and so this sounded more aggressive than she had meant it to.)

"*Stop it!* We have obligations too!" He paused. "I hope Matty never asks me to account for the way I treated his mother."

"Peter. Liddy was unfaithful and overambitious. She chose her path—"

"Don't say that! Whatever path she took I pushed her down it. She's not the person you think she is." He shook his head sorrowfully. "And I am not the person you think I am. You don't understand. I was a terrible husband to Liddy. Then she was alone. And I crucified her."

The muscle on Peter's face twitched and the tone of his voice made Rose want to cry again.

"Do you mean financially?" whispered Rose.

"Every way I could think of," he said.

At dinner parties in Williamsburg, and during workshops in the gender studies department, Peter had always enthusiastically espoused an ideal of equality in marriage, a model that proved that the personal could be political, whereby two adult individuals with a capacity for independence would enter and leave it, desiring nothing but good will from the other. Now he told Rose that when Liddy left him, the limits of his idealism became clear. Liddy had knelt before him in the library of Carroll Gardens, and confessed her sin, and begged. *She would do anything*, she kept saying, *if he would forgive her.* But he was wild with sorrow and anger and when he told her what she had to do, the only condition on which he would take her back, of course she could not. *It's a boy*, she told him, *I'm going to call him Cal.* So Peter told her he would never forgive her.

He gave her nothing; she gave him half of everything, from the 401(k) to custody of Matty, and an allowance for child support too (if Curtis Oates had known the very un-*shark*like way she negotiated her own settlement, he would never have hired her). But still Peter found his desire for vengeance to be insatiable. He adopted an unremittingly hostile attitude toward her. He announced he could not afford to buy her out of the town house, but refused point-blank to move, so, without protest, she signed over her share of the property to him to ensure that Matty would not lose the only home he had ever known. At one point she had said, "It's only money," which was wise because Peter was not quite done; after Liddy had agreed to pay Matty's school and college fees, there was nothing more he could take. But he had convinced himself he deserved it. After all, he had sneered at Liddy, quoting from Edith Wharton: "'For always getting what she wants in the long run, commend me to a nasty woman.'"

Despite all this, Liddy had never said a word to Matty against his father.

Rose gulped. No wonder Liddy had tried to warn her. Peter had a dark side, all right.

"She was so strong, you see," he said. "It drove me mad. I kept going because I wanted to break her, she hurt me so much I thought it was the only way I would feel better. But I've seen her broken now, and I feel nothing but shame."

Before Rose could say anything, he walked out of the room.

Rose finally allowed herself to cry and cry. Then, oddly relieved, she looked out the window at the redbrick buildings baking in the sun, and considered the appeal of the green fields, mountains, and fens of the Irish countryside, "the land of exile and redemption," as she had once heard it described in a lecture on James Joyce. Obsessed with the constricted world of her body, a growing baby, and a bed, she had forgotten the vast landscapes that lay both outside her room and within the power of her mind; she had chosen to abandon her interior life of thinking and books and art to fixate on the external, over which she had no control. This overload of passivity had changed her personality. In the four short months she had been removed from the stimulation of her work life, she had become fearful and negative and unempathetic.

Rose remembered a scornful debate she had participated in during her freshman year about women like Liddy, professional women whose lifestyles were balanced precariously on the subjugation of other women, women like Lucia, who were their servants. (For two and a half decades Rose had self-consciously scrubbed her own toilet bowls; the moment she was forbidden to, Peter had greeted with cash and open arms the two undocumented Eastern European maids who came for four hours every week.) But now she knew that Peter's unpaid sabbaticals, the renovations to the house, the new car, had all been lubricated by his ex-wife's salary, and the lifestyle Rose enjoyed was wholly dependent on the continued labors of Liddy. Rose's plan to give up her job for a peaceful, familial, stay-at-home existence had been contingent on Liddy continuing to pay for it.

She felt dizzy with a sudden rush of truth to the head.

Liddy and the boys emerged from the night flight into Dublin airport, in the haze between sleep and waking, after a couple of hours of snatched rest curled in the economy seats next to the toilets, the only three available when Liddy had booked the day before. She led them through passport control like a mother zombie, the flickering fluorescent lighting increasing her sense of apocalyptic strangeness. As the glass doors into Arrivals opened, she noticed Matty, who enjoyed his five-star childhood, involuntarily looking for a uniformed driver holding a sign with their name on it. She pointed toward another sign reading BUS TRANSFER TO CAR HIRE. As they staggered toward it, she thought of Vince and how she would miss him. She hoped Curtis would treat him well while she was away.

The car was the last available, a small two-door in bright orange, and was a stick shift, which Liddy had not driven for twenty years. But the staff reassured her with "Ah sure, you'll be grand!" and a young mechanic helped her load the trunk with luggage and stayed to fix the child's booster seat for Cal. (He had seen the expression on Liddy's face as she lifted a seat belt on the backseat ineffectually and peered at the instructions in despair.) After a quick three-minute refresher on how to move between gears, he waved her in the direction of the road going south, saying, "Remember to drive on the left!" She nodded, and as she took her foot off the clutch and lurched forward, he tapped the roof of the car.

"*Dia dhuit!*" he shouted.

"*Dia is Muire dhuit!*" she called back.

Matty stared at her.

"That's 'hello' in Gaelic, the Irish language," she said. "I had to learn it when I was a kid here. I thought I'd forgotten it all, apart from prayers."

He said nothing. He was too tired to decide what mood he was in, though Liddy could make a fair guess. His response to the news of the nonnegotiable Irish vacation with his mother had been to post a picture of Alcatraz on his Facebook page.

"Remind me to drive on the left," she continued with a breeziness she did not feel.

"Reassuring," he grunted, sticking his headphones firmly over his ears.

Driving over the toll bridge past the docks, although Matty was staring out the window and Cal was fast asleep, Liddy talked. As she drove past the wide strand at Sandymount, deserted in the morning apart from a few dog walkers and a couple of men hunting for razor clams in the sand, she remembered walking there with her father, her tiny hand in his, and afterward taking tea in a tumbledown cottage with his two elderly aunts, who had no television but sat on either side of an ancient wireless tuned to the BBC world service.

Matty, though pretending not to listen, surreptitiously turned down the volume on his iPod.

"And here is Blackrock," said Liddy. *"An Charraig Dhubh,"* and although she considered herself a resolutely unsentimental person, she typed a street name into the route map on her phone. Following insistent high-pitched instructions, she turned off the main road, away from the large Victorian houses painted white, into a winding maze of clustered housing estates. Finally she found what she had been looking for: a modest, terraced street first built in the 1950s, apparently unmauled by the rise and fall of the Celtic tiger, where washing still hung on lines in the back gardens and young children played soccer between the parked cars.

"This is where my granny used to live," she said.

"Which house?" said Matty, which surprised her, as she had become used to talking to herself.

Liddy thought for a moment of the black-and-white photograph pinned on the corkboard in the apartment, her parents standing proudly on either side of a large, old-fashioned stroller on the sidewalk outside one of these doors.

"I'm not sure exactly," she said. "I think it's on the right down the end. I know the street name, but I've forgotten the number."

"They all look the same anyway," said Matty dismissively, his eyelids fluttering shut as the sudden, disorienting dizziness of jet lag hit him. Liddy got out of the car and looked around, curious to see what memories might be evoked. But she found it impossible to distinguish anything authentic from the incidents she had reimagined out of photographs. Yet she had indeed been a young girl in this place—running around the puddles with a hula hoop, visiting her grandmother's neighbors next door, arriving for tea in her white dress and veil after her first Holy Communion.

She turned to see an elderly woman in a floral overall and thick support stockings staring at her from across the street.

"Are you looking for someone?" called the woman.

Liddy shook her head and approached her.

"No," she said. "But my grandmother lived here. Mary Murphy."

"The Murphys lived at number fifteen."

She pointed to the house that Liddy now recognized well enough to know it had a newly painted red door. The woman's leathery hand trembled slightly as she did so.

"And who do you be?" she asked.

"I'm . . . Lydia Mary. Patrick Junior's daughter."

"Ah. All the way from America. I should have known." She stared into Liddy's face. "You look like a film star."

Liddy laughed, but the woman did not. Liddy hastily took off her sunglasses.

"Will you be going to the graves?" the woman asked.

"Not today," said Liddy, and she waved and headed back to the car, where Matty was snoring softly with a high-pitched splutter that harmonized with Cal's unconscious exhales.

She sat still for a moment. She was glad Matty had not asked where her parents' house had been. For the answer was "a mile or so away" but ten years ago it had been flattened so a multistory parking lot could be built on top, and the symbolic implications of this disappearance without a trace were such that Liddy resolved there and then not to turn the trip to Ireland into some self-indulgent back-to-my-roots nostalgia fest. But still—

When she finally drove away, she tuned the radio to an eighties classics channel and turned it up loud to keep herself awake. She swigged cola from a can and sang along to songs that Matty and Cal, who both jerked awake too, had never heard before, like "The Way It Is," "Walking on Sunshine," or "Born to Run" (at this one Matty glanced sideways to see his mother acting out some intense lyric involving heroes on a last drive somewhere).

They headed along the coast to Dún Laoghaire, through the stage-set prettiness of Dalkey, and along the Sorrento Road, with its breathtaking views over Killiney Bay. The hazy sunshine glittered on the sea, the music played, and because of the daze she was in, the journey took on the quality of a dream. Liddy allowed herself to soar with a series of rising chords and felt that she was in the opening scene of a movie. Yes, an inspirational movie for the female audience about how a highly paid divorce attorney at the height of her professional powers might respond to the disintegration of that life by returning to the place of her birth to *find herself* or possibly *spend quality time* with things that matter (like the fractious six-year-old child who keeps a photo of Lucia under his pillow, or the morose teenager who has said little since being expelled from summer camp, apart from announcing in sarcastic tones how many more strangers have logged on to YouTube to watch the video of his mother's breakdown live on national television) with a reassuring conclusion of familial reconciliation, self-empowerment, and perfect hair.

Liddy was speculating on which film star might do her justice in this role when Matty moved his attention from iPod to iPhone.

"Thirty-nine thousand two hundred and twenty-five hits so far!" he shouted as they drove through Shankill.

"Oh, stop going on about it," said Liddy. "It wasn't that bad."

"Have you actually seen it?" said Matty. "It's *mortifying* for me."

"Good word. Have you managed to read a book recently?"

"No. That's what Dad said when you were lying in bed."

"What else did Dad say when I was lying in bed?"

"He didn't talk much because he was crying."

Matty spoke defiantly, but he had clearly been rattled by the scene. Liddy noticed the mustache on his upper lip, which grew darker by the day. She felt a primal pulse of intense love for him.

"Your dad's a good man," she said, more than a little rattled herself. She knew then that self-dramatization would be no use to her whatsoever, and, anyway, Liddy did not believe in Hollywood endings. She was well aware that the fantasy lives of women are not the same as the real lives of women, and too often involve surrender or subjugation or sadomasochism. Which was why she always preferred to watch action films, films where male heroes are trapped in space, or are captured by pirates, or have to cut their arms off with penknives to survive.

She switched off the radio as she turned toward Wicklow.

As a small child, Liddy had driven this road many times with her parents, and while it had been resurfaced and widened, the route remained the same. Once they had visited the Powerscourt Waterfall in Enniskerry, where they had parked next to a ramshackle caravan with a picture and a slogan painted on its side: HEAVEN WASN'T BIG ENOUGH, SO GOD CREATED IRELAND. Liddy's father had been delighted with this and repeated it many times, frequently when they were back in Silver Lake and he got a little drunk and maudlin late at night. Back then she had found it embarrassing and mawkish, but this day, as she drove slowly through Kilmacanogue and onto the winding road toward Roundwood, with the moors and fens stretching into infinity on either side and the green Sugar Loaf mountain rising behind her, she saw its beauty and she understood. In the rearview mirror she caught sight of Cal, his cheek squished against the glass of the window, entranced by the real-life animals he saw roaming the unmanicured fields around him. She smiled. She had never thought of the countryside as her *thing*, but as she stared into the wide horizon, she felt the freedom in the space here. She understood why city people reminded themselves of the earth by lovingly reclaiming small, secret gardens in the wells between tenement blocks, or nurturing their window boxes and tiny pots of herbs on window-sills, despite the showers of black soot that frequently rained down upon them.

She thought fondly of her fig tree in Carroll Gardens.

The iPhone beeped and told her she had reached her destination, a tiny shop called O'Toole's that nestled beside an enormous rusty red barn that was the spectator stand for the local Gaelic football club. Then, as Sebastian had said, she looked for a small blue sign saying PLEASE USE FOOT DIP PROVIDED and turned down the rutted road beside it. The car wove through a patchwork of stone walls and fields until she rounded a corner and the land-scape changed to woodland and water. From there Liddy crawled along in sputtering second gear until she reached a small waterfall trickling down a bank into a gully; then she saw the tall, black wrought-iron gates with the name STACKALLAN DEMESNE carved into one of the stone pillars beside them. She drove through, clat-tering over the cattle grid, and headed up the driveway.

Sebastian's gate lodge was built of stone and slate and sat on a small but perfect plot of land beside the lake. When Liddy pulled up outside, she knew from its unadorned exterior, masculine metal shutters, and the rickety wooden jetty that it was not designed for children or visitors, and that Sebastian most often stayed there on his own. The couple of photos he had sent her had shown only two bedrooms, one bathroom, and a small, dust-covered television straight out of *The Flintstones*. Although the living area was flooded with light from the windows and skylights, and looked large enough for the boys to run up and down, the galley kitchen was tiny, with an aged stove and no dining table. A wooden sign with lettering burned into it was propped up by the locked garage; the house was simply called THE GATE LODGE, with no indication of any mythical powers or imaginative space within.

She got out of the stale air of the rental car, her clothes reeking of pine air freshener and cheap upholstery shampoo, and stood in the cool breeze that came off the water. She stretched her arms above her head and then stopped, quite still, to watch a young deer that had come up from the road and was picking its way through the hazelnut trees, stretching its neck forward to sniff the leaves that carpeted an unkempt flowerbed. Without making a sound, Liddy turned and reached her hand back, tapping ever so gently on the car window. Matty looked up and nudged Cal. They all stared in absolute quiet until a large crow rose squawking from the hedgerow. The startled deer leapt down the driveway that continued through the ancient wood toward the big house, whose chimneys could distantly be seen above the trees.

Liddy looked around. A row of dark brown gnarly rosebushes lined the flower bed, each with a single brave bloom upon it. She walked over and smelled every single one. She knelt down on the ground and took a handful of earth in her hands and then let it fall through her fingers. She listened to the rhythmic lapping of the water, the insistent song of the lake tide. She felt the absence of the cacophony of noises that had become the sound track to her life. She became aware that the absence of these sounds was a presence; it was peace.

Liddy understood why Sebastian would never have given this place up.

She pulled open the passenger door to be greeted by an ear-splitting yelp from Matty.

"My phone's not working!"

He ran out of the car and clambered up onto a rock, waving the phone in the air.

"Yes, the owner told me the reception can be patchy," said Liddy, reaching back to help Cal out, and feeling nothing but relief that they could no longer witness her ongoing excoriation on the worldwide web. "There's a landline for emergencies."

"What good is that?" said Matty in horror. He finally took notice of his surroundings.

"*What the* . . . *!* There's nothing here. This is worse than I thought. What am I gonna do all day? Watch the freaking grass grow?"

Liddy walked away and started pulling bags out of the trunk and left them on the gravel.

"*Why did we come here?*"

As Liddy did not have an answer to that question beyond *So I could get a grip*, she turned to Cal in her best camp counselor tone.

"Shall we explore?"

"Where's the pool?" Cal said, for he too enjoyed his five-star childhood.

Liddy explained that there wasn't one and they would swim in the lake, to which Cal shouted, "Yuk!" and looked like he might cry. Matty came over, hugged him, and turned to Liddy.

"I get why you want to punish me for what I did at camp, Mom. I know it wouldn't be enough to take away all my electronic devices and ground me, and that's why I'm with you in this shithole for the summer. *But how could you do it to Cal?*"

At this, Cal did cry, so in the spirit of picking your battles, Liddy ignored Matty and chased after a tiny white feather that the breeze had lifted and blown toward her face.

"What's this, Cal?" she said to distract him.

"Look!" he said, pointing up ahead where a pile of tiny white feathers was strewn across the gravel as if two fairies had had a pillow fight. He ran ahead to investigate as Liddy looked for the rusty bucket Sebastian had described, under which the key was always left. She heard Matty's heavy footfall crunching toward Cal. She heard Matty start to laugh.

"What's funny?" asked Liddy, immediately worried.

"There's some bald bird running around here."

Oh, no, thought Liddy, but it was too late. Cal screamed; she hurried over to him and he leapt into her arms. Matty was peering at a young seagull's half-chewed carcass, the brown and red guts spilling out like worms. He picked up a stick and prodded it.

"A cat got it, I hope. Or else it's some other wild beast."

"Stop it!" shouted Liddy as Cal screamed again.

"What a good idea this was!" said Matty in his best camp counselor tone. "Isn't nature great?"

"I wanna leave!" cried Cal.

"So do I," said Matty.

"We are *not* leaving. I need a break."

The boys stared at her resentfully.

Liddy exhaled wearily. She could not deny it was an inaus-picious start to their great adventure. "I need a break from my job, from the city, from the stress. From everything apart from you two."

"Huh," muttered Matty. "Hashtag first-world problems."

She stared over the lake to the horizon and contemplated run-ning into the water and swimming away. She did not. She looked at him. "And while a lovely vacation in your ancestral homeland is certainly not a punishment, you, son, do need some time to re-flect on your behavior and *change it*! Inside. *Now!*"

He looked back at her, his nose wrinkled as if sniffing the piousness with which he reeked. "You ever thought about anger management, Mom?"

Liddy stuck the rough, rusting key into the lock, pushed her right shoulder against it, and fell into the house, Cal on top of her.

"Epic fail," sneered Matty.

Liddy pushed herself up, relieved to discover that the floor tiles were clean. She retrieved Sebastian's instructions, which she had slipped into a handy plastic cover, from her pocket. Matty stepped over her and headed for the small bedroom at the far end of the living room.

There was a pause, and then the inevitable *slam!*

"This is fun," said Liddy bravely. She leaned down to Cal, wiped his eyes, and kissed him on the forehead. Then she gave him a packet of pretzels she had stuffed into her bag on the plane, and they made their way hand in hand through the galley kitchen, into an adjoining utility room behind. After following a compli-cated series of instructions typed on the sheet taped to the door

(Sebastian had helpfully scribbled *Do not touch this or you will blow yourself up* on a Post-it note and stuck it on a red button at her feet), she switched the heating on, causing an alarming rattle from the boiler. Then she returned to the living area and unpacked. This did not take long, as she had only brought essentials: a few clothes, walking boots, freshly laundered white sheets, white towels—two bottles of red wine with twist-off tops wrapped within them—and the clothbound notebook Rose had given her, which she had grabbed as she headed out the apartment door.

She had also packed something called a "hitachi wand," apparently of vital importance to solitary ladies, which Lloyd had sent her in a gift-wrapped box after she had told him she would sell him her apartment when she came back from Ireland. He had tucked a handwritten note inside it with the message "Hope you're not missing me too much." Liddy walked into the master bedroom, pleasingly bare with faded blue wallpaper, empty shelves, a large double bed, and nothing else, and stuffed the wand under a pillow. She decided to lie down. The bedroom reminded her of her own apartment. She wondered if Sebastian had been waiting for a life to fill this place too. She closed her eyes—

—only to judder awake five minutes later to find Cal staring into her face. He was holding the half-finished packet of pretzels above his head and they showered over him onto her bed. Liddy stopped herself from snapping at him in protest but had absolutely no idea what to do about this. Disciplining him had always been someone else's job.

"I'm hungry," he said.

It was then she realized that she had not thought about food, for the feeding of Cal was also someone else's job. Over the past weeks, in fact, it had become her habit to eat less and less. The diet app on her Jawbone had confirmed her recent weight loss, although she had stopped telling it the truth, as on the day she had recorded dinner as three spiced pear martinis, a plate of eda-mame, and a Snickers bar, it had reported that she had a disorder. Her cheekbones were hollow and there was a reverse triangular-shaped gap between her thighs.

(In fact, before the funny turn, Sydney had assumed she was taking a secret admirer on a romantic desert island break and had asked her if she was getting "bikini ready.")

"Okay," she replied, walking to the kitchen and opening the two cupboards and the refrigerator that hissed. But they con-tained only something in a jar called marmite and another called swarfega, both of which looked similarly disgusting. She would have to drive back past the foot dip sign and hunt for a restaurant.

"Put on your shoes," she said to Cal, and he stood up, bits of pretzel crunching beneath his feet, kicking the shards across the floor as he walked. Almost physically appalled by the mess, she retrieved what was almost certainly a vacuum cleaner from the utility room. She plugged it into the electric socket and switched it on with a flourish. Nothing happened. She picked up the plastic nozzle and moved it around a bit. *Nothing.* She ineffectually stabbed at a couple of buttons on the handle and then gave up. Liddy had worked her whole life so she would never have to fix a domestic appliance. She did not intend to start now.

She piled the boys back into the car and headed to Roundwood, stopping at the small supermarket to buy milk, coffee, tea, bread, butter, canned tuna, and cereal. Then she found a pub with an outdoor garden where they sat at a wooden table in the sunshine and ate chicken strips and fries and ice cream.

"I like it here," she said, looking around.

"Yeah, it's okay," said Matty unexpectedly. "What d'you think, short stack?" he continued, turning to Cal.

Cal took an enormous scoop of ice cream and grinned. Liddy relaxed. On the table behind them a couple of seagulls, greedy for food, turned their black eyes on the abandoned plates of the previous diners and swooped down to grab half-eaten fish cakes.

"Hey, Mom," said Matty. "Is Dad coming to visit?"

"I invited him, but he can't because of the baby," said Liddy quickly. It was too late. Cal was looking at her over the top of his sundae with the same expression she had seen at his birthday party before he had asked her where *his* dad was.

Oh, no, she thought, *not now*.

Matty saw her desperation and started laughing. This made her angry.

"Why did you take that stuff from Josh's bag if you didn't know what it was?" she said. She instantly regretted it, but it was too late to stop, so she continued. "Why did you give it to those other boys in the summer camp?"

"It's none of your business," he fired back. "I made a mistake, okay? You ever made one of those, Mom? Remember?"

And he raised his finger very slowly and pointed at Cal.

"Don't ever say that again!" she said, exploding.

He laughed again, cruelly this time, and imitated the contorted shape of her furious face. Then the biggest and boldest bird came to a precarious halt on the bench beside them and, before Liddy could protect Cal's food, grabbed an enormous beakful of chicken strip. Cal's mouth fell open in outrage and fear and he began to wail.

"Bet you wish a cat had murdered that one," said Matty, and Cal wailed louder. Liddy scooped him up, although he struggled and beat his fists against her back, and hauled him to the car. Matty trailed behind, shuffling and occasionally kicking the curb for no apparent reason. Liddy worried people might stare, but in fact no one did. She was unremarkable, just another exhausted forty-something mother dealing with her exhausted and recalcitrant children. As she closed the car doors, she caught sight of herself in the side mirror; there, staring back at her, was a frazzled woman in dirty sweatpants.

Once in the driver's seat, she switched on the phone app to navigate back to the house. But it did not register the tiny roads and dead-end junctions and instead sent her in a circuitous route that, even in her wooziness, she could tell was wrong. There came a moment where she rounded a narrow corner and saw the house nestling in the distance. She headed onward but the device kept insisting "You have taken the wrong direction. Stop and turn back."

She did not. She pulled the car to a halt by a rough stone wall bordering the lake. She wound down the window. She threw the phone out.

It landed in the water with a satisfying splash.

Matty opened his mouth to speak.

"Don't say anything!" she hissed.

He shrugged and closed his eyes.

Back at the gate lodge, she sat Cal and Matty in front of the aged television to watch *SpongeBob SquarePants* dubbed into Irish, and wandered around the house to see what had been left behind that might teach her something about its owner. There was little: three copies of *Atlantic* magazine from 2010, a dog-eared paperback of *Eat, Pray, Love,* and two CDs left on top of the stereo—Keith Jarrett's *The Melody at Night, with You* and *The Art of the Song* by Charlie Haden. But there was something about the atmosphere of the house, whether it was the smell of wood and turf or the old-fashioned solidity of the furniture, which Liddy could only describe as kind. Sebastian was a kind man, however much he might pretend not to be, and when Liddy remembered the image of him here with Chloe, two ghosts of Google Earth, and his dream of walking this land with his children, she felt sad for him.

In the wardrobe hung a few of his shirts, which, if she were the leading actress in the movie about her life, she would have clutched to herself and sniffed. This struck Liddy only as unhygienic, particularly the armpit area, from which she concluded that her feelings for Sebastian were confused—or simply realistic.

Liddy knew that he would soon find a Chloe 2.0, this time one with functioning ovaries, and in the future Liddy would once again only meet him in court.

She turned to see the two boys wilting into the sofa, and as it was now late afternoon, she said they could go to bed, and they didn't argue. She carried Cal into her room, Matty disappeared into his, and she emerged with what was now a medicinal need of alcohol. She grabbed one of the bottles of merlot, untwisted the cap with her teeth, and swigged it straight from the bottle, reveling in the feeling of taboo. Then she filled a tumbler.

She picked up the CD of *The Art of the Song* and saw a version of a traditional hymn she had often heard Peter talk about. She put it in the stereo, pressed play, and the room filled with the melancholy beauty of the simple song.

> *I'm just a poor wayfaring stranger*
> *I'm traveling through this world of woe*
> *Yet there's no sickness, toil nor danger*
> *In that bright land to which I go*
> *I'm going there to see my father*
> *I'm going there no more to roam*
> *I'm just a-going over Jordan*
> *I'm just a-going over home*
> *I know dark clouds will gather 'round me*
> *I know my way is rough and steep*
> *Yet golden fields lie just before me*
> *Where the redeemed shall ever sleep*
> *I'm going there to see my mother*
> *She said she'd meet me when I come*
> *I'm only going over Jordan*
> *I'm only going over home.*

Liddy leaned against the wall. She tried to close her eyes and listen, but, without warning, a shivering more violent than that of exhaustion engulfed her, and because she was in the long-lost country of her birth, her mind writhed in the grip of the kind of intense introspection about the past she had designed her city life to avoid.

For more than half her years, Liddy had been emotionally estranged from her parents. She did not relinquish her responsibilities toward them, she assisted them financially, she called them on occasion, and she visited once a year. But she saw herself as a person effectively orphaned, not by death but by self-betterment. And they made it easy for her. When she spent a day in the condo in Orlando, Patrick sat glued to the TV, and Breda began washing the dishes the moment food had been put on the table. It seemed that her parents did not *like* her very much. Certainly, they had nothing in common. Liddy always felt that they were punishing her for that.

She remembered with a shudder how her mother had urged her toward a sensible life: a pensionable job, an appropriate marriage to a nice boy, a ranch house no more than thirty minutes' drive away, and, above all, no disturbing desire to be different. (After all, Breda used to say, look what happened to Janice McCrea, who went to Los Angeles to be an actress and got pregnant and took drugs and Mrs. Mulvey from church says is now a hooker.) Then how, having ignored all this, when her father lost his job and told her she could no longer continue her undergraduate studies at Yale, she had howled with rage and run outside to a phone booth and called her grandmother, who had been sitting in the tiny kitchen of that house in Blackrock, and asked for ten thousand dollars. And how her grandmother had said yes and not asked why. (When Liddy had got the job at Rosedale and Seldon, she had paid the loan back with interest, and also bought her grandmother a car.) On Sundays, Liddy had worked an unpleasant but highly paid shift in a plastics factory with three ex-convicts and a former US marine. They swore all the time and the marine leered at her. She cleaned houses and waitressed and tutored rich kids all the way through college. She never took a penny from her parents ever again.

When Peter first met her, he had found her history entirely understandable, even charming. He had pointed out that literature has always needed orphans, from Becky Sharp to Harry Potter, and that it was far harder to create forward momentum for protagonists if they have to get past their parents. But the moment Matty was born Peter's attitude began to change. It became important to him that his child have a sense of his wider family.

"What did they do that was so bad?" he would ask, insisting that Liddy was not beaten or starved and that his parents drove him crazy but he would never stop them from seeing their grandchild. He said that the narcissism of youth can feed false memories in anyone, and that Liddy *should get over it* for the sake of her son. Liddy was horrified. Peter appeared to have forgotten that, while Liddy had abandoned her religion long ago, there was one article of faith to which she was devoted. Of course she had not endured the gothic horrors of others' experiences, but her childhood was still something she had to survive.

Tough breeds tough; Liddy had learned that the hard way.

She had triumphed against the odds, of that there was no doubt. But this country, and her childhood home, and, yes, Patrick and Breda Murphy, were part of the petri dish in which her aggressively independent nature had been grown. She had come to America from somewhere, and that seemed like an important thing to be reminded of. *For hadn't Peter once shouted that she had spent so much time and effort making herself she had lost herself too?*

"Stop!" she muttered, jumping to her feet. She switched off the CD. It had been years since she had stayed still and listened to a piece of music for its own sake; now she knew why. Music could awaken feelings that she had put to sleep. She had relegated it to a backdrop for meditation, or a motivational tool for exercise, the relentless reinforcing of the awesomeness of everything. To calm herself, she began to recite law cases under her breath, exactly as she had done as a student when she was taking her exams, but it was no good. She began to pace up and down. *What the hell had she done? What the hell was she going to do?* She had children, responsibilities. She could not throw her life away like her mobile phone, which presumably now lay at the bottom of the lake (the seventy-three messages from Curtis unlistened to), never to rise again like the sword Excalibur.

And what about the resurrection of her work life, after such a spectacular and public disintegration? In the career game of Snakes and Ladders she had not just fallen down a ladder, an enormous boa constrictor had swallowed her whole. Despite her literary agent's assurances that "all publicity is good publicity," there would be no second best-selling book detailing how to break up without fucking your kids up, for, quite clearly, whether ten tips or seven signs, she had been too preoccupied advising others on how to spot them to take any notice herself. And while another woman, humbler or more attuned to the ironies of life, might take a kind of perverse pleasure in the dark humor of the situation, Liddy felt nothing other than coruscating self-hatred and humiliation.

In the background, she heard the sound of Matty's phone ringing. He answered it in his newly gruff stranger's voice and walked into the hallway to stand by a window. There was a low rumbling of generic conversation—and then she heard what sounded like a book being hurled onto the floor and a shout as the patchy reception went on and then off.

"Is everything all right?" she called.

"That was Dad," he called back.

Liddy stood up and went to find him.

"I'm sure you miss him and Rose."

"I miss my bedroom!"

"Oh, Matty—"

"Leave me alone!"

And he went back into his room.

Liddy turned and walked away, but as she reached her bedroom she heard a strange noise from the other end of the house. At first she thought it was the low humming of a harmonica, but as she approached Matty's room again, she heard him crying. She ran into him and held him in her arms.

"I've been such an idiot," he sobbed. "I let you and Dad down. I'm so embarrassed. Do you think they'll ever let me into the camp again?"

"Matty, don't worry. Just promise me you'll never do it again and we'll work it out. Your dad and I love you so much. We were so scared."

"My throat still hurts, Mom. I thought I'd never stop puking. Like, I honestly thought my guts were coming up." He looked up at her, his face wet and blotchy. "This isn't how I thought my life would be. I want to be happy."

Liddy hugged him harder. *Me too*, she thought. "Everything's gonna be okay," she said. "I promise."

"I'm straight edge from now on, Mom. Did you ever take drugs?"

Oh, the brave new world of parenting a teenager.

"Once," she said, completely truthfully, "but it didn't do anything for me."

She had indeed made one attempt to walk on the wild side and had rubbed proffered cocaine onto her gums late at night in a nightclub, where the drumbeat was so loud it seemed to be punching her in the chest. But it failed to have any discernible effect, so she headed home and had a mug of cocoa instead. She had awoken the next morning secure in the knowledge that it was another rite of passage she had passed, or failed, depending on your point of view.

"Trust me, Matty. There's a reason we tell you not to do certain things. It's our job to protect you." And she lay beside him and stroked his hair until he settled, curled on his side around a pillow.

Liddy pulled the door closed and hurried outside and down to the shore. The sky was cloudy and streaked with pink, the lake was glassy and gray. Almost in silhouette, a woman passed on a paddleboard with a large dog balanced behind her. She lifted a muscular arm in a cheery wave as she rowed. Liddy limply waved back, and waited for her to pass by. Then Liddy cried, bitterly and resolutely. First, for the loss of the life she had worked so hard to achieve, then for the loss of her marriage to Peter, for which she had never had time to grieve, and (last and most bitterly and resolutely) for the loss of her children, or rather, all the time with them she had given away.

Liddy had always taken pride in her ability to see the positive in every situation. "If it isn't terminal, it doesn't matter," she would say, and others either marveled or felt a bit scared and stayed out of her way. But there was no positive spin to be wrung from the sight of distraught Matty and no escape from the regrets that filled her now, the worst of which was clear. She did not know her sons, and they did not know her.

The first drops of a heavy rain splattered on her hair. She ran inside to find Matty still awake and told him to pick up his mattress and put it on the floor of her room. For one night they would all sleep in there together. He obeyed without a word—secretly he found the incessant hammering on the skylight above him far noisier and more disturbing than any air-conditioning unit in the city—and was asleep in minutes.

Liddy lay quite still next to Cal, her heart pounding, and listened to her sons' breathing and the deluge outside the windows. Peter would have told his students it was "pathetic fallacy" and said that the weather was mirroring her emotional turmoil.

All she knew was that it felt like hell.

The next morning, Liddy was awakened by an unusual buzzing a few inches from her face. She lifted her right hand and swatted back and forth in front of her nose, waiting for her eyelids to open. Only then did she feel the scratchy pain in her throat and the thick stabbing pressure in her ears and across her cheekbones. Her sinuses were bubbling with infection. When her vision settled, she rolled over to see Cal brandishing an object that could only be the hitachi wand.

"Gimme!" she said gruffly, grabbing it and peering at it to see how to turn it off. At the foot of the bed, Matty surfaced, sitting upright, his hair adorably ruffled, looking about six years old himself.

"What is that?" he said, and she muttered something about a foot massager, and stuffed it back in the paper bag, secretly thrilled that he was not yet as grown up as he thought. Pale morning light struggled through the window. Liddy swallowed, groaned, and looked at her watch, mentally computing the hour to Irish time. It was nine o'clock in the morning. She closed her eyes. She felt herself drifting into feverish sleep again, and in the distance she heard the sound of some pigeons calling a melodic, comforting *coo*—

—when suddenly a dog started barking as another sound, that of some sort of rattling vehicle pounding down the track, reverberated. There was a shriek of brakes as it hurtled to a halt, and then there was a relentless hammering on the wooden front door, which seemed to make the whole house shake. Liddy didn't move. She had momentarily forgotten that there was no one else around to answer it, and so had the boys. She pulled the duvet over her aching head to see if the noise would just go away. But instead it got louder and more insistent, until she wondered if it might be some intruder with malevolent intent. She grabbed the hitachi wand, although obviously there was little damage a vibrator could do to a violent attacker, and made her way slowly to the kitchen, Cal trailing behind her, his arms wrapped around her pajamaed legs. She peered out the window.

There in the driveway stood a woman of stocky build and unkempt appearance, in her late thirties or so, her hair an indeterminate shade of gray black and cropped short, nest-like and horizontal, as if she had been dragged through a hedge backward and forward.

"Hello? *Hello?*" the woman said, and as she clearly had no intention of leaving, Liddy opened the door on the latch.

"Hello?" said Liddy, before coughing violently.

"Who are you and what are you doing here?" the woman demanded.

"Who are *you?*" gasped Liddy in between gulping breaths.

"I'm Storm Stackallan. Sebastian's sister." (*Of course*, thought Liddy, blaming the ache in her head for her failure to figure this out immediately. Although through the gap in the door she could only see one eye, the corner of a mouth, and the side profile of Storm's nose like in a cubist painting, from the window she should have recognized the slope of the woman's body, which was exactly like her brother's.)

There was a pause, and used to the confusion her name often elicited, Storm continued by way of explanation. "My mother named me after her favorite horse." She paused. "Are you Sebastian's mistress?"

"*No*. I'm Liddy James. I'm staying here for the summer. Didn't he tell you?"

"No," Storm announced assertively. "Sebastian always comes here for the summer."

It was clear to Liddy that Storm was not about to blow away.

"Not this year," she replied, reluctantly opening the door. "He's on a remote island in Alaska, fishing."

Storm entered. "Alaska? No wonder he hasn't called me. And of course the Internet's been down for weeks."

Matty's strangled yelp of protest resounded from the bedroom.

"Who are you?" she said, looking at Cal.

"Cal," he replied, holding out his hand. Storm considered, held out her own, and shook.

"Where do you live?" she said.

"New York City."

"Oh. Are you one of those sad city kids who think milk comes out of a carton?"

"*No!* It comes from a cow," he said, chortling, "who lives on an organic farm in New England."

Storm turned back to Liddy. "Of course, Seb's running away from the divorce. He doesn't do failure. He used to make the teachers re-mark his exams if he got a B. Mind you, I never liked Chloe. She came here for one night, announced she was allergic to mold spores and that he had to take her to a hotel. It was never going to work out."

Liddy walked over to the kitchen area, where she swallowed three acetaminophen, plugged in the antiquated coffeemaker, and improvised a filter with a paper towel.

"He told Roberta it was horrid. Chloe fleeced him for everything he'd got."

"Well," said Liddy, "in fact, they settled by mutual agreement."

Storm looked over, curious, and Liddy leapt at the chance to get rid of her. With her avowed dislike of Chloe, Storm might not wish to spend time with the chief instigator of the "fleecing."

"I was Chloe's divorce lawyer."

There was a moment. And then Storm burst out laughing.

"*Really?* That's hilarious! And he invited you? That's *so* Sebastian!" She paused. "Good job Roberta's not here, mind. She's hopping mad about it all."

"Sebastian and I are . . . friends, we've known each for years. It wasn't personal, it was work," explained Liddy. "It sounds weirder than it was." Then she thought, *Nope, that's a line you could use in New York, but here, it sounds pretty weird.*

"Mom's also a writer," said Matty, who had appeared in the doorway. "She's been on TV. You should watch her on YouTube. When will the Internet be back on?"

Liddy flashed him a warning look.

"Dunno, kid," said Storm. "I'm waiting for Seamus to find the big ladder."

She looked out the window. As if on cue, a shambling, aged local straight out of *The Quiet Man*, in green boots, filthy woolen jumper, and bobble hat, limped past with his flea-bitten mutt and crooked stick.

"Ah, there he is. I'll have a word with him in a minute."

"Storm, this is my elder son, Matty."

Matty stood still for a moment. He stared first at his phone and then at the disappearing figure of Seamus, an expression of exaggerated horror on his face. Finally he grunted something unintelligible and went back into his room. That he managed not to slam the door was his only concession to the presence of a stranger. His remorse of the previous night had been short-lived.

"Do you want a cup of coffee, Storm?" Liddy said.

"Only if you're sure," said Storm, but as she had already thrown herself onto the couch, Liddy knew this was merely politeness.

"I'm knackered," Storm continued. "I couldn't sleep with the foxes barking last night. Did you hear them, Cal?"

Cal shook his head, and proceeded to deal her in to his dinosaur Top Trumps.

"I've always thought I could be a writer," said Storm. "When I tell people about my family, they say I should definitely do a memoir. And of course, Sebastian published a book."

"What about?" asked Liddy, returning with the coffee.

"Of his poetry," replied Storm.

"Brontasaurus!" said Cal, putting a card on the table.

"T. rex trumps him!" said Storm triumphantly.

She lifted her mug to take a swig and her sleeve fell down, revealing a vivid and large tattoo in red and black across her forearm. At that moment, Matty somnambulated out of his room for the second time, drawn to the mothership of the hissing fridge.

"What does that say?" he asked, peering over.

"I dunno, it's Sanskrit for something," said Storm happily. "But it was twenty years ago when I was living in Bali and I don't even remember how I got it. I think I was drunk."

Liddy decided to change the subject. "Have you always lived here, Storm? What do you do?"

"Yes. I was born here. Like Sebastian and our younger brother, Will." She paused, and Liddy, who excelled at cross-examination, could tell she was about to admit something that she then thought better of. "And . . . I do lots of things, but I told Roberta I'd keep an eye on the place for her while she's away. To be honest, I'm at a bit of a crossroads. Need thinking time."

For one moment Liddy thought this might be an invitation to spill deeply personal details and wondered how to convey that she was (a) not the confessional, therapy-loving, neurotic type of New Yorker, and (b) she was not looking for a friend. Fortunately, Storm stood up.

"So I'm off to Dublin now. Anyone fancy a ride?"

Matty opened his mouth, but Liddy interrupted, remembering Sebastian's e-mail. "We're fine, thanks."

She winced as the catarrh in her head began to set like green concrete.

"Do you need anything? How long will you be here?"

"Eight weeks and three days," said Matty mournfully. "Unless there's, like, some natural disaster."

He looked up. The patter of raindrops on the skylights had begun again.

"Does it ever stop raining?" he asked. (Liddy remained silent.)

"This isn't rain," said Storm, patiently. "This is what we call a *soft* day."

Matty thought for a moment. "Does the lake ever flood?"

Storm ignored this.

"I'm delighted you're here. It's a bit of a lonely old station rattling around up there on my own. Come to the house for tea. Three o'clock. I'll show you round the place." She looked at Cal. "You can feed the chickens." Then at Matty. "There's a pool table in the stables and a trampoline out the back, young man." Then she turned to Liddy. "And you can raid Roberta's medicine cabinet and see some really embarrassing photographs of Sebastian when he was a baby."

"I don't like pool," said Matty.

"Oh, give your mother a break," said Storm, heading toward the door. (Because she was not his parent, she had reached the limits of what she could ignore.)

"Okay," he replied. "Sorry, Mom."

Liddy nodded. She decided to relax into the comfort of her illness, which though unpleasant physically, was actually preferable to the mental anguish of the previous night. She liked the sound of the onsite children's activities. And she was curious to visit the big house, which was tantalizingly out of sight, and walk the Stackallan ancestral lands in order to understand what all the "home and history" fuss was about. She followed Storm outside into the intermittent drizzle to see a large scruffy dog sitting in the aged Land Rover parked outside.

Suddenly she heard the sound of music, distant but recognizable, and she turned. It could only be coming from a house on the far side of the lake.

"It's amazing how the sound travels over the water," said Liddy, but there was something in Storm's expression that made her pause. She noticed the muscular shape of Storm's arms and knew Storm had been the woman on the paddleboard the previous night.

Storm must have heard her sobbing.

"I've had some ups and downs recently," Liddy said, which was as far by way of explanation as she wanted to go.

Storm nodded. "Join the club," she said.

She clambered into the vehicle and, after reversing into a ditch, revved the engine so hard it screeched in pain and belched blue smoke over the rosebushes, then roared off onto the main road at about seventy miles an hour.

Liddy looked around. In the distance white sheep dotted the green pastures and two glossy-coated horses whinnied and cantered around the neighboring field.

The boys came outside looking for her.

"I'm hungry," said Cal.

"I'm bored," said Matty.

Liddy opened her mouth to retort, but wisely decided she had better get used to those two statements, as they were likely to reverberate constantly for the next eight weeks and three days, like the buzzing of the wasps on the coconut-scented yellow flowers of the gorse bushes. And while there was little at that moment Liddy could do about the latter, she dealt with the former straightaway by pouring bowls of cereal and making toast laden with butter, which they ate standing up by the open window. It tasted good. The pain in her throat eased. Then as she realized this was probably the last day she could send the boys back into bed without protest, she did, and they all dozed for another few hours. By one o'clock they were all starving again, and as Matty had already eaten everything that Liddy had not hidden under her bed, it was time to venture out. There seemed to be no way of securing the house to New York City standards, so Liddy stuffed the two thousand euros in cash she had brought into her jacket pocket and hid her camera and laptop in the rusty bucket beside the garage. Then they headed off. They bought sodas and hot dogs from O'Toole's shop, a note on the counter confirming that it had been PASSED FOR FOOD HYGIENE, and ate them on the jagged rocks that jutted into the lake.

Cal took off his shoes and dipped his toes in the water. Liddy remembered how to skim stones and even Matty was impressed by the one that leapt five times.

At quarter to three, they trudged slowly along the track through the dark wood, keeping their eyes down to watch for sheep and deer droppings, and trying to ignore the rapid scuttlings and strange rustlings in the undergrowth around them. Then, from deep within an ancient oak tree, a white-faced barn owl flew across their path, its great wings flapping in front of their noses, causing Liddy to shriek with fear and the boys to shriek with excitement. Thankfully, just as Liddy was beginning to feel she was trapped in a live-action nature special, they emerged from the tunnel of the dense overhanging branches.

There, right in front of them, was the house called Stackallan Demesne.

Liddy involuntarily raised her hand to her mouth. The darkened sky and the gray clouds gave the scene before her the appearance of a black-and-white daguerreotype.

The image would be called *Ruined House with Donkey in the Doorway*.

"What a dump!" said Matty contemptuously. "I'm not going in there—it looks dangerous!"

Only the external structure of the old house remained: the square gray-stoned shape of a small Georgian manor, two Ionic pillars on either side of the empty doorway. The window frames were empty too, and Liddy could see straight through to the mountains beyond. And while a shiny new roof had recently been put on, the only inhabitants were the couple of tame donkeys, who cheerfully munched grass in what had once been the hallway.

Liddy took Cal's hand and approached. They walked together up the stone steps and peered inside. In front of them were the charred remains of what had once been a magnificent curved staircase with individually carved railings. The walls of the great rooms to the right and left were a palimpsest of peeling wallpaper, moss, and huge streaks of black soot. All that remained of the furniture were the two crystal chandeliers hanging, miraculously unscathed, in their plaster rosettes in the center of the two ceilings.

"*Hey!* Liddy!"

Liddy turned to see Storm waving enthusiastically from the doorway of what might most kindly be described as an inelegant prefabricated bungalow, sitting beside the tumbledown stables to the right of the property.

"Kettle's on," she hollered, and they all came over.

Storm was smiling as she saw the expression on Liddy's face.

"I know, I know," she said. "Everyone thinks it's gonna be like Downton Abbey!"

(Liddy, who had most definitely thought this, tried to look more nonchalant.)

"When did it happen? Is it a . . . *historical* thing?" asked Liddy.

"You mean were we burned out by the Fenians?" said Storm, laughing. "Not at all! We're Catholics. We've been on this land since 1758, and swapped sides a few times to keep it. No, it was New Year's Eve eight years ago. Roberta left her curling iron plugged in and sent the whole place up in flames. Sebastian was staying, thank goodness, and he saved her, but he couldn't save the house. She lost most of her stuff, lots of inherited family things, and she hadn't ever increased the insurance so the roof is all it would pay for. All in all a Stackallan-style family disaster!"

They walked into the cramped hallway, only to be greeted by the pungent smell of pets and mothballs. An arthritic cat crawled toward Liddy and scraped her bony body against Liddy's ankles, purring.

"It was an awful time," continued Storm. "Mummy was in a desperate state, but then she got in touch with her witchy powers and became a druid. We had to call her Daffodil for two years."

Liddy snorted with laughter, but Storm looked serious, and so Liddy turned it into a cough.

"I know it sounds mad, but it saved her, to be honest. She did find some peace in the rituals, and it helped her to be close to nature and reconnect with the land." Storm picked the cat up and put it out the window. It screeched in protest as it jumped down onto an aged barrel. "Sebastian was shaken up for a long time too. We reckon he had that PTSD and that's why he married that ghastly woman. But now I think he loves the old place more than ever. He's always had a weakness for lost causes."

Liddy took this personally. She wiped the snot from her nose and stood up a bit straighter and attempted to do a better impersonation of herself, but then she looked around and gave up. The bungalow was like a junk shop; furniture was piled high in corners, and on every available piece of wall space hung an eclectic jumble of pictures, photographs, and books. Matty and Cal were dumbfounded. Liddy felt depressed.

"Boys, what are you staring at? In you come," called Storm. "The kitchen's down here. I made a cake."

"This place is very messy," said Cal.

That's my boy, thought Liddy.

"Nonsense," retorted Storm. "Every home needs some mess. A forgotten nook you can bring your book and no one will find you."

In the small, cozy kitchen Storm had rescued a collection of Sebastian's board games, their crumbling boxes clearly dating from his youth. Storm cheerfully told them that she had retrieved them from his secret hiding place. As a child Sebastian had been very particular about who played with his toys, so all the pieces were intact. Cal picked up a box of dominos and started to line them up on the wooden table like a long, wind-y snake. Matty went to the window and, seeing a basketball and hoop in the courtyard, took the proffered slice of sponge cake from Storm and headed out to play.

Storm handed Liddy a cup of lemon and ginger tea. She retrieved a bottle of whiskey from behind the breadbasket and poured a good slug into it.

"Kill or cure!" she said happily. "That's what the house used to look like." She pointed to a faded photograph propped up on the dresser that showed a striking young woman and her three small children, all wearing floppy hats and flares, standing on the stone steps in the sunshine. Wisteria and ivy crawled up the facade of the picturesque building behind them; a menagerie of pets sunbathed in the driveway. It was like a home in an old-fashioned children's storybook, or maybe a dream. Liddy stared at it.

"Is that Sebastian in the middle?" she asked.

Storm nodded. "Yes. That's me, obviously, and that's our little brother, Will."

Sebastian held a pet tortoise with pride. At ten years old, he had the same measured, slightly amused gaze as in his forties.

"Sebastian hasn't changed much, has he?" said Storm. "Mummy says he's always had this amazing sense of self. He's not always easy, but he's good and he's loyal. I just wish . . ." She trailed off for a moment before continuing. "I wish he smiled more. He never smiles anymore. How long have you been friends?"

Liddy thought about the "lost causes" comment again. "To be honest, Storm, we're colleagues. I had a . . . difficult episode and I think he felt sorry for me. I don't know if we are friends."

"Well, he's very particular about who he lets stay in his house, so you must be something," said Storm stoutly.

Liddy smiled. "You all seem very happy," she said, looking at the photograph again.

"We were," said Storm. "I mean you couldn't call it a conventional upbringing. The three of us have different fathers, not one of whom stuck around, and we have four stepbrothers too. Dear Gordon, the stepboys' dad, died suddenly of a heart attack in the conservatory, and we were broke whenever Roberta was between husbands, but . . . it was okay. *Good shot, Matty!*"

Liddy gulped at the amount of trauma and tragedy this sentence encompassed, but Storm did not seem to notice. In the courtyard Matty pumped his arms and ran to the window.

"Will one of you play with me?"

"Not now," said Storm. "But tomorrow I'm gonna whoop your ass!" She poured more hot water into Liddy's mug. "You look bloody awful to me, Liddy. Why don't you stay for dinner?" Without waiting for a reply, she pressed play on the stereo, walked over to the sink, and started peeling potatoes. "Tomorrow we'll find these boys a soccer camp, go shopping, and I'll show you the local sights," she continued, and when Train came on she began dancing wildly to "Drive By" and Cal danced around too.

So this is how it feels to have a wife, thought Liddy, gratefully sipping her tea. Storm was as kind a person as her brother, and it appeared they were to be friends (whether Liddy liked it or not).

And so Liddy James discovered what most parents do when on vacation. She became a chauffeur and cook and watcher of children's movies, and was asleep by nine o'clock every night. For "Liddy time" she would sit in the nearby Laundromat, reading dog-eared gossip magazines and watching the clothes go round and round in the dryer. Of course, she attempted a to-do list of self-improving activities—learn to conjugate Irish verbs! knit Celtic cable sweater! read *Ulysses!*—but she quickly abandoned it and decided that if she could dye her own hair with a drugstore kit and get rid of the cluster of stubborn plantar warts that nestled on her right heel, that would be enough. Then Storm opened up the garage and they found old surf gear and guitars and three bicycles. After a shaky and comical start where Liddy fell off her bike four times and was treated to a hearty rendition of a new song by Matty and Cal (with the rhyming scheme of "ass" hitting the "grass"), most nights she allowed them to chase her in the rain, laughing, up and down the driveway. The soft days turned into soft weeks, until, to her amazement, Liddy awoke one morning at the end of July to see that the sun was streaming through the window. The light made the room look shiny and new. She decided that she would agree to Storm's suggestion that they spend the day surfing on the beach at Brittas Bay, something she had been avoiding.

She had not been near surf, sand, or sea since Cal's conception.

She flipped pancakes and chivied everyone into their swim gear and soon they were lying on the wide sandy beach under stripy umbrellas. At a little distance, a glamorous German Frau and her two deeply tanned teenage daughters sunbathed in small bikini tops. Matty sat nearby, his wetsuit rolled down over his skinny white torso, rigid in a state of amorous confusion. He did not know which one to pretend was his girlfriend.

Two teenage lifeguards in red shorts were grinding flags into the sand to demarcate the swimming area and telling anyone who passed them to beware of the riptides farther along. Cal was digging a big hole with a plastic spade and Storm, resplendent in one of Roberta's caftans, had decorated its perimeter with pebbles and driftwood. With great satisfaction Liddy glanced at her watch; all this by ten thirty in the morning.

Around them, the beach was filling with other families, staking their claim to an area with soggy towels and plastic buckets; Liddy made a mental note that they must always get there early to guarantee a superior position. Suddenly Storm's mobile phone rang and, startled, she scampered off toward the dunes to talk.

It had taken time, and a series of intense withdrawal symptoms—she kept sticking her hand in her pocket for her phantom phone—but Liddy had finally got used to its absence. Now she actually gave thanks that she could not be similarly disturbed. When she glanced over, Storm was walking back and forth, arms gesticulating like an animated stick figure. She pulled her baseball cap down over her nose and the aged wetsuit up over her top, and enjoyed the feeling of the sun baking her and the faint odor of burning rubber. She lay back and ran her fingers through the sand.

It was considered impolite, Liddy often thought, to tell the truth about the intangible, magical privileges of wealth. She never lied about it to herself, however. *No sitting in a dingy kitchen playing pass-the-parcel for her sons. No mandarin orange and a Rubik's Cube for their birthdays.* She had promised that her own offspring would never be impoverished in their memories, experiences, and opportunities—whatever it cost her. Whenever she heard someone opine that such children did not live "in the *real* world," she would scoff and say, "You can't manufacture hardship." She would never wish the frustrations and deprivations of her own experience on them.

But lying on the beach that day, as Matty and Cal splashed cheerfully in the waves, Liddy saw that they were all far, far from the things she had convinced herself were vital to their happiness. And yet they were happy.

"*Liddy! Liddy!*"

She sat up to see Storm, her face drawn and ashen, crouched in front of her.

"Something dreadful has happened!"

Liddy sat up to check that the boys were safe. They were.

"That was Roberta from Brazil! She's getting married to this bloke she's been traveling with! She's flying back in a fortnight and wants to have the ceremony in the house. She's e-mailing me instructions as we speak. I knew I shouldn't have got the Internet fixed!"

"The Internet's fixed?" said Matty, approaching.

Liddy tried to look innocent. "Don't worry," she said. "We'll leave. Move into a hotel—"

"*What?*" shrieked Storm. "You can't leave, Liddy." She grabbed Liddy's hands in hers. "You have to help me!"

Storm's head was darting around from side to side like a terrified meerkat. Liddy quickly said she would.

"I have to start calling people. She said some names to me, actors she used to work with at the Abbey Theatre. I thought they were dead!"

A thought occurred to Liddy. She paused to consider how she felt about it before saying it aloud. It turned out she was no longer tired and no longer confused.

"Will Sebastian come back?" she said. (She felt excited.)

"Not a hope," said Storm, reassured of Liddy's friendship and her offer of organizational assistance. "He said last time he was never going to another of Roberta's weddings."

If Liddy had any doubt about the witchy powers of Roberta "Daffodil" Stackallan, they were removed by the fact that the weather remained fine, and the morning of the wedding dawned exquisitely rose pink and fair.

Liddy stood by the window in her bedroom, cup of coffee in hand, happily watching the gentle mist rising over the fields. She listened to the birdsong; she was beginning to distinguish between the blackbird and the robin and the song thrush. She had come to love these brief moments of meditation during the days, moments where she was able to stop and stare. It was positively *mindful* she said to herself. Her life coach would be so proud.

She glanced over at Cal, still fast asleep on a blow-up mattress in the corner of the room—now that they spent significant time together during the days he had abandoned the practice of sleeping on top of her legs at night—and took a moment to consult the handy day planner she had prepared and distributed to the relevant parties to ensure smooth running for the day ahead. Individual duties, detailed with color-coded stickers, were listed in half-hour increments. Liddy and Cal were starting at 8:30 a.m., meeting Seamus and his big ladder beside the nineteenth-century sundial at the foot of the stone steps that led up to the house. (After an evening spent researching pagan wedding rituals, Liddy had suggested it as the venue for the ceremony, in the absence of any nearby woodhenges.)

Underneath the day planner were two plastic folders; one contained a printout of important druidic principles and a glossary of terms, the other a police background check on Roberta's husband-to-be, a certain Harvey Browne, which Liddy had organized. Liddy had felt the details of his backstory were somewhat vague (there appeared to be a series of missing years in his forties). But as he was the same age as Roberta, appeared to be employed, and, most important it seemed, was neither a Romany sculptor named Jorge nor currently married to someone else, Storm was relieved, particularly as they wouldn't meet him until the ceremony. Roberta and Harvey had flown into the airport from Rio the previous morning, made one phone call to check on the progress, and, reassured, immediately booked into the nearest luxury hotel for extensive spa treatments. Whatever her choice in men, Liddy had to admire Roberta Stackallan's ruthless ability to delegate.

The now-familiar sound of a vehicle rattling down the track and a screech of brakes signaled the start of the day. The front door burst open to reveal Storm, significantly more rumpled than usual.

"Where are you, Matty?" she shouted, brandishing her day planner, but to Liddy's amazement, Matty appeared in the doorway fully dressed.

"And Will hasn't arrived!" screeched Storm, to no one in particular. "I can't bear it when people don't do what they say."

Liddy shrugged sympathetically. This was not an accusation that could be leveled at her. She was also still in her meditative state.

"Chill, babe," Matty said cheekily. "Bye, Mom." He kissed Liddy, who felt a tuft of his baby beard on her cheek, before following Storm out the door. They headed up to the bungalow to start cooking.

Liddy lifted her arms above her head and stretched. She suddenly realized she was doing a yoga sun salutation. She stopped immediately. *Enough is enough.* She glanced down at her day planner: *7:30 a.m. shower, wash hair, bleach mustache.* Dutifully, she headed toward the bathroom.

By two o'clock, the sun was dappling through the arch of willow and white flowers Liddy and Cal had woven with the help of Seamus, who had proved unexpectedly creative at floral design. Liddy stood beneath it in an aged T-shirt, rolled-up jeans, and a white panama hat. Up at the bungalow Storm was finishing the buffet dinner and Matty was preparing the playlist for the party on his laptop.

Liddy looked over to see Cal sitting on the lawn brushing the large, scruffy dog.

"Hello?"

It was a man's voice, a deep, melodious Irish lilt she recognized. Liddy did not move. She paused to enjoy the moment, which was completely unexpected but completely thrilling.

Then she turned—

—but standing before her on the lawn was a younger, shorter, and more rotund version of Sebastian (as if Sebastian were reflected in a side mirror where objects appear closer than they really are), a burning cigarette stub hanging off his lower lip.

"Hi. I'm Will." He looked at her with an expression in the sexually interested range.

"I'm Liddy," she said, trying not to look too disappointed. "I'm a friend of Sebastian's."

"Bugger!" said Will. He took a final drag on his cigarette before hurling it into the ornamental fountain, ignored her outstretched palm, and opened his arms to embrace her, extravagantly kissing her on both cheeks. To her surprise, despite this uncomfortable invasion of her personal space, she immediately liked him.

"Good to see Seb's back in the saddle again! Where is he?"

"Alaska," said Liddy, but she was saved from further explanation by the agitated arrival of Storm.

"Will! Thank goodness. Better bloody late than never. Liddy, show Will the day planner. What time is it?"

"Time for the druidic priest to arrive," said Liddy, glancing at her watch.

Will looked at Storm. "Oh, no," he said. "Not the one Roberta met on the retreat in Clonakilty—the one that married the woman to the dolphin?"

Storm rolled her eyes and nodded.

"Is it legal?" asked Will, looking at Liddy.

"It is," said Liddy. "Roberta and Harvey, that is. Not the woman and the dolphin. The druidic priest is a solemnizer as well as a white witch."

"Oh well, there goes another chunk of the inheritance," said Will.

"What happens if you wanted to divorce the dolphin?" asked Storm, turning to the expert among them.

"Human-animal marriage is not recognized by law in any country," said Liddy. (Curtis had once raised it in a partners meeting under the heading of new business.)

"Yeah. Imagine trying to divide the marital assets!" said Will. "By the way, I hear Chloe *fleeced* Sebastian!"

"Don't say that in front of Liddy. She was Chloe's lawyer, but she was only doing her job," replied Storm.

Will looked confused for a moment, but given that today was already full of confusing things, he decided to let it go.

"And honestly, what did the apartment mean to Sebastian apart from bad memories?" Storm added.

"An awful lot of money, I expect," said Will. Storm elbowed him.

Liddy consulted the day planner.

"One of you has to pick up your mother and Harvey from the hotel. And we still need a broomstick for them to jump over," she said.

"Oh, Storm, get the one you use every full moon!"

"Ha bloody ha!"

The two siblings dissolved into childlike giggles.

"Greetings in the bounty of Mother Earth!"

A gray-bearded man in white robes was approaching.

"Jesus Christ, it's Gandalf," muttered Will, reaching for his cigarettes.

"Remember the elven greeting!" said Liddy. She nodded at Cal, who walked forward with his right hand outstretched, his fingertips to the sky.

"Blessings, friends," said the man. "I am Brian the Druid."

"I am Liddy . . . the lawyer," she replied. "Here are Roberta's children, Storm and Will, and my son Cal. We were just talking about broomsticks."

"Any twigged besom will do," said Druid Brian. "I have brought my own handfasting. Storm and Will, does your mother intend to be monogamous?"

"Until she meets husband number seven, I guess," said Will.

Will and Storm burst out laughing again. Liddy shot them a cold-eyed look. She was beginning to find the sibling hilarity rather challenging, particularly as there were still ten trays of sausages to be cooked before four o'clock that afternoon.

"For a monogamous coupling we use a tight handfast," continued Druid Brian. "A polyamorous or open couple will opt for a loose handfast."

He stared hard at Liddy. "I am polyamorous."

In all her research, Liddy had not discovered the correct way to respond to that. She tried nodding understandingly. Druid

Brian was still staring. "Do not be afraid of your shadows, Liddy the lawyer. Your aura tells me you are at one with this place, a true Being of Light, a friend and follower of Nature."

Liddy was gratified. She always liked being the best in any group.

"Now I must bless the sundial with oil and water."

He lifted his robes to reveal socks and sandals and walked off. Will and Storm were now laughing so hard they were barking like foxes.

"Honestly, you two," said Liddy, exasperated. "How are we going to get everything done if you don't take it seriously?"

"Yes," said a male voice behind them. "I mean, our sixty-four-year-old mother's getting married for the sixth time in the charred ruins of our ancestral home and she's asked a druidic priest called Brian to officiate a ceremony that includes the fertility ritual of jumping over a twigged besom. The problem is definitely that we're not taking it *seriously*."

"*Sebastian!*" screeched Storm, leaping into his arms and hugging him.

"Hello, Sebastian," said Liddy, stung. When she had imagined the completely unexpected but completely thrilling moment of seeing Sebastian again, this was not how it was meant to go. Disoriented, she flipped into her default settings. "Come on, I've got a schedule."

"Sounds like a military operation," said Sebastian.

"Well, my ex-husband did once compare me to a Sherman tank!" said Liddy brightly, then immediately wished she hadn't.

"When I saw you just then I couldn't decide if I recognized you or not," he said. "Now I definitely do."

"Oh," said Will cheerfully. "The two of you *are* friends. Not *friends* friends . . ."

"Don't be such an idiot, Will," said Storm. "How could Liddy be Seb's *friend* friend? She's a top lawyer like him. She's not his type at all!"

"Good news for me," said Will lasciviously. "Right, I'm off to collect the happy couple!"

Cal came over and took Liddy's hand.

"And who is this?" said Sebastian.

"This is my younger son, Cal," said Liddy.

Sebastian leaned down and offered his right hand formally to shake Cal's.

"Yes, he looks like you," he said.

"He looks like my father, actually."

"He must be a good-looking man."

"My mother says he was 'the handsomest buck ever came to Belmullet.'" Her accent was spot-on. Liddy glanced at Storm, who laughed.

"By the way, Liddy," said Sebastian. "I don't think your phone's working. The line's dead."

"I threw it in the lake."

"That seems rather . . . uncharacteristic."

"I know," Liddy said, resisting the urge to say, *See, I can be a spontaneous person.*

"Are we staying in your house?" asked Cal.

Sebastian nodded politely.

"You need a swimming pool," Cal said.

Liddy noticed Sebastian was wearing jeans and a white linen shirt, unbuttoned at the neck. The sight of the top of his chest and the line of his collarbone and the strands of dark hair below it distracted her.

"How do you feel about giving a speech, Seb?" said Storm.

"Don't push it. I'm here, aren't I?"

"Sausage rolls?" said Liddy, thinking, *I'm not spontaneous about the cooking times of raw meat, of course.* Storm, sensing a change in her brother's mood, dutifully scuttled off.

Liddy looked at Sebastian. He looked away. She turned back to the wedding arch, where Cal had run and was preoccupied, tying ribbons around the dog's collar.

"Why does my mother have to keep making such a fucking mess of her life?"

He spoke very quietly. Liddy could only just hear him above the sounds of the water and the wind and the birdsong that were silence in this place. She walked toward him and he reached out his hand. And as she took it and felt the warmth of his palm, she experienced the disorienting state of erotic excitement she had felt the first time she had ever met him. She shook her head a little. Who could have guessed the banal yet bizarre truth about aging, that fifteen years later she would still feel exactly the same way?

"I can't lecture anyone on that. Can you?" she said.

Sebastian stared at her. "I told you I was a pessimist."

"How was your trip?" she asked.

He answered with a noncommittal grunt, then curled his fingers into hers. "How are you?" he said.

Because she felt nervous, she had to suppress the urge to jump around manically with her hands clamped to her sides as if in a straitjacket.

"I've got over my funny turn, thank you," she said, instead.

"You gave me a bit of a scare. It wasn't the pain-in-the-ass Liddy James I'm used to."

"Some people find me very accommodating. We've just always rubbed each other the wrong way," she said.

"Don't be daft."

"Sebastian . . . you're the one who called me a *nasty woman*."

He opened his mouth to speak, but she shook her head. "It's okay. I know what you meant."

"That's good," he replied. "Because I bloody well don't." He looked around. "Do you remember being here when you were a kid?"

"I do, actually," she replied, although she was finding it difficult to concentrate.

Now he tilted his head and smiled his roguish smile. "Maybe we walked past each other years ago? Maybe we snogged each other at the youth hostel disco?"

"I wasn't a very snogging type of young woman," said Liddy. "You should have seen me."

"I bet you were beautiful."

"No," said Liddy. "I was five foot eleven at age thirteen, with braces and a concave chest."

"I got my tongue stuck in a girl's braces once."

"Ouch!"

"Yes. Sorcha Lennon. Unforgettable, for the wrong reasons."

He turned and walked a few paces, still holding her hand. On the lake, two gray herons rose in the air and called to each other, the distinctive croak echoing.

"I knew you would like it here," he said.

"Is that why you invited me?"

He didn't reply. She looked down at her feet. She flicked her hair behind her ears.

"I thought maybe you had a bit of a . . . *thing* . . . for me?" she said.

He looked at her. "Maybe I do?"

I'm flirting, thought Liddy delightedly. She seemed to be getting it right this time. She was more mature, of course, and her life had taught her how to have sex for fun. Then it occurred to her that she was quoting his ex-wife and stopped.

"This is surreal," he said. "I feel like I'm here but not here. Like the walking dead."

Liddy knew exactly what he meant. When she had arrived in her state of shock and exhaustion, and walked along the narrow paths beside the water and beneath the sky, she had felt it too.

"I need to clear my head. I'll stroll round the lake or something," he said.

Reluctantly, she pulled her hand away. They stood very still for a moment. The herons croaked again.

"Don't be too long," said Liddy.

"Why?"

"The ceremony's at four p.m." Liddy looked down to consult her planner, and when she looked up he was standing in front of her.

He lifted her chin with his left hand and kissed her.

"Why did you do that?" she said.

"I thought you needed kissing," he replied.

It was only after he had walked away without another word that Liddy realized she had kissed him back.

With the elven greeting and the surprise guest, not to mention the unexpected kissing, it took all of Liddy's Liddy-ishness to get herself showered, changed, and standing beneath a willow tree— her handsome boys on either side of her—in time to watch Roberta Stackallan and Harvey Browne pledge their troth under the wedding arch. Druid Brian blessed their union in the three realms of sky, sea, and land, and told them to run down the lawn between the box hedging and jump the broomstick, which Matty had balanced on the heads of two ornamental stone frogs.

Roberta, clear-eyed and sinewy in a white pantsuit (a testament to Gyrotonics and an irrepressible love of life) gamboled off, but Harvey's hip replacement failed him at the critical moment and they ended up in a tumbled heap next to the pet graveyard. As a concerned throng gathered around them, Roberta leapt to her feet, a champagne bottle suddenly in her hand. She ripped the gold foil off the top and ceremoniously unscrewed the wire, sending the cork flying through the air, straight at Liddy, who ducked and fell into the delighted arms of Druid Brian.

"Only chorus girls cringe, dear!" exclaimed Roberta in Liddy's direction. Then she turned to Harvey and kissed him on the mouth for an embarrassingly long time to the extravagantly thespian whoops and bravos of the guests, a varied group of all ages and sizes with the four stepbrothers and their families, druids, and actors, including one dressed like a geriatric Ophelia, who was running around the lake throwing flowers in the air. When Roberta came up for breath, she shouted, "Where's Sebastian!"

Liddy extricated herself from Brian's beard (to his obvious disappointment), and watched as Sebastian moved into the engulfing embrace of his mother. He towered over her, her arms reaching around his waist, then spun her round as if she were a child.

"You've lost weight, but it suits you," Roberta said firmly in her magnificent voice, a combination of English actorly pronunciation with the soft inflection of her native brogue beneath it. "How d'you think I'm looking?"

She glanced around, pouting a little.

"You look marvelous, Mother, and you know it," said Sebastian. "'Age cannot wither her, nor custom stale, her infinite variety.'"

He leaned down and kissed her on the cheek.

"Darling Sebastian," she said. "I know you think I'm a silly old fool, but I truly love him. That's why I'm marrying him."

"Of course."

Now Roberta looked at him with the intense gaze that Sebastian had inherited from her. "You should try it sometime."

"I'm never getting married again," said Sebastian.

"I meant, truly loving someone."

Sebastian's eyes filled with tears. Roberta rested her hand on his heart for a moment, then she turned.

"You must be Liddy?"

Liddy nodded.

"How do you two know each other?"

Sebastian and Liddy took a breath simultaneously.

Then Sebastian spluttered "we're friends" as Liddy spluttered "we're colleagues" and then Sebastian said "friends and colleagues."

"Liddy's one of us, Mum," he said like a nervous teenager. "Lydia Mary Murphy."

Liddy nodded. She didn't mind being called Lydia Mary Murphy anymore. But Roberta's eyes went beady and cold and her nostrils flared imperceptibly. She looked at Liddy with an expression that said *You're not one of us yet.* (Roberta had extricated Sebastian's tongue from Sorcha Lennon's braces, and tended to feel that his romantic exploits always ended similarly.)

"C'mon, Seb, have a drink," she said briskly. "Let's celebrate. Isn't that what you Americans do, Liddy? You have divorce parties, don't you?"

"I didn't," said Liddy. "But some people do, when the separations are amicable."

"It's a shame for you, son," said Harvey, clapping his hand on Sebastian's shoulder. "But it's not like there were any children."

Liddy, concerned, glanced over at Sebastian, but he betrayed no emotion whatsoever.

Suddenly, from behind them, Matty pressed play and the air was filled with the sound of Peggy Lee singing "The Folks Who Live on the Hill."

Roberta turned.

Liddy, Storm, and a reluctant Seamus had spent days chasing the livestock out of the ruined house; they had shoveled the shit out of the front reception rooms, scraped the moss off the walls, and scrubbed the black-and-white marble tiles clean; then Liddy had hung long white drapes against the empty window frames and decorated the rooms with flowers.

She didn't need to paint the walls with Mist on the Heather; she had the real thing.

Now Will lit a series of tapers that burst into flame along the stone stairs, illuminating the entrance to the house and the sweeping, shattered staircase beyond. The effect was romantic and magnificent.

Roberta gasped. "The old house just came back to life!"

She looked at Storm. "Storm, this is the most beautiful gift you could have given me."

"I couldn't have done it without Liddy," said Storm, throwing her arms around Liddy's shoulders and planting a sloppy kiss on her cheek. "Liddy can do anything. She's the most amazing person I've ever met in my life."

"Then thank you, Liddy," said Roberta. "Harvey, let's dance!"

Someday, went the song, they would build a house on *a hilltop high.*

Liddy felt Sebastian's gaze upon her.

She turned.

But suddenly Storm intervened with a cheery "Sorry, Liddy" and dragged him off. Sebastian, Storm, Will, and their four stepbrothers surrounded their mother with happy hugs and kisses, and Roberta pulled them to her with a fierce love.

Liddy looked at Cal.

"Shall we dance?" she said and held out her hands. He took them as Peggy Lee sang about families and changes. And then Matty ran over and for a couple of minutes the three of them swayed and twirled together, until Matty saw one of Sebastian's teenage stepnieces loitering under the chandelier and hurried over to her.

"Shall we go back to the house?" asked Liddy, and Cal nodded.

The sky was streaked with dark blue, orange, and pink.

"Can I join you?" said Sebastian, returning.

He lifted Cal onto his shoulders, and they walked together down the track.

With Cal safely asleep in bed, and Matty ensconced at the party enjoying the attentions of the stepniece, who marveled at his accent and giggled prettily whenever he spoke, Liddy and Sebastian stood outside the gate lodge. They both agreed it was their favorite time, just before sunset, the hour when the light takes on a particular warm glow that enhances everything around it, as if by magic.

Liddy had often spent this time by herself, outside on the jetty, looking at the colors around her and thinking about landscape paintings by Cézanne. She had not been conscious of wanting to share this with someone, but as she stood beside Sebastian she realized she had.

She told him of her love of art, that in a different life she might have been a teacher of art history. She felt safe because she knew he had published poetry and, once upon a time, might have envisaged a different life for himself too.

"Do you paint?" he asked.

"No. I wish I could. I used to take photographs. I had a wonderful manual camera that I learned to use, but it broke eight years ago and I never replaced it."

"Maybe you should."

They walked down to the shore. A couple of guests had escaped the wedding party and were gently rowing a wooden boat called *Serene* across the water. In the distance music played.

"I never took a photograph that told the story of the moment, what it *felt* like to be somewhere. That's why I wish I could paint. I think when you look at a painting you can experience something beyond the image. You think that sounds mad, right?"

He shook his head, so she said, "I don't want to take photographs of here. I want to live it. For the first time in ages I feel that I'm *in* my own life, Sebastian, not watching as some person I don't recognize lives it for me."

She took off her sandals so she could feel the ground beneath her feet.

They talked about the land and the lake and the mountains and, now that Liddy was most certainly not immune to Sebastian's Celtic charms, whether their shared DNA, born from the primordial soup of turf and water, was why they both felt at home there. *It came to me late, this love of the land,* she wanted him to know, *but it had come.*

She looked down to see a perfectly round white stone beside

her foot. She picked it up, wiped the water off it, and put it carefully in her pocket for Cal.

They turned and started clambering back up to the path, which bristled with heather and bilberry, and as they reached the top an extraordinary sight greeted them.

The hedgerow was filled with hundreds of orange-and-black butterflies.

Liddy gasped in awe. In the magic hour, the translucent wings glowed.

"They're Painted Ladies," whispered Sebastian. "Someone once told me that Lough Dan is on their migration path, but I've never seen anything like this."

"It's incredible," she said.

Neither moved for fear of ending the moment. Then a sharp breeze blew and the butterflies flew away, the orange-and-black cloud of wings rising above them.

He pulled her into his arms.

They had kissed for a long while, but they had not made love, because, while they had both considered it for more than a fleeting moment, as they tumbled down onto the grass the sharp ends of a thistle bush dug into their backs, and they had laughed and agreed they were too old not to care (in truth Liddy had always been too old not to care) but too young not to have tried. When they walked through the door of the gate lodge, Liddy, in her full tousled, bruised-lipped state, accidentally caught sight of herself in the mirror.

"You scream sex," said Sebastian fondly, and Liddy did not argue.

She quickly smoothed her hair. She rearranged her dress. She wondered how much time they would have alone before Matty returned.

Sebastian followed her to the door of her bedroom and they both looked at Cal, who was sleeping softly, like an angel. Then they walked back into the living room and he put wood and turf in the stove.

Liddy poured them both a whiskey. They raised their glasses. She waited for the "Just so you know I couldn't fully commit to someone who had children" bit. It didn't come. *He would make a brilliant father*, she thought. Then she glanced at the red-hot coals in the grate, the sparks sizzling and dancing, and she knew she was playing with fire.

"*Sláinte!*" he said. He sat down on the couch.

"Well, here we are, Ms. James. Who'd have thought?"

"Indeed, Mr. Stackallan."

"I like seeing you in my house," he said happily.

He patted the seat beside him. She joined him obediently. He slung an arm across her shoulders. This made her happy. She kissed him again. *And again.*

"Hey, hey," he said. "What about Cal?"

"He never wakes up. Honestly, an earthquake could go off!" *I hope*, she thought.

But, playfully, he held her at arm's length. "Listen, I've got something to tell you."

She looked at him.

"I'm not going back to New York, Liddy," he said.

"What do you mean?"

"I spoke to Gillespie and Ross last week. I'm setting up a European office. There's nothing left for me in the city."

Liddy said nothing. She lifted her glass and glugged down an enormous swig of whiskey. It burned her throat.

"And the thing is, Roberta and Harvey are going to live in his house in Dublin. Neither Storm nor Will is interested in staying on the land, so Roberta's giving it to me. I'm going to restore the old house and live in it."

Liddy smiled. She did not take it personally. She knew him better now and she was happy for him.

"That sounds like a wonderful thing to do."

"You think?"

"Yes. It must be nice to have your past be part of your future. I guess that's what it means to have roots."

There was a pause.

"In fact," she continued, "I think I envy you."

Now he glugged down an enormous swig of whiskey.

"Then why don't you stay too?"

Liddy was quite sure she had misheard him, but when she looked at him, his face was calm and resolved in the flickering light.

"What have you got to go back to?" he said. He stroked her shoulder with his fingers.

Sixteen-hour days with a personal life as an optional extra, thought Liddy.

"I mean, I know it's sudden, and it might not work out, but, Liddy, even if you stayed for six months, or a year, we would have tried to have a new life together in a new place. And who knows, we might just live happily ever after."

"What about the boys?"

"The more the merrier."

She rested her hand on his knee. He lifted it and kissed her wrist.

"You know you feel something for me," he said.

She nodded. "I do," she said. "I think I always have."

He grinned. "Do you still believe in love?" he said.

YES! YES! she thought. *I could rebuild that house and make it beautiful again, the boys could go to local schools where no one has a private jet or a painting by Rothko in the games room, by day I'd be one of those feminist housewives, by night I'd go to bed with this incredibly sexy alpha male, and back in New York, people would say, "Whatever happened to Liddy James?"*

And then the landline started ringing. *NO! NO!*

"Hadn't you better get that?" he said.

"No," she said.

"Liddy, it might be an emergency."

She dragged herself away from him. She lifted the phone off the hook. She heard nothing but a high-pitched crackling noise. She held the receiver away from her ear. She moved to put it down.

"Liddy?"

The crackling subsided.

"Liddy? . . ."

"Rose?" said Liddy. "Is everything all right? Did Matty call you?"

"No," said Rose.

"I told him to. He's at a party tonight. I'll make sure he does tomorrow."

"Thanks, Liddy. I'm sorry to bother you."

"Don't worry about it. Believe me, I understand."

She craned her head and looked for Sebastian. He was standing outside, looking up at the night sky.

"How are you?" she said.

Rose mumbled something that disappeared into the ether.

"How's Peter?" said Liddy, but Rose changed the subject.

"How's the vacation, Liddy?" she said.

"Brilliant. I'm doing restorative yoga."

"What?" said Rose. "I thought you only did the fast, sweaty kind so you could lose lots of weight and get fantastic arms."

"I'm trying to relax, Rose. Don't you think my arms are fantastic enough?"

Rose did not sound like herself at all, but she managed a laugh at this. Liddy was glad.

"When will we see you?" Rose asked.

"I'm not sure exactly—" Liddy replied, and her heart beat faster for joy.

"Right," Rose interjected. "There's a letter from Matty's school here."

"A bill, you mean? I bet there is. I bet Peter hasn't opened it either," said Liddy. Now she laughed. "I'll deal with it. *Rose?*"

"Yes, Liddy?"

"I want to thank you, Rose. For everything you've done for Matty, and for me, over these past years. We're all so lucky to have you in our lives."

She paused.

"Thank you, Liddy. You sound so . . . calm." (Liddy knew Rose had been about to say "different" but had thought better of it.)

"I am calm, and it isn't because I'm bored out of my skull— once I gave up trying to find sushi, I've been fine. I've gotten really good at sleeping and cooking proper meals, and we're having fun."

"What do you do all day?" Rose was genuinely curious.

"I don't know. We get up, the boys do some sport in the village, there's always an animal to look at. We've made some friends. But mainly we hang out. You know, I think I'd actually forgotten that simple things are worth doing. Just lazing around has value, or chatting to a person you don't know."

She looked at Sebastian again.

"Staring at the stars has value. I'm enjoying . . . no, I don't mean that. I mean who in their right mind *enjoys* endless cooking and washing and arguing about bedtime, it's just . . . it feels good to spend this time with the boys." She paused. "It's like Peter said. I need to be their mother."

Rose paused too. "I know, Liddy," she said finally, "but I miss you."

The crackling came on the line again and Rose hung up.

Liddy stayed very still for a long moment.

"Is everything all right?" said Sebastian, walking back inside.

She came over to him and kissed him hard like it was the last time. Then she sat down beside him.

"I can't do it, Sebastian. I can't stay here—much as I would love to. If I was on my own I'd do it in a heartbeat, but . . . my life is very complicated and I can't just decide to make it simple."

He exhaled a little. "You are the sort of person who can decide to do anything you want."

"No, I can't," she said. "I learned that lesson a long time ago. Matty has a father in America." She thought of Rose, back in Carroll Gardens. Rose had sounded lonely and afraid. "And another mother too."

Sebastian stood up and moved over to the fire. "We can't nearly get together every fifteen years, Liddy. Next time we'll be in bloody wheelchairs. I can't wait."

She pulled a couple of stray thistle flowers from her hair. A relationship in your forties is like sex in a field, she decided: you might fantasize about it, but painful thorns pierce your butt and you end up shivering in the cold with itchy regrets, like dirt in your underpants.

"I know," she said. "Why would you?"

Slam! The door of the gate lodge burst open. Matty and Will tumbled in.

"I'm squiffy," Will announced, "but I promised I'd get this young man back to you before he started having too much fun. That's the kind of chap I am, Liddy, responsible, reliable. You can trust me, you know. I'm a doctor!"

Resigned, Sebastian drained his glass. "Believe it or not, that's actually true," he said, drily. "Unsuspecting patients allow him to remove their internal organs. Good night, Liddy."

He kissed her perfunctorily on both cheeks.

"Good night, Matty!" he said, then he looked at Will. "Come on, you reprobate, let's get you back. I am a bit drunk, and I intend on getting drunker. We're about to send Mum and Harvey off."

And without a backward glance he grabbed Will's arm and they walked out the door. It was as if the magic hour and the butterflies and the flickering firelight had never happened. In fact, as Liddy watched them leave she wondered if she had imagined it, imagined Sebastian as a hero of romance and herself as, well, a completely different person. Or rather, the person she might have been if she had taken the road more traveled.

"Call Rose," she said to Matty, and as he went to his room, she sat down again.

She poured herself another drink.

Liddy was woken early the next morning by a car driving fast down the track, scattering gravel as it passed the gate lodge, rattling the cattle grid. She tried and failed to go back to sleep, so she walked along the jetty and stood looking out at the water with only the dragonflies and the sunrise for company.

She heard the soft *kerplunk* of an oar and turned to see Storm on her paddleboard, minus the large dog. When Storm saw Liddy she paused and said, "Hey there!" and even though she was at quite a distance, Liddy heard her perfectly.

"Morning!" said Liddy as Storm came closer. "You're up early."

"Yeah," Storm replied. "Sebastian woke me as he left."

"Oh," said Liddy, remembering the revving of a car, the driver desperate to get away. "He woke me up too."

Storm floated to the shore.

"It's none of my business, Liddy, but Sebastian can be an imbecile sometimes."

"It's okay, Storm," said Liddy, but she could not keep the disappointment out of her voice. "It's just bad timing."

"He wasn't the reason for, you know, the way you were that first night?"

"No!" said Liddy. "That was a whole other thing."

Storm shook her head. "I don't understand, Liddy. Whenever you were together yesterday, he never stopped smiling."

Storm pushed the board back out into the water. She raised her arm to paddle and Liddy saw under her strappy vest a livid stripe of scar where a scalpel had cut away her left breast.

Liddy took an intake of breath in a way she thought was imperceptible, but Storm had heard the sound, which had traveled.

Storm paused.

"I was going to do the reconstruction," she said, "but it got infected, so I have to wait."

"Why didn't you tell me?" said Liddy.

Liddy deeply regretted her "bad timing" comment, not to

mention the "ups and downs" of before, but Storm understood. She looked over at Liddy.

"I don't like going on about it," Storm said. "I'm going to be fine. And you will be too."

Liddy nodded. She sat down on the rocks, and the vivid yellow glow of the dawning sun illuminated all around.

"*Mommy!* Where are you?"

She turned to see Cal running out of the house toward her.

"I'm here, baby."

He came and sat beside her, his head heavy against her arm. Then they heard a movement from the woodland and they turned to see a small group of last night's revelers swaying slowly down the driveway toward the main road.

Storm waved at them; then she lifted the oar to start paddling.

And as Liddy watched her friend drift away, she thought about the wedding and marveled at the shared, convivial energy of this ragtag bundle of relations and friends. She saw that Roberta Stackallan's greatest performance was in this place. Roberta had created a family despite everything; she had smothered love, like gloopy icing, over the messes she had made, the traumas and tragedies she had lived through, and the convoluted relationships that they had all survived.

Their home was not the grand house but the people in it and the life they shared. No fire, storm, or tempest could destroy it.

She put her arm around Cal's shoulders. "Cal," she said. "There are all different kinds of families in the world."

"Yes, Mom," he said.

"Matty has me and Peter and Rose and their new baby, and you have me and Matty," she continued.

"And Peter and Rose?" asked Cal.

"Yes, of course," said Liddy.

"But I don't have a dad," said Cal.

"No," said Liddy. "Your dad and I had a lovely time together, but he went away before he knew I was having you and I haven't been able to find him."

"He's never seen me?"

Liddy shook her head. She leaned over and put her hand on his cheek.

"I was at school and a man came and looked at me through the door and went away. I thought it was him. I thought maybe he didn't like me."

"No," said Liddy. "That wasn't your dad."

"So it's just us?"

Liddy nodded. "It's not your fault, Cal. Lots of families have just mommies or just daddies. It's okay," she said.

"Sarah Jayne in my class has two mommies. And Arun lives with his grandma," said Cal calmly.

"Exactly," said Liddy.

"Where's my grandma?"

There was a pause.

"Your grandma Breda lives with Grandpa Patrick in Orlando, remember? Would you like to go and see her when we get home?"

Cal nodded.

"You know that they were born in Ireland and I was born here too."

"I like Ireland," Cal said.

"So do I," said Liddy.

"What was my dad's name?" asked Cal.

"Gavin," said Liddy. "You and Matty are the greatest gifts of my life and I love you both very much."

"I love you too," said Cal. "Do you want a wonder hug, Mama?"

"What's that, my precious Cal?"

"It has all the hugs in the world in it."

"Then I would like that very much."

They wrapped their arms around each other.

"I miss Coco," said Cal.

"So do I," said Liddy. "And when we get home I'm going to get us a new little house with some outside space for Coco to run in. But you and Matty are going to have to promise to help look after her."

He thought about this for a moment. "I don't like picking up dog poop."

"I'll do that," said Liddy. "I was thinking you could brush her every day."

He took her hand and, side by side, they looked over the water.

Because Liddy had been brought up a Catholic she had a sudden impulse to pray. She whispered the Irish blessing Druid Brian had recited at the wedding.

> *Deep peace to you*
> *Deep peace of the running river to you*
> *Deep peace of the flaming sun to you*

Deep peace of the silent earth to you
Deep peace of the shining stars to you.

Liddy gave thanks she was alive.

She kissed Cal's hair and thought of Matty, snoring exuberantly, inside the house.

She knew what kind of love she still believed in.

CURIOUSLY OPTIMISTIC

The C-section was booked for August 25, but the baby had other ideas, wriggling and announcing its impending arrival eight days before while Peter gave a workshop on *Portrait of a Lady* at a summer school upstate. Rose called her doctors, picked up the small bag she had packed, and got a cab to the hospital, where, in complete contrast to the various emergencies of the previous months, she was quickly and naturally delivered of a healthy baby, who lay sleeping peacefully in her arms when Peter finally arrived.

Afterward, people asked her if she had minded giving birth alone, and although Rose dutifully expressed her disappointment that Peter had not been there, at the time she had been so overwhelmed by the experience that she did not notice. She had closed her eyes and panted and imagined herself retreating into a dark, deep cave, like an animal with a job to do. It was only when she emerged, a mother at last, that she looked for him, and his absence reminded her of the strange tension that had arisen between them and her fear that birth might be an end rather than a beginning. But the moment Peter met his child he seemed to relax.

"She's so precious. What shall we call her?" said Peter, entranced by the perfect face under the tiny cream cradle cap.

"Grace," said Rose.

"Perfect. When did you decide that?"

"I just thought of it. It feels right."

He nodded. "Hello, Grace," he said. "Welcome to the world."

Now that the pregnancy was finally over, Rose delighted in becoming herself again. Barbara had warned her about the "baby blues," and to expect a dramatic and inexplicable darkness to engulf her in the week after she gave birth, but this did not happen. Rose was tired, of course, but she had been bedridden for so long that walking down the road to the coffee shop practically made her whoop for joy. This return of energy and love of life came at a price, though. Her thoughts no longer muddled through her head like splotches of ink; and so the vulnerability of her situation came into focus with horrifying sharpness.

Rose would come upon Peter in the library holding Grace in his arms. She would sit on the footstool beside him and in those moments they would talk in shared awe about sleeping and feeding. Then they would count Grace's eyelashes. She learned firsthand how children are a glue that sticks parents together, not always on a deep emotional level, but often on a more practical one—that there is always something to talk about or some mess to clear up.

But after a short while, Peter would stand up, the veil of silence and preoccupation returning, and leave the house, often for hours at a time, apparently to visit the library or walk in the park, although Rose never knew if that was the truth and she never asked him.

The morning they had brought Grace home, Rose had stood by the window in the nursery and looked out at the redbrick houses and the green trees. Below, Peter came into the little garden and she had tapped on the glass so he would notice her and wave, but the builders working on the house to the right had turned up the radio so he did not hear. She watched as he collapsed on the stone bench by the fig tree. What caught her attention was not the somnambulism of his movement, but the sadness on his face. He leaned over and wiped moisture off his cheeks with his fingers.

Rose told herself this was sweat, not tears, because she could not bear to see him cry.

It was Peter, not her, who needed bed rest all the time these days, and when Rose saw this, she felt empathy for him and clarity about the situation. Peter had looked forward to spending more time on his own studies. Now he would be eighty years old when Grace finished college.

The following day, a beautiful bunch of yellow roses had arrived from Liddy. Rose stuck them in a vase in the downstairs cloakroom, disappointed and ungracious about the gift but refusing to acknowledge why. It was Barbara who verbalized it at their next appointment, as they sat together in her office, keeping the windows closed as the stale late-summer air was hotter outside than in.

"I thought she'd give you a stroller," Barbara said, deftly peering into Grace's ears. "One of those top-of-the-line Stokke ones that you can jog behind."

"I wouldn't be jogging."

"Or at least a complete set of babywear. Tasteful organic cotton. Ribbons on the boxes."

"Those days are gone, Barbara. Liddy's flying back tonight, but I . . . *we* . . . don't have much of a clue about her plans."

This was true. During their daily calls, Rose had attempted a gentle inquisition of Matty on the subject, but he had demurred and merely told them another funny story about something Liddy had done. (The other day apparently she had accidentally locked herself in the woodshed and had escaped using a shovel and ski pole. Afteward, she had laughed so much she went cross-eyed.)

"All we know is that she's rented a small place in Prospect Heights—she got a Skype tour and made the broker hold an iPad out the window so she could check the noise levels—and she's been doing restorative yoga. You have to hold the positions for twenty minutes. I've never seen Liddy be still for twenty seconds!"

Saying this out loud, Rose's brain whirred into life, and tension spiraled through her body, stirring Grace awake. Grace mewled like a kitten and unfurled her tiny paws one by one, the inevitable precursor to an almighty scream.

Rose lifted Grace up and tried to feed her but was unsuccessful because Grace was confused and agitated, and they both ended up in tears of frustration.

"There's a legal agreement between her and Peter, isn't there?" Barbara continued, as she helped Grace to latch on.

"No. They never had a formal settlement, and if they did, it wouldn't hold up in court, apparently. Liddy was far too generous."

"Guess you can't get blood out of a stone."

"I was going to say you can't kick someone when they're down. But, yes, you're right. No blood. No kicking. It doesn't matter what Peter and I think about the situation. If she decides she wants more time off, that's it. I just wish I knew."

Rose relaxed as Grace began to feed.

"Looking after kids isn't exactly time off," ventured Barbara, typing Grace's notes into the computer.

"She made this big point that she needed to be Matty's mother. Why did she say that?"

"*She is.*" Barbara was refusing to commiserate with Rose and Rose knew why. And for once, Barbara was on Liddy's side, which made it worse.

"It's just I thought I knew what kind of woman she was," Rose said, for she wanted Barbara to understand.

"I know," said Barbara calmly. "You thought Liddy was different from you."

Rose's eyes filled with tears of shame.

"I thought she was invincible," Rose said, remembering their previous conversation about *Coriolanus*. "Who'd have guessed? 'Like a dull actor now, I have forgot my part, and I am out.'"

"I like her better now that I feel sorry for her," said Barbara. "But I think that might mean I'm a terrible person."

And they both thought about what Barbara had once said about Liddy's hubris, and what Rose had said about nemesis. Now that it had struck, what on earth could happen to Liddy next? Rose reached out a hand to grab a pen and the pad on Barbara's desk. She scribbled a note (something she had not done for months), as she had an idea about the course on Shakespearean tragedy, and a new question for the students: Should hubris always be considered a negative flaw?

"What happens to a tragic hero after they fall?" said Barbara.

Rose shuddered. "Mostly they end up dead. Or alone."

"That's not good," said Barbara, and she rested her hand very gently on Grace's head to check the fontanel.

Afterward, Rose pushed her secondhand stroller to Carroll Park, where she sat under a shady tree. She picked Grace up and held her to her breast, watching as small children ran laughing through the water sprinklers. She saw one sandy-haired boy, an energetic seven or eight years old, twerking vigorously in the center, his floppy fringe falling over his eyes. She decided she would visit Liddy tomorrow. She would scream, *I love your son, don't take him away from me.*

But of course, Liddy might well scream back at her.

Rose pulled her phone from her pocket and dialed Peter to find out where he was. It clicked straight through to voice mail, so she left a neutral message about Grace's weight. She stood up, settled Grace back in the stroller, and headed home.

She called for him as she came through the door, but there was no answer. Grace was asleep so she parked the stroller in the hall and walked the rooms, searching. But it was to no avail. Once again, Peter was out.

Deflated, Rose went into the library, the coolest room. She sat down in Peter's armchair and closed her eyes for a moment. When she opened them, she saw that the red light on the answering machine in the corner was blinking on and off. It was such an unusual sight that for a moment she thought she was back in 1990. She walked over and tried to remember how the machine worked. Fortunately there was a button labeled PLAY, so she pressed that. It was Liddy, looking for Peter, her tone short, sharp, and strange. She said she'd listened to some garbled message from him on Matty's phone about meeting them at JFK, but they were about to get on the flight in Dublin. It ended with Liddy demanding, "What's going on?"

I have no idea, thought Rose. This realization made her both laugh and curse bitterly.

"I wonder what will happen now?" she said.

Suddenly there was a genteel but firm tapping on the front door.

Quickly Rose ran toward it, expecting Peter and a story about lost keys, but instead she pulled it open to reveal the unexpected sight of Sophia Lesnar. Sophia had adopted the long, white, and flowing approach to New York summer dressing, with a straw hat perched on top, so it was as if an energetic Edwardian lady explorer from England had appeared on the doorstep.

"Darling Rose," said Sophia. "How are you?"

She held out her arms and kissed Rose on both cheeks, and

Rose got a glimpse of her Edwardian-style abundantly hairy arm-pits. For some reason this made Rose even more nervous.

"Fine," she said.

Sophia paused and stared at Grace for a moment. "Adorable!" she whispered, then crept silently away saying, "Let's not wake her," which Rose now understood and felt grateful for.

"How are you?" said Rose.

Sophia followed her into the kitchen. She made herself com-fortable at the table.

"Oh, very good, thanks." Sophia inspected the room curi-ously as if searching for important artifacts, like a laptop or a few pages of research. Then she turned her piercing stare back toward Rose. Rose experienced the uncomfortable sensation of being pinned against a wall, like a moth on a canvas.

"Tea?" asked Rose, wriggling. "Lemonade?"

"A quick lemonade, please," she said. "I'm on the clock! So how's the writing going?"

Rose carried a glass of homemade lemonade to Sophia and handed it to her. Sophia sipped it approvingly.

"Delicious!"

"Thank you," Rose replied. "I use lime and lemon."

Rose knew she sounded dispirited and nervous and thought that Sophia could not fail to notice. But she did not. Rose won-dered if Sophia's husband, whom she had never spoken to but with whom she had often felt solidarity, sounded nervous all the time.

"I understand completely why you haven't been in touch, what with the pregnancy this and the bedridden that, and of course Peter's ex cracking up—don't tell him I said anything, by the way, he'll think everyone's been gossiping. Which of course they have!"

Sophia paused for breath but only for a moment.

"Anyway, I've told Charley at the *Literature Review* that I will be sending them a ten-thousand-word piece by November twentieth. Then a week before, I will say I have a family emergency and that you're filling the slot instead on behalf of the department."

Rose poured her another glass. "I don't want you to lie for me, Sophia."

"*Mmmm . . .*" Sophia slugged the lemonade down approvingly.

"I've got three kids, Rose. I have a family emergency once a day, twice a day if you include things like plumbing. Okay? Where's Peter?"

"I don't know," said Rose.

"Typical!" exclaimed Sophia, standing up. "Can't take the swollen breasts and the various discharges. But we both know men are redundant at this stage of the game. That's why in ancient cultures pregnant women retired alone to a secluded place for confinement and recovery."

They also died of postpartum infections, thought Rose, whose experiences had made her impatient with the "squatting over a pit is better" school of birth advice.

Sophia was now marching toward the door. "Bye, Rose. You know one of the best things about having a baby—you're not pregnant anymore! Call me when you have your subject."

She paused. "I have complete confidence in you."

Rose looked straight back at her. "Thank you, Sophia."

She closed the door carefully and turned to see her bag on the floor, beside her baby in the stroller in the hall.

She opened it and pulled the pad out of it. She saw her scribbled idea on it. She thought of the quote she had alluded to with Barbara.

> *This Achilles / He'll pay the price for that great courage*
>   *of his*
>   *Alone, I tell you—sob his heart out far too late—*

She walked into the library. She switched on the computer.

She thought of Liddy.

She asked herself, *What is the difference between arrogance and courage in a tragic heroine?*

She began to write.

Peter was not a creature of impulse, a trait that Liddy had always admired, so when she spotted him walking toward them through the crowded terminal building, she assumed she had made some sort of mistake and he was about to berate her for a misremembered plan. But when he saw her he waved cheerfully.

Matty ran straight over to him and they hugged each other hard, but because Cal was sitting on top of the bags on her trolley, Liddy made more cautious progress.

"Have I missed something? Did we make an arrangement?" she asked, genuinely curious. Then she looked at Matty.

"Did you make an arrangement?" She paused. "Peter. Why are you here?"

He ruffled Cal's hair, then moved behind the trolley to push it himself.

"I'm in the green parking lot," he said. "How are you?"

"I'm fine, actually. Well, more than fine. I'm good. Very good."

She somewhat stuttered through this answer, because, in truth, the combination of Peter smiling happily at her and the fact that he did not answer her question rattled her.

"That's a relief," he said. Then he paused, not for long, but long enough for Liddy to notice that there was no tremor in his voice, no loaded comment, no pain.

"I need to say something to you."

He stopped outside a small snack bar. He lifted Cal down from the trolley, took a twenty-dollar bill from his wallet, and handed it to Matty.

"Boys, get something for the journey home."

Matty took Cal's hand and ran toward the doughnuts.

"Well, I've been meaning to talk to you about future arrangements," said Liddy.

"It's not about that. Well, it is a bit about that."

His phone rang. He looked at it. "It's Rose," he said, but did not answer it.

"I'm confused," said Liddy. "Are you bringing Matty home to meet Grace?"

He did not answer her.

"Did you tell Rose you were coming?" said Liddy accusingly.

"*I'm sorry*," he said. "For everything. That's what I want to say to you."

Liddy did not think it would be possible for her to be more astonished. She peered at Peter. She did not recognize him.

"What happened to me wasn't your fault," she said quickly, because she felt a familiar protective urge toward him rising within her. She stopped this. Last time she felt this way they ended up married. "And I'm sorry for everything too," she continued.

They both exhaled. Peter's phone beeped with a message from Rose.

"What will I tell her?" asked Peter, as this had not occurred to him as he zealously planned his mission that afternoon.

"Tell her you decided to come and get Matty as a surprise. It was a spontaneous thing."

"That's a good idea, but she won't believe it."

"Tell her the truth, then, I don't care." Liddy grinned mischievously. "Just stop her panicking that you've come to declare undying love to me."

For a moment she felt twenty-five years old again, Lydia Mary Murphy, full of brightness and grit and inexperience, sitting in the storytelling salon in the Cornelia Street Café.

"What if I have?" he said, a particular expression on his face that scared as well as reassured her. It was Peter, all right.

"*Don't*," she said, suddenly serious. They were still standing far apart, so she reached out her hand to him. Peter took it.

"Get over it, Peter. For all our sakes. Our story ended. It shouldn't have ended the way it did, but—"

"Do you want anything, Mom?" Matty shouted from the register. Liddy shook her head.

"What do you mean?" Peter asked.

"I mean, I think," said Liddy, "that in real life we can't force things to have a beginning, a middle, and an end we always like. And I've tried, God knows. I love to be in control. I am a woman who has a spreadsheet for packing."

Cal trotted back to them and clambered back onto the trolley, a doughnut as big as his head in his mouth. Liddy linked her arm through Peter's and they walked on, Matty at a little distance ahead.

"You know, Liddy, I have dedicated my professional life to the analysis and understanding of literature, with its stories of heroes and villains, happy endings and often reassuring morals. But the day we brought Grace back from the hospital, I went outside to be alone for a moment and there, sitting on the bench by the fig tree, I thought about everything that has happened over the last few years, and I experienced such an overwhelming sense of the randomness, the chaos and shapelessness of existence, that I burst into tears. I understood that such structure can never be duplicated in real life."

"Maybe we wouldn't want it to be," said Liddy. "Peter, you're a good man."

"Not good enough, Liddy. Within the chaos we can live with purpose and ethical rigor, and on many occasions I have singularly failed to do that."

There was a long pause. What had needed to be said had been said and they both considered it.

"Don't mess things up with Rose," said Liddy. "To lose one . . . something . . . may be regarded as a misfortune; to lose both looks like—"

"Carelessness," finished Peter. "*The Importance of Being Earnest.*"

"Exactly, Oscar Wilde, right?" said Liddy.

I miss Sebastian, she thought, so she decided to mention him to make herself feel better.

"My friend who owns the house in Ireland is Irish. He's a divorce lawyer too."

Peter turned toward the car with a little dismissive grunt.

"And a published poet," said Liddy, thinking, *Take that,* because she couldn't stop herself reacting to that grunt.

They had reached the parking lot now. Peter had forgotten where the car was, so he clicked the button on his key and a set of lights, three rows over, flashed at him obediently. Matty ran over to it. Liddy lifted Cal down.

"What are we going to do about him?" said Peter, looking as Matty clambered into the back of the car and beckoned for Cal to follow. "I'm terrified. And we've got at least another four years of him walking around with a permanent erection."

"I'm terrified too," said Liddy. "And remorseful. Do you think it's payback for what I put my parents through? I look at Matty sometimes and I think, *Why are you speaking to me like that? Where did you come from?* And then I remember my father calling me a changeling."

Peter smiled. She turned to him.

"We're going to ride the roller coaster beside him and try not to shout too much."

"Good," he said.

They got into the car. Liddy found the lever to push back the passenger seat to make room for her legs.

"I have this incredible urge for a drink," said Peter. "We could go to that speakeasy on Grove Street if it's still there."

"We can't. You're driving and we all have to get home," said Liddy. "Call Rose."

"Didn't we have a terrible argument there one night?"

"Yep," replied Liddy. "It was about Barry Manilow. You impugned my taste in music with specific reference to 'Mandy.'"

Peter shuddered and said, "Don't start singing it," but she did anyway, and they leaned over toward each other and laughed hard.

Matty and Cal looked at each other. Matty put his fingers in his ears and Cal, giggling, followed suit. Liddy stopped on a high note.

"Call Rose," she said again.

Rose had stayed awake and kept writing, waiting for Peter and Matty's return, but when Grace had fallen unexpectedly and deeply asleep at about eleven o'clock, Rose took a short nap on the floor of the nursery beside her. It was there that Peter woke her.

"What time is it?" she asked blearily.

"After midnight. I dropped Liddy and Cal off in Tribeca. I've put Matty in bed."

He sat beside her, and she propped herself up on her elbows.

"I would have been a useless lookout in the Wild West," she said.

"Yes," agreed Peter. "Or pilot in the dawn patrol in World War One."

This was not how Rose had imagined the conversation beginning at all.

"Why did you go and meet Liddy?" she said.

Peter did not answer for a moment. This did not frighten Rose because Peter always took time to reply, as he liked to speak in proper sentences.

"Big changes are upon us, my love," he said slowly.

Now Rose felt a pulse of pure terror, for she knew how he ridiculed those who spoke in banalities (*"That wins first prize in a 'stating the obvious' competition,"* he had shouted at her once), and so what he was about to say would be unexpected.

"I don't care," she said defiantly. "We'll manage. I just wrote a thousand words of my article."

"It's more than that," he replied. "I've been to see a lawyer." He saw the expression on her face and stopped. "What's wrong?"

"You tell me," she said, thinking, *Is this it?* Why hadn't she listened to Liddy? Why hadn't she got him to sign that "Couple Cohabitation Agreement"?

"Rose, my love. You know I did not greet the news of my impending second chance at fatherhood with . . . shall we say, unbridled enthusiasm. I didn't want another child."

"Do you want this child?" she whispered, so upset she could not use Grace's name, but he seemed not to hear. "Is that why your marriage broke down?" she said, a little louder.

"Liddy really wanted another baby, and if I had agreed she would never have done what she did. I mean, if I'm honest, when I look back I see how unhappy we were, but she wouldn't ever have left me."

At this moment, there was a loud *crash!* and muffled swearing from upstairs as Matty fell out of bed, which he sometimes did while dreaming.

"Sounds fun, doesn't it?" Peter said ruefully.

"Do you want this child?" Rose asked again, because he had not answered her the first time, and when he said yes immediately, she smiled and fell silent, deciding to quit while she was ahead, but Peter had not finished.

"This time it's different," he said. "I was enough for you without it."

Her anxieties vanished. Rose relaxed. She was safe, secure, she could be Rose again, Rose for whom enough was enough, Rose whose faith in life and Peter James, which to her were the same thing, had not been misplaced, and she rejoiced. He lay back on the floor and she cuddled up next to him.

"The moment I saw our beautiful daughter, so perfect, so new, so full of grace, I was overwhelmed by the desire to make her life as unsullied as I could. I have wasted so much time feeling angry and bitter toward Liddy and I don't want to feel like that anymore."

There was a new purposefulness and peace in Peter's expression that Rose liked. She knew it meant that he had no more desire for revenge.

"I know we won't get any more money from her," said Rose. "I know I have to go back to work. My article may be late, but it'll be great. And I have an idea for a book about the 'good' stepmother in nineteenth-century literature."

Peter paused to consider this. "Like Isabel Archer?"

"Yes. I was thinking that there are so few models of successful stepparenting in fiction. I'm sure I can do something interesting with it."

"Sophia will love that," he said with the sort of intonation that Rose knew was not a compliment but a grudging recognition of her resourcefulness. "If it works you'll finally get yourself on tenure track."

Rose grinned. "I hope so. I called Sophia and she says she's excited. She also said that one of the adjuncts was caught on security camera this afternoon in a closet with a graduate student, so the dean is looking favorably on my . . . maturity."

"I never heard about that," said Peter, for a moment thinking wistfully of the escapades of his presurveillance younger days.

"So," she said, "Liddy? . . ."

"I want to sell this house and give her half the proceeds. That's what should have happened when we separated."

Rose stopped. Even restored to her old saintly self, this was a shock. "What will we do?"

"Turns out it's worth a frankly immoral sum of money, so even with half, we can happily buy ourselves a very pleasant place a little further outside the city—commuting distance for us both, of course—and make our own home. We can also invest a little nest egg and plan for my retirement."

She stopped and looked at him. Despite his talk of retirement, in this moment of heroic generosity he had never appeared stronger or more manly or *younger* to her.

"What about Connecticut?" she said quickly, for her brother Michael lived there and he had flower beds and chickens in his yard and talked about the excellent public schools.

"Sure. I want you to be happy. I want us all to be happy. And I want to cease being . . . *cangled* . . . with my ex-wife. You and Grace have made me a better person."

Tears welled up in Rose's eyes and the yellow light of the street lamps outside blurred and surrounded both of them like a halo. It was the final miracle of her life, she could ask for nothing more. But there was more, for, to her amazement, Peter stood up and then, creakily, got back down on one knee between the sippy cup and the discarded toys.

"Will you marry me, Rose?"

If Curtis was annoyed that Liddy had ignored his repeated summonings to meet in the office, he gave no sign of it. He made no comment on Liddy's explanation that she had hurled her phone into a lake by the side of a road, and accepted that she had not wanted to speak to him. They knelt in silence, side by side, in a pew in the small chapel on Lisbeth Dawe Bartlett's estate in Montauk, at the simple and moving family service to mark her death.

Chloe Stackallan, visibly distressed in her immaculate black, read Psalm 23, the King James Version, "The Lord is my shepherd . . ." She returned to her seat and clutched the arm of the handsome, broad-shouldered man sitting beside her. He leaned over and pulled her closer to him.

Curtis stood up to read the poem "If" by Rudyard Kipling, as Lisbeth had asked him to. When he returned to Liddy's side, his hands were shaking, so she held them.

She felt the collective sorrow of the congregation. Like Curtis, many people were no doubt remembering the incomparable Lisbeth, her flamboyant life and the many generosities that had touched them. But some others bowed their heads in grief and remembered other losses, their own regrets at chances missed and words unsaid.

Liddy watched as Lisbeth's three elderly sons lifted her featherlight coffin and proceeded out of the church. The organ played "Jesu, Joy of Man's Desiring." The incense rose toward the stained-glass windows. Liddy sat still; she had learned how to be still, and she listened to the music. She thought of her death.

What will Matty and Cal remember of me when, in fifty years, or ten years, or one year, or one day, I am gone?

Outside, the mourners huddled together in the graveyard, under a canopy of black umbrellas, as Lisbeth was buried next to her assorted husbands and animals and it rained an insistent fall rain.

Liddy thought of her life.

What do I want them to remember?

Afterward, Curtis was waiting for Liddy, as arranged, in a coffee shop in the town square, perched on a stool at the counter in his black suit and tie. As Liddy entered, Curtis was sipping his Americano and nibbling on a granola muffin while staring at the other pastries. Liddy knew he was wondering how much better they might taste, and she experienced a feeling of momentary disorientation. It was exactly as if they were back in the Viand Coffee Shop on Madison, meeting surreptitiously outside the office to discuss things like an asset division strategy, or how to let go of an unsatisfactory associate. She felt the quickening within, her intellect sharp like a steel rake cutting through mud or, yes, a shark's fin rising through the water. She lifted her right hand in a confident wave and marched over to him, kissing him damply on both cheeks.

"What would be your position on a premium payment over and above a prenup for serial infidelity?" he asked, characteristically avoiding unnecessary pleasantries, as if the funereal start to the day had never happened.

"We have numerous precedents of renegotiation for confidentiality, so in the case of a high-profile client, or one embarking on a subsequent marriage, I'd go for it."

Liddy ordered a coffee and a bagel, surprising the girl behind the counter with the rapid-fire *rat-tat-tat* of her speech, aware that Curtis was scrutinizing her to see if she was still fucking nuts. But in her slim navy skirt and crisp white shirt, she looked exactly the same, and as she scraped black currant jelly on top of her cream cheese, she felt relief condense off him like steam off a wet dog.

"How are you feeling?"

"Not fucking nuts." She looked at him. "The funeral was done beautifully."

"Lisbeth planned every detail—apart from the weather, that is."

"I'm sorry, Curtis. I'm sorry for your loss." Liddy nearly reached her hand across to touch him, but the moment for physical connection had passed. "'If you can meet with Triumph and Disaster,'" she continued, and Curtis allowed himself a small smile. (This surprised him because he had expected he would have to fire her. But here she was, Liddy James again, and he was mesmerized by her, a woman unlike any other he had met, a woman who was just like him, *only wearing a skirt*, a thought that as always both repulsed and excited him.)

"So. What's going on?" he said.

Liddy had hired a car and driven from the city to the Hamptons early that morning. On the way, she had listened to the Keith Jarrett CD she had stolen from Sebastian's gate lodge and stopped to look at the ocean, before visiting Springs and the Pollock-Krasner House.

"*Liddy!* Wake up," said Curtis, and in exasperation he pulled out his iPhone and started to check his e-mails, a gesture that Liddy found poignant. Part of her had pined for the rush of busyness; the hours apportioned into thirty-minute increments between 5:30 a.m. and 11:30 p.m.; the ability to measure exactly what had been achieved in a day.

"I'm not coming back, Curtis," she said.

As she had passed Shinnecock Inlet, the wind had howled and risen, whipping the rain into swirling sheets that thundered onto the windshield. Liddy had pulled into the parking lot by the beach and watched as a group of maverick surfers towed themselves out to ride the enormous, rolling waves. In their midst was one woman, her blond hair blowing over her black wetsuit. *"You go, girl,"* whispered Liddy, with admiration and a little fear. She had turned on the heater and was happy, safe in the car listening to "My Wild Irish Rose."

Curtis put the phone back in his pocket. *"What?* I've spoken to the publicists, they have ideas about how to rehabilitate your image. In fact, it could work for you, the power of vulnerability, you've heard of that, right? It's very now. You could do a TED talk."

He stared at his feet, appearing to take an extreme interest in the tips of his shoes. Then he looked up.

"I have plans for you, Liddy. Val's getting soft. You must have noticed."

Val Tynan, the managing partner, had recently had a triple bypass.

"Curtis, I'm not coming back."

As a child, Curtis had always won the "don't blink" game as, at age seven, he had perfected a technique to hold his eyes wide by biting the top of his upper lip. This had proved surprisingly useful in the course of the next fifty-three years, but today he didn't bother.

"Okay. You win. What d'you want?" She knew he was bracing himself for a list of Scandinavian-style demands, no doubt including "working from home," which he considered simply a cover to sign for furniture deliveries.

"I can be flexible. Look, I've been giving everyone Friday afternoons off for the summer."

Typical, thought Liddy, *the pioneers get the arrows, the settlers get the land*.

"This isn't a negotiation," she said.

"Everything's a negotiation."

Liddy shook her head.

In the house in Springs, she had stood in Jackson Pollock's studio as the rain beat down outside and had stared at the floor, which was covered in multicolored splatters of paint, overlayed into a deep pattern that made no and yet total sense.

"What will I tell everyone?" he said.

"That I'm spending more time with my family."

"Then *everyone* will think you've been fired. You should come back for six months. Facilitate the transition."

"If I come back, I won't want to leave."

And it was true. At the thought of anyone else in her files, Liddy found herself worrying about her poor little job in its designer room (despite the toile de Jouy and cashmere throws). *No one can look after it better than me, no one is more devoted to it*, she thought, and then she countered with, *but I don't love it anymore*. She had been a high priestess of the cult of overwork, and she did not underestimate what leaving would do to her. She had promised to give herself a year to get over it, but she knew it would be one day at a time. *I am a recovering workaholic*.

Curtis stared at her uncomprehendingly, so much so that his mouth drooped open ever so slightly and he instantly aged ten years. "God help me, I don't understand. What do you want?"

"I don't know."

He rescrutinized her. He had wanted to forgive her, but he had made a mistake. She was serious, and she had clearly lied earlier. She was *totally fucking nuts*.

"What I do know is that I have to spend more time with the people in my life to whom I am irreplaceable."

"What about me?" he wailed.

"I am not irreplaceable to you."

They both thought of Lisbeth, and then of her three elderly sons, bowed with grief, carrying her coffin out of the chapel.

"If you take any clients, I'll have you disbarred," he said.

"Understood."

"I wanna buy back your share options."

Liddy didn't blink. "We'll do a deal. I need the health insurance."

Curtis admired her style, and because he didn't want to lose her, he was furious.

"You should promote Sydney," she said.

He drank the last of his coffee with a savage slurp. He slid off his stool (with an embarrassing trip at the end). He slapped a ten-dollar bill next to the charity box. He walked out of the shop and into the street, where the sun had come out and was blazing. Liddy followed him.

Waiting at the curb was a large black car, and standing beside it was Vince. He hastily pulled on his jacket despite the heat and opened the door. When Liddy saw him she waved, then turned to Curtis.

"Here comes the sun," said Liddy cheerfully, and then, "Look," for in the distance there was a rainbow arching across the sky. "My son Cal, he asked me the other day what happens to the pot of gold when the rainbow goes into the water."

Curtis was unmoved by the idea of the cozy motherly chat or the image of the rainbow. "It doesn't mean anything. It isn't a sign that you've done the right thing. In fact, you've just done an incredibly stupid thing."

"I'll call you next week. Then I will call my clients. And I will help facilitate the transition."

Curtis paused before he began his final soliloquy, more in sorrow now than in anger.

"It's all so *unoriginal*, Liddy. The only thing you haven't said is some bullshit about work/life balance. I thought you were different. I thought you were like me."

"No, Curtis. It turns out that I am like *me*."

Curtis got into the backseat. Vince closed the door.

Liddy looked at Vince. "He's gonna miss me."

Vince grinned. She reached out a hand to him, and after a moment they embraced.

"How are you? How are the boys?" she said.

"All good. Vince Junior got into Harvard."

"You must be very proud."

"We are. How are Matty and Cal?"

"All good too."

Curtis momentarily stopped seething in the backseat to hammer on the inside of the window.

"How's he treating you?" asked Liddy.

"Easy." Vince turned to go, then paused and looked back conspiratorially. "He works less hours than you."

Liddy nodded, stepped back, and watched as the car pulled away. *So that was that*, she thought. She found herself looking up again at the rainbow, which was fading, washing out like a watercolor. Her phone rang and she grabbed it, knowing Rose would be calling to see how the meeting had gone.

But instead there was an echo on the line, a pause and then, "Liddy? . . ." Another echo and then again, too loud, "LIDDY? . . ."

"Don't shout. I can hear you."

Liddy had summoned all her formidable resources to expunge Sebastian Stackallan from her day-to-day thoughts, and had largely succeeded, but now that she heard his voice she was more delighted than she would have guessed to hear from him.

"Where are you?" he asked.

"I've just been to Lisbeth's funeral."

"Ah," he said. "I heard. She was a magnificent woman."

"Where are you?" she said.

"I'm standing in the field behind the wood with Seamus, trying to wrangle a runaway cow."

"And you thought of me? How touching!"

"Don't start!" he said, and even though he was thousands of miles away, she knew he was smiling.

"How did you get my new number?"

"Sydney. Now, *there's* someone who's got a thing for me."

Liddy ignored this. "I'm looking at a rainbow."

"How very *Darby O'Gill and the Little People*. How are you?"

"I'm going to try journaling to find out."

There was a pause, then a peal of laughter.

"And I just told Curtis Oates I was quitting my job."

"Holy God, I wish I coulda seen that. Why?"

"I can't do it anymore. Or for the moment, certainly."

In the background the wind blew and the cow mooed.

"So," Liddy said. "Were you calling for a reason?"

"Yes," he replied. "I'm sorry I disappeared like that. I . . . Look . . . I was thinking about everything . . . the moving to Ireland business and the not-waiting wheelchair stuff and so forth. . . ."

Liddy said nothing.

"I think we'd better have a proper date first."

"Sorry, I can't hear you . . ." she said, but she had heard him perfectly.

"Will you go out with me?"

"How? On Skype?"

"No! I still have to visit New York. I've got a board meeting next week."

She grinned. "I'm not a lost cause, you know," she said.

"Pardon?"

"You don't need to save me."

"What on earth are you on about?"

"Nothing, nothing. Call me when you get in."

"Good," he said calmly. "I want you to know I feel curiously optimistic. What are you going to do now?"

"I don't know. That's the truth, but it's not good enough, is it? What do I want? How shall I live? How can I do the best for my boys and still be me? All these questions and I find myself saying the same thing over and over again. *I don't know.*"

In the field behind the wood, Sebastian Stackallan thought for a moment.

"Then 'I don't know' is the answer," he said.

NEW YORK CITY, OCTOBER 5

Tonight is my last night in this apartment and, as I sit here surrounded by crates and cardboard boxes and color charts left by Lloyd's interior designer, I suspect this will be my first and last go at journaling.

I can already tell it's not my thing.

I've organized enough work to keep the family afloat for the foreseeable future, but it'll be a three-star life for the boys from now on. I'm going to consult for Marisa at Rosedale and Seldon, and I'm giving a few lectures at Columbia University. I'll be working from home too, in the new place in Prospect Heights, which is good because I have a lot of furniture to be delivered.

Cal has started at the local school there.

Peter has put the house in Carroll Gardens on the market and soon he and Rose and baby Grace will be moving to Connecticut. (Rose has already found a cottage with a shed in the garden for him to escape to when baby Grace is crying and Matty has friends to stay.) I have accepted his offer of half the proceeds—my pride left me, along with my dignity, in front of three million TV viewers. I am glad to be secure.

Matty will live with me during the school week and he will see Peter and Rose on the weekends. Things with him are no picnic, that's for sure, and I strongly suspect it will all be rather messy, and I hate mess because I am a Virgo, but I know it's time to embrace the random and the chaotic and the shapeless, because my attempts at overcontrol did not work. The unfortunate truth for those of us who rely on force of will and extreme organization to get through the days is that, in the end, you might be lucky, or you might be me.

I talked to Marisa the other day about it and she surprised me. Out of the blue, she said that she believes every woman who wants a career and children is carrying an unexploded bomb around with them, and while the consequences of it might not be quite as dramatic as mine, each of them will have their moment in the hurt locker. It was a bit melodramatic for my taste, but I do know what she meant.

You cannot spreadsheet your kids.

I called my parents yesterday and spoke to Mum. She was in the communal garden and I told her all my news and my plans, such as they are, and I said I wanted to bring the boys to visit whenever it suited them. I could tell that this made her happy, but she didn't embarrass either of us with any great display of overemotionalism. She said, "What about next weekend?" as if it was a completely normal occurrence. I was happy too. How else were we to do it? (Now I just have to brace myself for the sight of the dotty neighbor's bush.)

I told her I had spent the summer in Ireland and that I had brought the boys to see Grandma's house. She asked me if I had knocked on the neighbor's doors, or visited my cousins, and when I said no she seemed disappointed. I said I would be going back soon, that I had met an Irishman, and when I told her his name she said, "He sounds a bit posh," but she laughed.

She only irritated me once. At the end of the conversation she said, "I never thought you'd be able to do this, Lydia. I never thought you'd walk away from everything you worked so hard for."

Afterward, though, I realized she was admiring, not critical.

I have been the slave of my own life force—the restless force within me that has always had something to prove. I have kept moving, and allowing things to happen, and I have never questioned my decisions or my feelings. This is what has made me the woman I am today. But I know there is something unfinished about me.

I said to my mother, "I'm not walking away from everything, Mum."

She thought for a moment and then she replied.

"I see that, Lydia Mary. You are walking toward your life."

ACKNOWLEDGMENTS

Thank you to:

Amy Einhorn, Kate Parkin, Liz Stein, Nick Sayers, Helen Richard, and all at G. P. Putnam's Sons and Hodder & Stoughton.

Nicky Lund, Allison Hunter, Harriet Moore, Jennie Kassanoff, Dianne Festa, Katey Driscoll, Alison Jean Lester, Eimear O'Connor, and my mother, Monica Casey, who gave me particular help, encouragement, or insights at different stages of the manuscript.

My friends in Ireland, England, and the United States. My family, Casey and O'Connor. My sons, James and Marcus.

And Lizzy Kremer, David Forrer, Rosamund Lupton, and my beloved husband, Joseph O'Connor. Quite simply, without you, I would never have got to the end . . .